THE FIRST MARAUDER

THE FIRST MARAUDER

I OF III

LUKE RYAN

DEAD RECKONING

20   17

COLLECTIVE

Publisher: Dead Reckoning Collective
Book Cover Art: Tyler James Carroll, Kenna Milaski, Joshua Ryan

Printed in the United States of America

ISBN-13: 978-1-7338099-7-9 (paperback)

"With strong, clear prose, Luke Ryan shows us what happens when the veneer of safety that society provides disintegrates. As we follow Tyler through his journey through the untamed wilds of Florida and humanity, Ryan forces us to reckon with our own humanity."

-Michael Ramos, Creative Writing Professor for UNCW

"While I hope Luke Ryan will never forget his poetry roots, *The First Marauder* is a phenomenal fiction debut. A coming-of-age novel set amid the rubble of a nation ravaged by "the Red." Ryan weaves a story that is engaging, entertaining, and thanks to his years as a U.S. Army Ranger, tactically sound. You'll root for 15-year-old Tyler Ballard as he negotiates an eerily familiar post-apocalyptic America fractured along ideological fault lines and hope that he possesses both the training and moral courage to face the real enemy when it presents itself. You'll be glad this is just the first novel in a trilogy."

-John Daily, USMC, retired

"Post-Red America is a place where chaos reigns, and those willing to resort to violence have the upper hand on everyone else. Despite this being a world where tragedy is the new normal, Tyler's resolute determination leads to a feeling of hope that pervades the story. While there's no such thing as a happy ending post-Red, *The First Marauder* leaves a sense of optimism that whatever Tyler faces next, he will find a way to endure."

-Mac Caltrider, founder of Pipes & Pages

"A stunning debut. Ryan builds a rich and vibrant apocalypse, stitched together with so many threads of realism that it becomes impossible not to live through these characters. I'll continue to read whatever Ryan puts in front of me.

-Kacy Tellessen, author of *Freaks of a Feather*

Dedicated to those who were shaken by violence in their youth.

1

"101.7 FM, the last radio station to adorn the airwaves and grace your ear canals. Brothers, have I got a playlist for you today — it's got soul, it's got fire, but it'll break your heart into a million tiny 'lil pieces. I'll make you love rock, I'll make you love pop, and I'll make you wish you hadn't heard either of them 'cause you're so torn between the two.

"And don't forget, you heard it here first — and last — on 101.7, the soundtrack to the end of the world."

"MEN from Lakeland murdered my brother. They came last night and shot him dead in our parents' old room." The boy's voice shook. It shook with red-hot rage, it shook with confusion, and it shook with a grief so large he couldn't see the end of it.

He was a lanky boy in his mid-teens, at the stage where his proportions were all racing at different speeds. Amidst his mess of dirty blond hair, his awkward limbs, and the slight crack in his voice, the boy's eyes were dark. The spark of youth had been replaced with something else, something that didn't belong in a teenager. A lot of boys had eyes like that in those days.

He stood in the East Tampa Militia's recruiting office, an airless room where dust hung in the air and moisture stains ran down the walls. The militia's initials E-T-M were spray-painted on the back wall just beyond the desk in front of him. On the desk blared the radio with that voice everyone was familiar with, the self-proclaimed soundtrack to the end of the world.

The boy's eyes were fixed on Major Kessler, a man who, though sitting behind the desk, towered over the boy. Kessler puffed a cigar through his bushy mustache that had only just begun to gray in recent years.

The Major reached over to his radio and turned it down. Every movement the colossal man made was deliberate, as if it were a coordinated effort requiring the attention of every body part involved. He turned the volume knob down to exactly 2, diminishing the music to little more than a distant buzz.

The boy had heard the whispers from the roving neighborhood teenagers: Kessler had fought in some now forgotten war before the Red. Some said he took shrapnel to the left leg; some said he killed ten men after getting shot in the arm. The Major simply leaned back in his chair and smoked his flawless home-rolled cigars, allowing his mythos to grow in any direction it pleased — such things were of no concern to him.

Even if the Major had done nothing more than flip burgers before the Red, it was his actions after that rang in the boy's head. Kessler had fought in the first "Expulsion of the Bandits," as they called it, when anyone who had been caught stealing from the living was removed from the East Tampa city limits. One organized group had fought back, and Kessler led the charge against them. People were also endlessly whispering about the wall-of-a-man's actions on the Great Casino Raid, when some militia from the neighboring town of Lakeland holed up at the casino and the ETM flushed them out under his leadership.

The other East Tampa boys hadn't memorized those stories with quite the level of detail as this one. They were etched into his consciousness and he revered them like hieroglyphs telling tales of ancient and glorious battles.

The boy imagined he had performed some heroics last night.

Last night. When my brother…

He had spoken the words when it was necessary, but now even just the thought was too painful to finish.

The boy forced himself to hold the unrelenting gaze of the older, rougher man. Though it was the Major's job to find new recruits, he often tested their enthusiasm by ominously hinting at the horrors of war.

"You look like the type that would shrivel up at the sound of a gunshot," he would say, his gaze penetrating the cigar smoke between him and a potential recruit. Any other day, this boy would have been like the other boys and girls wandering into that station — trembling in fear of the mere presence of Major Kessler.

But today was different. Today he had his brother's blood on his left pant leg.

"I heard about that," Kessler said at last. "They hit several houses on the edge of town, didn't they?"

"Yessir. It was two men and one woman in a red truck. 4th Platoon drove them off, but… they didn't kill them." The image of the red truck idling just beyond his front lawn was seared into memory.

"4th Platoon is a good group of guys."

"Yes sir."

"We're not the police, son. We're not here to arrest folks."

"I know."

"We're not the National Guard either. You know why they dissolved so quick after the federal government? Because they were trying to keep a peace that couldn't be kept. We're not in the business of riot control or trying to befriend fellas who just want us to live under their thumbs.

"I know."

Major Kessler leaned forward, piping out a pillar of smoke. "So, you're out for blood?"

The boy didn't know what he wanted. He knew his heart wasn't supposed to yearn for violence, but it seemed to him that violence had kicked down his door anyway.

"I just want to help. I'm tired of not helping."

"Alright, sure. I think I ought to clear something up first. I say this to every hot-blooded recruit with some certain pre-existing objective on their mind," Kessler said.

"Sir?"

"This war, there are a lot of moving parts to it. A lot of good folks like your brother have died, and there are a lot of strategic and political considerations. But at the end of the day it all comes down to a struggle for resources in the end. You understand? Resources that are growing more scarce by the week."

"You mean copper, sir?"

"You've heard about that."

"I've know all the stories, sir. But not much beyond that."

"Well, you'll learn soon enough, but when there's something of value in this world you have some folks who aim to share and build, and you have others who want to take and destroy. We are far, far from perfect, but we like to think we're the prior. And you know who the latter is?"

"Lakeland, sir."

"That's right. So, while a healthy thirst for the blood of the enemy is important as a young warrior, understand that there are larger objectives at play. Those always have to come first."

"I understand, sir."

The Major leaned back in his chair, eyeing Tyler closer now. He pointed to some scribbles on the wall, tenets of the ETM painted with crude, broad brush strokes. "Read the second line."

"'No man or woman under the age of sixteen shall enlist in the ETM,'" said the boy.

"And are you sixteen?" Kessler said doubtfully.

"Yes sir."

"Can you prove that?"

The boy's heart beat faster in his chest. He would turn sixteen in three months and something about Kessler's eyes told him he knew. A man like that knows everything. "N-no sir. I was twelve during the Red, I didn't have any papers."

The Major nodded and retrieved a ledger from under his desk. "You're going to be assigned to my platoon."

2nd Platoon. The boy tightened his lips in excitement. They had conducted twenty-six raids and only lost three men since the conflict with Lakeland had started. They were feared. They were capable. Blood was indeed on his mind, and 2nd Platoon, East Tampa Militia would help him find it.

"Name?"

"Tyler, sir."

"Full name, son." The Major's voice was stern. Even small mistakes were met with tired disappointment.

"Oh uh, Tyler Ballard, sir."

"Well, this here ledger with your name in it is the only record we've got at the ETM. Your enlistment is entirely based upon your word and myself as your witness. Now, that may not seem like much, but the reality is that we don't have much. Don't get it confused, though, your oath is as serious as an oath can be in these parts. Do you understand?"

"Yes sir."

"I have to ask you this next question, don't take offense. Standard procedure. After the Red, were you in any way affiliated with Lakeland or any enemies of East Tampa, known or unknown?"

"No sir."

Major Kessler rose to his feet, a giant to the boy.

"Raise your right hand."

He did.

"Do you volunteer your services to the East Tampa Militia and the City of Tampa?"

"Yes sir."

"Do you swear to execute the orders of Mayor Whitley and those that he has appointed over you?"

"Yes sir."

The Major grinned through his thick mustache, like Tyler had instantly transformed from a scared little rabbit to a young brother in need of mentorship. "Then you're in. Welcome to the militia, son. We're going to bring some pain to those boys over at Lakeland — they poked the wrong bear. I'm sorry to hear about your brother."

Anthony.

Tyler's slain brother — could he really be gone? The night before seemed like a thousand fractured memories stitched together by muzzle flashes and whimpers. Each second lingered in the forefront of his mind, like it had happened only moments ago, and yet, it all seemed like something that happened so long ago. It was a dream. A nightmare only made more terrifying by the knowledge that it was real and irreversible.

He had lost Anthony. The same Anthony who was out building water filtration systems around town while Tyler was still grieving their parents, lost to the Red. The same Anthony who taught the countless orphans of East Tampa how keep the orphanage from flooding during hurricane season. Anthony was scouring his mind for clever ways to put his high school science–level knowledge to good use while Tyler was lost in his sadness.

Not anymore, he said to himself. *Enough sitting around.*

"Bring the sights up to your eye, don't move your head down to your sights." Sergeant Santana was the only other man in 2nd Platoon with prior military experience. Kessler had charged the rough-mouthed sergeant with training Tyler for two weeks before they would take him out on missions.

Has it been three days already? Tyler wondered. *Maybe four. Doesn't matter.*

He gently squeezed the trigger. *Click.* Tyler lowered his rifle. His arms were sore from what felt like hours of lifting his rusted M16, firing, listening as the hammer slammed forward, pulling the charging handle back, and doing it again. And again. And again.

"Can't spare the live ammunition," the Major had said. "So, we practice with dry fires. You'll be shooting live ammunition soon enough."

Tyler gripped his rifle tight, gritted his teeth, and lifted it again. He told himself that personal comfort was now forfeit. He figured vengeance wouldn't come easy, and a few sore muscles weren't going to get in the way of putting a bullet in some Lakeland soldiers. Particularly any Lakeland soldiers driving a red truck.

But for all his brazen thoughts, his muscles were still sore, and his aim was still wavering.

Sergeant Santana was a short, muscular man. His left arm was covered in tattoos, sometimes difficult to distinguish from his deeply tan skin. He kept his hair buzzed short and his sentences shorter.

"Don't drop your weapon so quick. Keep it up and keep it shooting until you know he's fuckin' toast."

Tyler was aiming at an "X" spray-painted on the side of a wall. The wall used to be the side of Munson Grocery, his parents' first choice for organic foods — now reduced to a single wall. After the Red, someone had holed up in there, trying to horde all the food for themselves. Someone else had driven a semi-truck through the wall, gained access, and a storm of gunfire followed — both parties ended up in the dirt. Hurricane season barreled through a month later, found a foothold in the hole in the wall, and tore the rest of the place down.

Tyler squeezed. *Click.*

He tried to keep his mind off such things. Off the way they used to be. Off his parents. When they crept their way into his mind, he lifted the rifle and — *click.*

"Better." Sergeant Santana was pacing behind him with an M4 slung across his chest. A reflex sight was mounted on the top of the weapon and there wasn't a spot of rust on the thing. Tyler envied such a weapon, and wondered why he got stuck with the long, cumbersome M16, especially when his wiry frame wasn't used to holding a rifle at all.

Santana caught Tyler's eyes wandering across his rifle. "It's the same damn weapon, mine's just shorter. You put in the time; we'll get you somethin' better."

Tyler nodded. He didn't want to seem ungrateful for what he had.

"Alright, put your weapon down. We'll dry fire more tonight. Next we hit the park to go over react to contact."

"React to contact?"

"What you do when you get shot at."

Tyler slung his M16 over his shoulder and walked with Sergeant Santana down the street. His makeshift rope sling dug into his skin, and it was too tight against his chest.

They strolled past the endless rows of vacant houses, some torn by weather and many reduced to rubble by the first waves of panic from the Red — the mass graves, the abandoned buildings and the ensuing destruction from looting and harsh weather were all part and parcel of an apocalypse. Now it was just home.

"Four years... I feel like yesterday I was back on leave, slammin' beers and chasin' tail." It was Santana's rare attempt at conversation.

"I can't really remember what it was like." Tyler repositioned the sling, moving it from one sore part of his shoulder to another. "Seems like another lifetime."

"Maybe that's a good thing — ain't no use bitchin' about the past now."

They walked in silence as the edge of the East Tampa Marketplace approached. It was a mess of shanty stores and buildings that had been gutted and repurposed as a place of barter. Since the Red, Tyler had never seen a place with so much commotion — sometimes he needed a reminder that there were more than just a few dozen survivors in East Tampa, there were thousands. There was still life, and the East Tampa Marketplace was teeming with it. Other times he would find himself lost in the mayhem of sweat and raised voices, and he would rush out of it in search of a few moments of precious silence.

The entry point to the marketplace was marked by the McCallister General Stores — an elderly couple that had found each other after the Red. They sat out on the front porch like they did every morning, and Mrs. McCallister smiled at the sight of him. She raised her hand to wave, but paused — she saw his weapon, his present company, and the smile faded off her face as she tried to justify the boy she knew with what appeared to be some kind of soldier. Tyler resisted eye contact until they had passed completely. He had only ever spoken a handful of words to her, but he needed to focus on Sergeant Santana and every kernel of knowledge the man had to endow upon him.

"What happened to your brother?" Santana asked. Like Kessler, he was not known for mincing words.

"The other night — you know when they came through and shot up some houses on the edge of town?"

"Yeah, I heard about that."

"Well, it happened then. I don't know what they wanted, though. I remember they were driving a red truck, two men and a woman. Couldn't see them too well in the dark. They started shooting, I don't know why, killed my brother and my dog. My dog's name was Lacey, she ran out into the yard because she was scared. She was always scared of loud noises."

Tyler didn't want to talk about his brother. The fire, the righteous indignation all boiled up because of his brother's murder, but he didn't want to talk about it. Talking about it meant really thinking about it, and the violent murder of dear Anthony was more than his mind could bear. Like filling a balloon with too much water — at some point it would probably just burst. So, he talked about his dog. Poor Lacey, whose crime was that she was afraid of loud noises.

"They killed your damn dog too? Jesus, kid." Santana unslung his rifle and carried it casually in one hand. "Well, Mayor Whitley isn't letting that raid slide. Did you hear his last statement?"

"I heard that he said he was gonna do something about it."

"He said a lot more than that, kid. You wanna fight, you gotta pay attention to the politics. Ya hear me? Lakeland started this whole war, killin' those boys in Plant City over canned food and beef jerky and shit. They're chomping at the bit to snatch up all the copper in the Tampa Bay area for themselves, and you know how valuable copper is these days. That woman they raped up in the old fire station? Hard to believe guys like that were your neighbors your whole life, then the Red comes along and bam — they're animals. I don't know what's in the water over there, but they need to be put in their place."

"Why can't they just keep to themselves? Like we do."

"Some people just want what you have, man. They'll take your food, your home, and shoot you in the face as a thank you. You can't talk to 'em because they're not interested in what you've got to say, only what you've got. The local government used to keep people in line, cops and lawyers and whatever, but that whole dog and pony show turned to dust with the Red. Then it was the National Guard for a bit, but you remember them bouncin' to the four winds too, I'm sure. When Kessler and us boys fired up the 'Expulsion of the Bandits' as it's so lovingly been called, no one made us do it. We all got off our asses and pushed through East Tampa block-by-block because it had to be done, and no daddy government was there to do it for us. It's up to us now, to stop any-one from walkin' all over the shit we love, understand?"

"I understand, Sergeant."

"Good. Now enough yappin', let's get this shit done so we can go eat."

They reached a grassy field and Tyler turned his attention to learning practical things.

There were twenty-two men in 2nd Platoon of the ETM. Only Major Kessler and Sergeant Santana were military veterans, and the rest were electricians, plumbers, accountants, and marketing specialists. One by the name of Desmond Long had never left Hillsborough County in his life until the Red. He had to make a trip to what was left of Miami when his sister fell into trouble with some roving merchants, and the ETM allowed a small contingent to accompany him. The sister didn't make it, and Desmond lost interest in ever leaving the county again.

That mission was one of many written in the pages in Tyler's mind. Every raid carried out by the ETM, every sporadic firefight — he listened to the whispered stories throughout East Tampa as attentively as he studied history in school. But he kept that to himself. *Best to just watch and learn*, he thought. *Watch and learn.*

Tyler shifted uncomfortably as he sat on the floor in the East Tampa Militia barracks. It was an old law office and chairs were scarce. As the newest member of the ETM, he was the last candidate to receive any type of comfort.

Several ETM militiamen were huddled around a radio plugged into a solar powered battery that was one of ten provided to the platoon. The static was almost louder than the music, but the militiamen soaked it all up anyway. Every so often a tune would bleed through, or the running commentary of the radio station DJ who never failed to earn a few laughs.

There was one radio tower left in the world — well, one operational tower within old Tampa's broadcast range anyway. Still, the militiamen called it the last radio station on earth, and they always traded horror stories about those who tried to go up there to take over the airwaves for their own purposes.

"I heard a bunch of blood-thirsty psychopaths are up there guarding it," one would say.

"It's surrounded by mines, and that's not even the worst of it," said another. "He's got pits with spikes and will leave you there to bleed out."

Sergeant Santana would chime in at some point, "Look, one day we're gonna have to take that tower and y'all better be ready. East Tampa is gettin' big quick, and having the Mayor stand in the middle of town square yellin' out orders ain't gonna cut it forever. Mass communication — that shit is key."

The radio station was nestled on top of one of the highest points in the area. That wasn't saying much, dead center in one of the flattest parts of the continent, but it was enough of a tactical advantage that any attempt at taking would surely end in high casualties, whatever manner of threat lay up top. Tyler didn't know much in the way of strategy, but he knew there was value in holding the high ground.

Until that particular raid arrived, Tyler put it out of his mind — he pushed that worry down with all the rest. Besides, they had enough to worry about as it was. The need to commandeer the town's primary source of entertainment had not yet bumped high enough on the Mayor's priority list.

"Hey kid, where were you when the Red hit?" Sean Ford had turned to him as the radio delved back into static. His midsection was always threatening to pour over his belt, and though he was in his early twenties, his cheeks were just as red as Tyler's. Until Tyler came along, Sean was the newest member of 2nd Platoon — Tyler could tell that he yearned for a chance to look down on someone else. "Kid" stumbled as awkwardly out of his mouth as he had stumbled around his weapon earlier.

"I was home for the weekend when everybody started getting sick," Tyler said. "My dad got it first, started getting the bumps everywhere, was dead in about ten days. My mom started showing symptoms soon after that."

"Anyone's parents make it? Any family members?" another soldier asked. Everyone was quiet. *Anthony made it*, he thought. *But there's no use in bringing that up now.*

The memory of his parents, riddled with grotesque bumps across every inch of their skin, crept its way past the walls he had built in his mind. How they squirmed and writhed with a deep, fading sorrow in their eyes. *Their eyes. The lungs fail and the skin falls off, but the eyes — the eyes always stay healthy. Until the end they stay healthy.*

Anthony was always the optimist, and at first he said their parents would make it. Then he said their mom would make it. Then he cried. And he cried and cried again. Tyler cried too, though he never felt like he could pour his soul out the way that Anthony could.

It was a miracle that his own brother made it. The occupants of the ETM barracks weren't the only people with no surviving family members. Tyler had yet to meet anyone who was as lucky as he was, to have Anthony after the Red.

"Y'all never say it," Santana grunted. He had a manual for an M240B machine gun in his hand, but Tyler could tell that he hadn't read a word of it. His eyes were focused just beyond its pages at something unseen.

"Say what, sergeant?" Ford asked, not sensing the seriousness in his voice.

"Smallpox. 'The Red' is a big scary name, I'll give it that, and it was a big scary disease, but y'all don't have the balls to call it what it is was… and I ain't sure why. Why is that, Ford? You're the one who likes to talk so much, why don't you speak those words?"

Ford's eyes fell to the floor, and he shifted in his seat at the sergeant's attention. "I… I guess it doesn't quite do it justice, sergeant."

"Weaponized smallpox that was engineered by suicidal terrorists, all evaporated in the storm they brewed up. There ain't no 'justice' to be had in that kinda thing, and you know it. No, I think that maybe your little brain just has a hard time graspin' the thing, so givin' it a big, scary name seems better than understanding that it was all just a couple assholes in some random part of the world who decided it all oughtta end." Santana cleared his throat. "And now we're up against a couple of assholes again. A lot more, actually, just without an apocalyptic virus on-hand. Only a few guns and a taste for blood." Silence filled the room as Santana's words drifted through it.

To Tyler's relief, Major Kessler poked his head in the side door. "Santana, get the boys ready. Mayor Whitley's making a statement in five minutes."

"Yes sir." Santana's eyes snapped back into focus and he tossed the gun manual to the side. He whipped his head toward the rest. "You heard him. Get your shit, let's go."

The platoon straightened their uniforms — plain, olive jumpsuits with ETM lettering stitched on the left shoulder — and they left the barracks and walked in two parallel files to the center of East Tampa. Most of the buildings in that part of town were little more than piles of bricks or stacks of splinters. The few structures that weren't damaged were simply unoccupied. It only took one plague and four years to almost desert the place entirely.

As they marched toward the town square, Tyler gazed past the shoulders of his comrades and considered the skyscrapers in the distance. They stood now as monuments to the Tampa of the years long past, dusty obelisks that held no practical value.

Even ghosts would get lonely up there.

They reached their destination: an unassuming roundabout before the Red, now adorned with a plywood stage and a matching pulpit. The Mayor had addressed the residents of East Tampa countless impassioned times before; Tyler had gone to a few, but he and Anthony mostly kept to their own neighborhood. There was always so much to do when you lived on the fringes of the city, and there was little time for a trip to the center of town to hear a speech, no matter how significant it may have been to your future.

The name "John Whitley" was inscribed into Tyler's memory alongside all the ETM's losses and victories — his would be a prominent name in the history books of the future, Tyler thought. Whitley was a former music producer who had served as a uniting force after the Red. When the government dissolved and crime ran rampant, it was Whitley who brought Major Kessler and a few other ex-military men together to form the East Tampa Militia. The Mayor sought out the remaining engineers and healthcare professionals in the Tampa Bay area and united them to rebuild the city from east to west. Expansion had stopped when they simply didn't have enough people to continue west, which was now largely populated by the occasional scavenger, the odd bandit, and a whole lot of empty spaces.

Anthony said the mayor complimented him on his water filtration systems once. He was beaming when he said it.

Tyler knew that people in charge were generally politicians of some sort. And like his father always told him, politicians wanted power above all else. But everything he heard about this John Whitley painted a very different picture, a picture of a man with raw charisma and intelligence. He wasn't a brute-force, hard-headed hillbilly like Mayor Hatch from Lakeland. Her infamy may have even outweighed the love people had for Mayor Whitley — infamy often has that effect.

They arrived at the square and positioned themselves in a rectangular formation, facing the platform and pulpit. Santana stood in front of 2nd Platoon, planted in the ground like a statue of immovable muscle. Tyler wondered if he would ever stand with such unyielding strength.

Five other platoons stood in formations to either side of them. 1st and 2nd Platoons were typically chosen for offensive missions, while the other three rotated through defensive positions around the city. Some wanted to take the fight to the enemy, and envied the men and women from 1st and 2nd Platoon. Others found pride in defending their homes, staying in and among the people for whom they fought.

The rest of the town square was flooded with civilians, and Tyler guessed there were about five hundred. He noticed a dog sitting quietly next to a middle-aged couple. He wondered what her name was.

As Mayor John Whitley emerged from the crowd and stepped onto the stage, the crowd erupted in applause and cheers. Whitley had jet-black hair and wore a wide, infectious smile. His sleeves were rolled up and his shoes, though scuffed, were clean. He stood on the platform and admired the sea of survivors before him.

Tyler stared in awe at the man. He wasn't a legendary hero like Major Kessler or an intimidating grunt like Sergeant Santana; here was a very ordinary man who had lost what they had all lost. His wife and children were taken by the Red, and yet he stepped up and took charge when no one else would. He took chaos by the neck and molded it into something livable for everyone. Tyler's ears burned as he waited for the man to speak.

"Friends. Lakeland has been relentless in their offensives against our people. Their aggression knows no bounds. Despite our constant attempts to negotiate, they continue to prey on the weak — to hit us when we're not looking. They don't have the military manpower to take us on directly, so they use cowardly tactics and they target our civilians. I wanted peace. We all wanted peace. But Lakeland... I think they want something else."

Mayor Whitley paused for a moment, shouldering an invisible weight upon his back. "My brother-in-law grew up in Lakeland. I used to go there every other weekend with my wife, God rest her. And now those same men and women who I sat with, ate with, laughed with..." The mayor's voice faltered, and he cleared his throat. "I don't know what happened. The Red took so many of us... and it took a piece of all of us with them. I know I've never been the same since..." He lifted his stoic gaze to the horizon. "But for all the Red has taken from us, I refuse to let it take my humanity as well. I wish I could say the same for our brothers and sisters in Lakeland.

"They're backing us in a corner here. That's the truth of it. They don't want total war because they know they can't win, we don't want war because it's not who we are. But at the end of the day, they want what we have and they're going to keep hitting us, raid after raid, eroding us until the mighty boulder that is Tampa is little more than a pebble. That's when they'll wage open war, and that's when they'll win. The question is... can we afford to wait for that to happen? Will we stand by as they pillage our homes and set fire to our infrastructure?"

The mayor took a couple quiet steps as his audience held their breaths. He turned his head and seemed to look every single person right in the eye.

"If it's a fight they're after, then it's a fight they'll get. But I'm not waiting around for the next explosion or bout of gunfire. Unlike them, we will refuse to lurk in the shadows. Unlike them, we will stand tall and look our enemy in the eye. Unlike them, we will have the courage to call this what it has already become: WAR."

The crowd erupted in cheers and applause. Tyler clapped, his heart teeming with righteous indignation. Here was a man who wouldn't only avenge Anthony, but all the others that Lakeland had snatched from this earth. Tyler knew he wasn't the only one who had lost someone he loved to the jaws of their Lakeland neighbors.

"I have pleaded to meet with Mayor Hatch. If I could just meet with her, I'd fall to my knees and beg her — for the sake of her people as much as ours — to do anything in her power to prevent war. But it seems that basic negotiations are off the table. Not only is she actively working to fuel the fires of war, but she seems gravely unconcerned about the fact that — given enough copper — we could potentially start expanding our electrical grid after the initial National Guard copper seizures. Hell, if we've got power, I'd be more than happy to expand and offer Lakeland a helping hand!"

As Whitley spoke, his voice grew in excitement for the dream of a partnership with Lakeland. But in the same moment, the dream dissolved, and his eyes returned to the mud on the ground.

"But Hatch's eye is fixed on petty things: any copper she can get her hands on, all to herself and leaving none for the rest of us. Not to mention the stockpiles of canned food that we need to feed our surviving children. That greed — it's cost the lives of forty East Tampa residents in the last month."

Forty. Tyler's brother was among that sacred number. *Survived the Red to be slaughtered by your own neighbor. What a waste.* He felt his pulse quicken.

"But if we must be pushed to war — what does that look like?" Whitley continued. "Well, we plan on redoubling our efforts, pushing further east. Our hands are going to get dirtier, folks. The resistance we've encountered at Plant City will continue to deteriorate as we push more of our elite and brave ETM militia men and women through their chokeholds. We will persist. We will survive, and we will overcome, just as we always have: *together*."

Applause. Cries of praise. Whitley stepped off the platform and disappeared back into the people. Tyler's heart was full. It only took minutes for the command to trickle down the official channels — from Whitley to Kessler, from Kessler to Santana, and from Santana to 2nd Platoon. They were scheduled for a mission in Plant City. When Santana read the manifest, Tyler's name was the last one on it. They had a job to do, a special assignment from the mayor himself — but his eyes would be peeled for a red truck, two men, and a woman.

2

"Today we got a little jazz for ya, brothers. You think a tune is gonna go one way, bam! Yer faced with a change in keys. You think a tune is gonna push another way, bam! Drummer decides to take a walk down memory lane. Predict the unpredictable and it just becomes predictable again — not so with the smooth jazz in my library.

"All here on 101.7, the soundtrack to the end of the world."

THE platoon's enthusiasm for war was much higher twenty miles ago. The Lakeland Militia were not known for their effectiveness in brute force combat, but word was that they had an eye behind every tree and an ear behind every wall — a convoy of trucks would hardly get two miles before every talking head in Lakeland knew which direction they were moving. If 2nd Platoon wanted to travel into Plant City without anyone noticing, they would have to strap on their rucks, tighten their boots, and walk in the old-fashioned way.

As the miles added up, even the strongest men dragged their feet. The gaps from soldier to soldier began to widen, threatening the integrity of their formation. Of course, they didn't want to be within arm's length of each other, but if they were too spread out and someone started shooting at them — executing a coordinated counter-attack would be difficult.

"Disappointed in some of you men. Get your act together and get your ass in gear — we've got a real fight ahead of us," Kessler said as they waded through a sea of saw palmettos. Their sharp teeth reached up and kissed the curtains of soft, curly Spanish moss that hung from the trees making it difficult to see more than twenty feet ahead. "Keep this formation tight. Do NOT lose sight of the man in front of you."

Santana was bouncing from the front of the formation to the back as they weaved along the same trails he had grown up exploring. "Get your ass up there. This is 2nd Platoon, we don't need pussies slowing us down."

Tyler's shoulders burned, unfamiliar with the weight of his pack. His long, cumbersome rifle bounced against the tattered vest he wore across his chest, banging softly against his scraped up magazines. There was a certain rhythm to the pain that made it less bearable, but he demanded that his mind made it bearable. He promised himself that he would push until his legs buckled and his face slammed into the earth. And so, he gritted his teeth and kept at the front of the formation, alongside men who had been rucking under heavy weight for years.

"You're a good kid," the Major said as he secured the tip of the long radio antennae through a piece of webbing on his upper shoulder. "This is a hard way of life. You need to get used to it."

"Yes sir."

"Why are you here?" Kessler often asked cryptic questions, and Tyler wondered what bout of wisdom would follow.

"…we're here to back up 4th Platoon, sir."

"Yes, good. But I meant, why are *you* here? In the ETM?"

Tyler took a few seconds to catch his breath, buying time to think of an appropriate answer. "I wanna help with the war against Lakeland."

"Bullshit. Why are you really here?"

After a moment: "They killed my brother, sir. They killed my dog. I don't know the difference between revenge or justice or… something else. I don't know, but I want whoever did that to my family to die."

"You're angry."

"Yes sir."

"Good. You're going to need that anger today." Kessler moved ahead to speak with the man on point. Santana made his way back up to Tyler.

"Well, at least you're not fallin' out. Pussies, man. I'd kick 'em out if it were up to me. Ten useful men is better than fifty useless assholes."

It was there, trudging through that jungle and listening to Santana curse those who lagged behind, that Tyler realized his whole life was filled with people who had spoken to him gently, like he was an egg to be transported with care lest he crack and spill open. Pleasant tones and soft voices. Growing up, that was how everyone around him communicated — they spoke to each other so gently, so frequently, that the idea of speaking in any other way seemed foreign. It was a soft language, which would have worked if Tyler was fated to live in a soft world.

"Fuck, man, get your ass up here, it's not that hard," Santana said.

Tyler thought he ought to be repulsed by someone speaking that way, but he wasn't. The crude, casual speech didn't make him uncomfortable; in fact, a part of him liked it, or at least, a part of him thought he did. After almost sixteen years, here was someone willing to treat him like an adult. It wasn't pretty, it wasn't fun, but something about it seemed honest.

"Just remember what we taught you, kid. War is a tricky fuckin' thing — you could train your whole life just to take a ricochet to the head. But trust me, the chances of that happening go way down if you do what you're told, when you're told. Are you an idealist?"

The question took Tyler off guard. Again, he wasn't sure how to answer.

Santana didn't wait for a reply. "You strike me as an idealist," he said. "That ain't me, but I don't give a shit. Just figure out all those moral dilemmas before the shooting starts, alright? Because when it does, the moral decision part of your brain ain't gonna be in control. If you don't know what you're doing, you're just gonna freeze up and get your dick shot off."

"Roger, Sergeant."

"Alright. Keep pushin'. We've got another mile or so before we set up shop."

Tyler forced one foot in front of the other. Images of what might happen next flashed through his mind. He saw a familiar red truck in a clearing. He imagined shooting one of the men as Major Kessler and Sergeant Santana shot the others. Maybe one of their men would get shot in the process, and maybe Tyler would drag him to safety under a wave of bullets. He told himself that he didn't want any of that to happen, but he thought that maybe it would.

His thoughts were interrupted by a blister, forming on his left heel; he could feel the skin starting to rub away against his sock.

"4th Platoon started taking fire about fifteen minutes ago. They've taken two casualties, but as far as I know they're both still alive."

Most of the men were huddled around Major Kessler under the burning, summer sunlight. Tyler and four others were kneeling facing outward in a stretch of cookie-cutter houses, tasked with keeping a watchful eye on the abandoned homes of Plant City as the platoon leadership developed a more updated plan. Tyler glanced back at the group every few seconds, as if he were required to look at them to hear them.

"Pull security, Ballard," Santana hissed and Tyler snapped his head back outward.

Tyler's knee had become tender and sore, so he switched knees. He saw a man and a child dash away into the brush, but they were gone just as quickly as they had appeared. Santana told Tyler to keep an eye out, but that was the last he saw of them.

4th Platoon. They fought off the trio in the red truck, and Tyler swore that he wouldn't forget that. They were in trouble now, and they needed him. They needed 2nd Platoon.

Santana scraped a crude map of the northern section of Plant City into the dirt with his knife, but Tyler's eyes were peeled for movement among the buildings ahead of them.

"You hear that?"

Tyler paused for a moment and devoted each of his senses to his ears. Distant pops echoed in the background, like pieces of plywood slapping together over and over again. Something in him told him it was gunfire, but it didn't have the same thundering bass he had imagined.

"That's 4th Platoon," Kessler said. "We're going to support them by flanking here." Tyler heard the sound of a knife stab into the dirt.

"From what I heard over the radio, it used to be a suburban area so expect a lot of abandoned houses. If we enter and clear any of these houses, watch your step. I don't want us to be tripping over furniture like last time. 4th Platoon will be here, firing north. They have a small support by fire element right here, but their fire hasn't been too effective."

Tyler had learned terms like "support by fire" and "enter and clear," but the last few weeks had been a blur of phrases and training events, all of which he understood in the moment, but very few of which really nestled into memory. On top of that, Tyler couldn't see where the Major was pointing, and he didn't know the area very well. He was about to ask for clarification when —

"Alright, let's go. They can't wait on us any longer." Kessler led the platoon further into Plant City.

As the gunshots grew louder, Tyler began to doubt his two meager weeks of training. *Am I really ready? Could anyone be ready in two weeks?* He trusted Kessler and Santana, even the other soldiers of 2nd Platoon, but he didn't want to make a mistake and become a liability. If he was injured, lost, or ineffective for any reason, he would be hurting 2nd Platoon — perhaps even responsible for the injury or death of another militiaman. He wanted to be an asset, not someone they had to "deal with."

I will NOT be a problem for these guys, he said to himself, over and over. But as soon as he asked himself exactly *how* he would prevent himself from becoming a problem, his lack of training returned to his mind, and all of that doubt overshadowed any false confidence he may have had.

The shots in the distance became increasingly sporadic, until they ceased entirely. Tyler couldn't imagine either side had the amount of ammunition required for a long firefight. He only had 75 rounds for his rifle — two and a half magazines. Kessler had told him to shoot slowly and accurately, no barrages of automatic fire, no wild suppressive fire. "Shoot what you can hit, son," he told Tyler.

Major Kessler turned down his radio, but if Tyler was close enough he could hear a faint crackle that would prompt the large man to press the device against his ear. Santana ordered the rest of them to keep their mouths shut and eyes open.

A faint voice bled through Kessler's radio. The large man listened for a moment and turned to whisper into Santana's ear. Santana went down the line and relayed the information: "Hey man, 4th Platoon shifted over to an abandoned high school just south, we're gonna head that way. Just under a mile from here."

"Roger, sergeant." Santana moved to the next man.

They trekked down the neighborhood streets, past vacant homes and abandoned cars. Hurricanes and tropical storms had sheared off shingles and torn away doors that were left open; weeds crept up streetlights and most grass blew knee-high in the breeze.

Places like Plant City made Tyler's stomach turn. Before the Red, he had seen apocalyptic movies and television shows depicting mass devastation and rubble. East Tampa fit that description to a certain degree, but places like this were simply vacant. If it weren't for his fellow soldiers around him, he felt as if the emptiness might swallow him whole.

2nd Platoon made its way down the street, one man on each side of the road carefully searching each passing window. At any second, a Lakeland Militiaman could leap around a corner or cut through a door, spraying bullets into their column. But the town remained silent, save for the cicadas.

Kessler bent to one knee and the men followed in suit behind any piece of cover they could find. Tyler lowered to a knee, resting his rifle on his leg. He kept watch over two nearby houses with thick vegetation growing behind them.

His feet were throbbing, and his shirt was soaked with sweat. His pack dug into his shoulders, full of extra food, water, and spare clothes. The small vest, also dripping in sweat, held two of his magazines, two bottles of water, an extra pair of socks wrapped in a plastic bag, and some iodine tablets for purifying water. If he had to leave his pack, his vest would allow him to survive long enough to make it back to East Tampa, or so Santana told him.

The sergeant knelt next to him. He pointed past Major Kessler, across a short clearing, and toward the rear of a large building. The back wall was littered with rusted air conditioning units, stained walls and upward climbing weeds.

"That's the backside of the school. We're gonna move two at a time across this field, 4th Platoon is waiting for us there. They know we're comin', and they know from which direction. You're gonna roll with Major Kessler first. Don't fuck it up."

"Roger, Sergeant, I won't." He was going to show Major Kessler and Sergeant Santana that he was an asset. That he was useful.

After a few moments, Major Kessler beckoned him over.

"You and I will take lead, son." His gruff voice inspired a certain grit within Tyler. "I believe that everyone should dive into the fire headfirst. Besides, I need my best shots covering our movement. You ready?"

"Ready, sir."

A mirror flashed across the clearing. Kessler nodded to Santana and the others, pointing their weapons across the field to cover their crossing.

Major Kessler began to run, and Tyler scurried at his side. Their labored breathing and rustling gear pounded through Tyler's head, but the great emptiness of Plant City swallowed every sound into its vast emptiness.

After what felt like an eternity, Tyler and Major Kessler reached the cover of a large air conditioning unit that seemed to be composed entirely of rust. Tyler could feel his heart pumping blood to every corner of his body. All the soreness, pain, and dehydration were long gone.

Be useful.

Not a second had passed before Tyler was pointing his weapon to the sides of the clearing. Major Kessler cracked a smile under his bushy mustache. "Good work, son."

Two by two, the remaining platoon crept across the open field and spread out against the wall behind Major Kessler and Tyler. A middle-aged redhead with a scraggly beard poked his head out of a nearby window.

"Major," he whispered. "Good to see you guys. The door's around that corner. We just unlocked it."

"Roger that."

The last man moved with Santana, and they began to crest the corner and file inside past Tyler and Kessler who stood guard at the door. Kessler looked carefully at the long tree line outstretched before them.

"I wouldn't count on staying here too long, Ballard," he said. "Things change. 4th Platoon has been moving around all day. I need their men to —"

Tyler wasn't sure what he saw or heard first. There was a series of bursts, the flickering of muzzle flashes from a secluded part of the tree line in the corner of his eye, and then the zipping and cutting of bullets spitting past him and slamming into the high school wall.

A bullet ripped through Major Kessler's skull, spattering blood and brain matter onto the wall behind him. The Major fell like a bag of rocks.

Tyler's mind froze, and his body froze with it. Kessler's mangled, lifeless body lay right in front of him. This monster of a man was reduced to — he didn't know what, exactly. It felt like a dream, and Tyler's gaze drifted up beyond the fallen Major to where he could see Santana, his rifle blazing back at the tree line. Brass was flying gently out of the side of Santana's rifle, pattering against the wall and onto the grass.

Santana whipped his head toward Tyler and extended a hand, yanking him across the wall and out of his dream-state. Tyler scrambled just inside the door, clutching his rifle close to his chest.

Santana fired several more shots out the doorway and ducked back inside.

"What the fuck, Ballard?! Next time someone shoots at you, shoot back."

The redhead was shooting out the same window. The shots were loud outside, but in here the sound bounced off the walls with a vengeance, hammering his eardrums unlike anything he had ever heard.

His mind was racing, but it wasn't exactly fear that had him frozen up out there. Or was it? He didn't know why his limbs had been turned to stone, but he knew he had to do better. He rose to his feet.

"Where do you want me, Sergeant?" he asked, and it felt as if his heart almost leapt out of his throat alongside his words.

"Pull security out of that goddamn window." Santana pointed out another side window, away from the shooting. Tyler did as he was told.

Tyler berated himself in his mind. *You knew things were going to go sideways. You didn't know how, but you knew. And you still froze like a dumbass.* Tyler pointed his rifle out the window, determined he would shoot if a bush so much as twitched in the wind. The image of Kessler laying with his head in pieces threatened to creep into his mind, but he pushed those thoughts aside with a squint down his sights.

"Slow your fire down, don't waste your ammo." Santana was taking charge of the other men. "Hold your fire unless you see movement."

"Roger, Sergeant," a militiaman said.

After a couple more shots the air went silent. Tyler suddenly became very conscious of his own breathing. Every inhale reminded him that he was just as "invincible" as Kessler; every exhale reminded him that those bullets could have just as easily ripped through his head instead.

"Ballard, you ready to fight now?"

"I'm ready, Sergeant." The words couldn't have come quicker out of his mouth.

"It's about fucking time. Come with me." Santana led him deeper into the school. He pointed the ETM to key positions around the building — a window here, a doorway there. "This place is too goddamn big to cover with our tiny-ass platoons," Santana said. "Stay tight as we move through."

Tyler's brother had a couple basketball games in this school before the Red, but it was the first time he had set foot inside its walls. It was a confusing maze of hallways, lockers, and doors, and yet Santana moved with confidence and speed. If Tyler didn't know any better, he would have thought that Santana had gone to school there. Maybe he had.

"Post up here. This is the back end, none of our guys are gonna be comin' around these corners. You see someone, smoke 'em. Understand?" Santana pointed down a hallway.

"I understand." Tyler dropped to a knee, peeking out around a corner with the muzzle of his M16.

"Good. I'm gonna be talking to 4th Platoon and figure out what our next move is."

Sean, the newcomer senior only to Tyler, was breathing hard on a knee just ten feet from Tyler, peering down another hallway.

"Did someone get shot?" His voice trembled.

"Major Kessler. He's — he's gone." Tyler kept his eyes on the hallway ahead, drawing every ounce of his strength to keep his eyes from misting and his head from clouding. Every door, locker, and corner in the abandoned hallway was under his barrel, and that's where he kept his focus. There was an opening to another hallway halfway down his own, forming a three-way intersection over which he presided. The end of his corridor only led to another hallway, perpendicular to his own.

"Major Kessler? No way."

More words would have meant more thought on the subject, and though Tyler didn't know much, he knew that thinking about things would have to come later. He watched his sector in silence.

But as he built the dam in his mind to one thought, another crept in. A memory, from before the Red. He remembered glancing at a television with a breaking news banner and a reporter standing outside of a school, painted with the red and blue lights of police cars. He remembered something about a shooting, or several shootings perhaps — the memory was gray now, only patches of the real thing. His father had shed a tear at the news, and his mother stared out the window and used words like "senseless" and "awful." He could feel the sadness of the event weigh in their hearts.

Such things were a way of life now. He thought that ought to break his heart, but he kept his attention on the hallway in front of him.

Gunfire erupted from somewhere in the hallways. The shots thundered through them, bouncing off every wall and making it impossible to tell which direction they originated from. Tyler wanted to whip his head around, to double check his surroundings for any movement.

Watch your sector, Tyler. He said it over and over, eyeing the hallway ahead and hoping Sean was doing the same to his flank.

The gunshots roared through the empty spaces, like a lumbering giant was clamoring his way closer and closer, each step a deafening boom. As the sounds grew louder, incoherent voices echoed with them.

In that moment, Tyler's life was dedicated to that hallway. He learned to walk so he could take a knee behind the corner overlooking the intersection in hallways. He learned to speak so he could communicate movement. And he learned to grasp things solely for the purpose of grasping that rifle in those quick minutes, ready to pull the trigger at any sign of movement.

Tyler flipped the safety off with his thumb and his finger caressed the trigger. He gazed at the lockers that lined the right side of the wall, and the papers strewn about the floor. He eyed the fire extinguisher hanging on the wall just across from the intersection's opening.

And then it happened: movement. A blur. A shuffle.

Tyler's heart sunk, raced, and stopped all at the same time. A tall man in a black windbreaker toting an AKM crested the hallway. He turned the corner and was facing the opposite direction from Tyler. Had Tyler been navigating these hallways alone, he knew there was a fifty percent chance that he would have made the same mistake.

Tyler raised his M16 to his eye, took a quick second to aim down his rusted iron sights, and pulled the trigger.

The lurch of the rifle surprised him, but the first bullet screamed through the man's lower back. Tyler pulled the trigger twice more, both rounds slamming into the wall behind his target. The man fell to the ground and writhed in pain, though he did not scream. He reached for his rifle, but Tyler took another quick second, aimed, and pulled the trigger again. The round went through the top of the man's head. It was not clean — the sculpture of his head was torn off, his skin and hair instantly turning into a seared mess of skull fragment, brain matter, and unrecognizable flesh.

A woman toting a shotgun came running into the same hallway, her eyes locked on the fallen man. Momentum had carried her sliding on her heels a bit further into the open than she probably anticipated. Tyler pulled the trigger again. Several rounds ricocheted on some lockers behind her, but the last round cracked through her leg the second she dove for cover. She wedged herself on the far side in a narrow gap between two lockers.

"What've you got?" Santana's voice appeared behind him.

"Two of 'em. I got the first guy. There's someone hiding behind those lockers on the right. I got her in the leg."

"Motherfuckers!" The woman screamed, half in agony and half in anger. She stuck her shotgun around the corner of the locker and let out a blind shot. Bits of cement rained down on Tyler and Santana's heads as pellets from buckshot scattered across the ceiling, far too high to pose any real threat to the two of them. Still, the shot caused Tyler to wince so hard he felt like he would implode, though the same feeling was what kept him from moving.

Both Santana and Tyler pulled their triggers, unleashing a wall of lead at the woman pinned behind the locker.

"Cover me, kid."

Santana moved forward with his rifle to his cheek. His body was like a tank, every movement deliberate and powerful, his legs moving forward and his hips square to the cowering shooter, but his upper body was fluid, making minor corrections to his aim as he moved.

"You're both fucking dead!" She screamed. "Your friends too
—"

Santana fired just as he had gotten a glimpse of her other foot, and she fell crashing beyond her cover. With another pull of his finger and a splatter of blood and bone, she was dead.

As if it were the next move in a dance of death, Santana didn't hesitate to grab the shotgun off her body, sling it on his back, and then grab the AKM and an extra easily grabbable magazine off the corpse with the black windbreaker.

Still keeping his eyes peeled down the hallway, Santana crept back to Tyler's position.

"Keep doin' what you're doin'. It's gonna be a long day, kid."

And with that, he was gone. Tyler shifted his attention back to the hallway. His hallway, once again still and lifeless.

His eyes kept drifting back to the carnage — at the man he had killed and the woman he had helped kill. They were living, functioning human beings with personalities and ideas only moments ago; now they were little more than piles of broken flesh on the ground. He wasn't sure if he should be sick to his stomach or proud that he did his job —

His ever-wandering mind was interrupted by another barrage of gunfire echoing through the school's hallways. *No time to think about any of that.* Tyler thumbed his safety, ready to flip it off once again.

"Let's go!" Santana and the redhead moved past Tyler with their weapons up. "We're gettin' the hell outta here." A long line of soldiers pushed past him, following the two leaders. Two stretchers carrying 4th Platoon's wounded bumped past him, two men on

LUKE RYAN

each side with their weapons slung across their backs. Tyler got up and moved with them, Sean right on his heels.

They maneuvered corner after corner. Someone sprayed a handful of rounds in their direction, but several of the militiamen fired back and the Lakeland shooters kept to their cover. For all the stories about Lakeland's weak militia and the indomitable strength of the ETM, Tyler felt that Lakeland had both the numbers and the firepower to push the ETM around. Their only disadvantage was that they were too spread out, but he knew that wouldn't last long.

In minutes, they reached the school's main entrance. There were broad windows across the front, but there wasn't an intact piece of glass on them — some were riddled with cracks, others were shattered entirely. Tyler and several others took cover behind the front desk, a long counter that stretched halfway across the room. Santana was speaking quickly to the redhead, both nodding with a mutual understanding of what steps would need to be taken next. Tyler admired their cool-headedness, superior tactical knowledge, and confidence despite losing Kessler.

Santana turned his attention to the militiamen itching their safeties. "Okay, 2nd Platoon is gonna move out first, using that line of cars as cover until we can get to those houses over there." He pointed out through a shattered window, down a line of cars and toward a cluster of houses. "4th Platoon will cover our movement. When we get there, we're gonna turn around and cover them. Any questions?"

There were none.

"Let's do it. 2nd Platoon on me, two man bounds. Remember they've got dudes in the tree line to our west."

"Um, Sergeant?" Tyler cleared his throat, almost afraid to ask.

"What?"

"Which… which way is west?"

Santana rolled his eyes but held his tongue. "Ford," he pointed at Sean. "Which way is west?"

"Uhhh, I don't know Sergeant."

"Then why the hell didn't you ask?" Santana jerked a hand in the direction to the right of the line of cars. "It's that way, get your asses moving."

They streamed out of the broken window in pairs. The sparse line of cars was relatively straight, but the gaps between them varied from almost-touching to a good-sprint's worth of open cement.

Once again, Tyler found himself with Sean. Now that they were neck deep in a fight, Tyler understood Santana's indignant anger at all the militiamen who struggled during the walk in. And though Sean didn't seem to be struggling so much with adrenaline in his veins and bullets in the air, Tyler desperately hoped that Sean wouldn't fall behind now.

For a split second, the air was thick with silence. The humidity was causing sweat to pour down every inch of Tyler's body, and in the silence he became aware of how thoroughly soaked in sweat he was.

Two militiamen took point and bounded forward, and Tyler and Sean were close behind them. They moved to the first car as soon as the cover was vacant.

That silence was short-lived.

The gunshots were distant and might as well have been shooting elsewhere, but Tyler caught a glimpse of the muzzle flashes along the tree line, and he felt the rounds whiz past his skull. Dust and bits of metal exploded into the air as several bullets struck the sedan he was using for cover. Sean cowered low, hiding behind the rear axle of the compact vehicle. Tyler swung his rifle over the top of the car and started shooting as accurately as he could toward the muzzle flashes. He felt his rifle click and paused a moment. He stared at his rifle in confusion, his mind turning at why it could have stopped functioning —

Another round of muzzle flashes erupted from the trees and Tyler felt bits of metal pepper his face as more rounds slammed into the car. One zipped through the car and exited just inches from his hip. It was a sharp reminder to take cover, so he did. He looked into the chamber of his weapon and ejected his magazine — empty. *Duh.*

Tyler stowed the empty in his back pocket as Santana had instructed him. He threw a fresh one in and was about to swing back over the top and start shooting again.

"Ballard!" Santana's voice cut through the gunfire and Tyler turned his head. He was taking cover one car behind him. "Bound up to the next car and shoot under from behind the wheels!" Tyler yelled in affirmation, but his soft voice was drowned in the gunfire. Santana glared at Sean. "Ford! Get your ass up and start shooting!"

"Come on!" Tyler grabbed Sean's collar as Santana had earlier grabbed his, and they dashed to the next car. Tyler threw his body onto the ground behind the front axle, aimed his rifle at the tree line and started firing. He knew it would be a miracle if he hit anything, but the muzzle flashes were spreading out and lowering in frequency, so their fire was doing something.

"Bound again!" Santana said. They bounded to the next car. Tyler slid low and fired. Sean managed a couple shots where he could.

When they reached the houses, they had a near perfect view of the terrain surrounding them. A toppled truck served as good cover overlooking the tree line, and the three houses were clumped together facing out with windows in each direction. 2nd Platoon flooded the houses, Tyler moving to the second floor of the one furthest east and looking out over a nearby street.

The room he occupied had been a nursery once, but the windowpane had broken, and the world had inched its way in. The walls and carpet just inside were painted with water stains and mold. Two stuffed animals remained in the windowsill, stuck there in the clutches of growing mold; Tyler nudged them off with the barrel of his M16 and poked his muzzle out the window down the street.

"Someone get on that street down south!" Santana's voice boomed through the house's thin walls.

"Already got it!" Tyler said.

"Roger. McKinney, Dawson, hammer that tree line!"

More scrambling, more yelling, more gunshots; Tyler focused on his street. On the bushes to the left and the oaks to the right. On the bent stop sign at the four-way intersection. He knew now that *this* was what his life led up to.

A handful of figures came dashing across the left side of the street, heading for the concealment of vegetation on the right. Tyler immediately pulled the trigger and sent rounds screeching toward them. One woman shot blindly back, but the rest focused on sprinting across the street. Tyler couldn't tell if he hit any of them, but he was pretty sure his shots were all too low.

"I've got five people running over toward the tree line!" He yelled back into the house. Santana was already moving through the doorway.

"Roger that, keep your eyes on that road. And pull your muzzle back from that window." With that, he was gone. Tyler shuffled a bit further back, keeping his muzzle from poking out the edge of the window.

More barrages of gunfire from 2nd and 4th Platoon, ripping through the forest like a hellacious bulldozer of fire and lead.

As Tyler kept a watchful eye on his street, he lamented his inability to shoot well. He wondered if the rest of the platoon was in such need of more training, or if he was alone in his incompetence.

Focus on the street. This is your street. That's what you have control over right now, and that's all that matters right now.

Tyler heard voices behind him — Santana and the redhead with the scraggly beard.

"We've got them pinned down. You guys head south and flank their asses, I think we can get the upper hand here."

52

"Roger that, I'm going to keep Pruitt and Leblanc here, they fucking suck. I don't want to be dragging their asses through the woods."

"That's fine, just don't forget to pick 'em up before you leave. I don't want 'em." They chuckled under their breaths and Tyler heard their footsteps shuffle downstairs.

"Alright, 4th Platoon! On my ass, we're rollin' out."

"2nd Platoon: on my mark, start layin' into those shit-heads. I want at least one window firing at all times, understand?" Santana yelled.

"Roger, Sergeant!" the house cried back.

Tyler felt Santana's hand on his shoulder. "Hey kid, 4th Platoon is gonna be rolling down this street here in a sec —"

"Yeah, I heard you guys. You're hitting them from the side, right?"

Santana almost smiled. "That's right. Don't shoot 'em. And when I say fire, no need to shoot. Got it?"

"Got it, Sergeant."

Santana moved back to the main firing line. "FIRE!"

The front of the house erupted in a bombardment of terrifying firepower as Tyler sat in the upper back side of the house. He watched as the majority of 4th Platoon left through the back door, down the street, and into the forest. They disappeared among the trees to take Lakeland's scattered militia by surprise.

Before long, Tyler could hear the groups trading volleys of gunshots in the woods. Screams of anger, terror, and pain drifted through the trees and into his window.

"Cease fire!" Santana commanded, and all shooting from the house stopped.

It occurred to Tyler that this entire time he had not once thought of his brother or his dog Lacey. No thoughts or hopes of seeing the red truck with Anthony's killers. Every decision, every movement, and every thought had been dedicated to each moment as it occurred, and each one seemed more important to him in those seconds than anything had ever seemed to him his entire life.

It wasn't long until all was quiet, save for the cicadas.

Tyler's blister had returned with a fiery vengeance. His sweat glands were going haywire, itching and turning red after a day of relentless summer heat and movement. His makeshift sling had spent the entire day digging and cutting into his shoulders.

The sun was going down, sending its final rays through the tiny gaps in the canopy leaves, and Tyler tried to think of that instead of the pain.

2nd Platoon was in the lead with 4th Platoon in tow. Major Kessler had been their only loss, but besides the initial two casualties, 4th Platoon had a man shot in the stomach and leg during their final flanking maneuver. They carried him on one of 2nd Platoon's litters that they had recently scavenged from a hospital in downtown Tampa; 4th Platoon was able to carry the others.

The platoons were not able to recover Major Kessler's body, and Tyler couldn't help but picture it under the Floridian sun, dissolving into the dirt like he had seen the bodies dissolve in the mass graves after the Red. He wondered, if he went back to look for it, if he would smell that same godless, wretched smell.

As feet turned into miles, Tyler's thoughts wandered back to shooting that nameless man in the black windbreaker. Should he feel pleasure for avenging his murdered brother? Shame for abruptly ending another human life? He felt neither, and he wondered if that ought to concern him too.

Another movie played in his head over and over: Major Kessler and the bullet cutting through his face. His strong, mustached head bursting open like a watermelon. The thought made his stomach turn over.

Tyler had held Major Kessler in high regard ever since Henry Warren, a nine-year-old orphan down the street, had told stories of him with those wide, brown eyes of his. Those stories, each of Kessler's heroic battles, had been ingrained in Tyler's head from the moment heroics were required after the Red.

And though Kessler had become a mentor and a respected leader to Tyler, there were no tears to be shed. And he wasn't sure why he didn't cry. He had watched war movies with Anthony, where soldiers would fall to their knees and cry until they had no tears left. Tyler cried when his parents died. He cried when his brother died; he even cried over his slain dog. He wasn't crying now. But it was a long walk, so he chalked it up to exhaustion.

"Friendlies comin' up from our front. Don't shoot 'em." Santana's voice gave rest to his busy mind.

Ten soldiers were headed in the opposite direction. They were well equipped with clean rifles, plate carriers with ceramic plates, and up to six magazines each. The packs on their backs were worn but well-kept hiking backpacks, which Tyler had looked far and wide to find when the Red first hit.

None of them spoke and they all kept their eyes on the ground or on the surrounding, darkening forest.

"Who's that?" Tyler asked after they had passed.

"Gray Platoon," Santana said. "They work directly under orders from Mayor Whitley. They're gonna go see if any of those dickheads are still rollin' around in Plant City."

"I didn't recognize any of them."

"They pull from central Tampa mostly. And they keep to themselves. Tactically they're okay, but they do a lotta badass shit. They'll finish off anyone still movin' out there."

Tyler had not realized there was a tactical military unit outside of the regular ETM. Something in his mind felt uneasy at the thought of a unit like that, outside the influence or even knowledge of the average East Tampa citizen.

Santana must have sensed his internal wheels grinding away. He took a long look at Tyler. "They're a good bunch of guys, man. They're prolly gonna be the ones that smoke the dudes who got your brother. If we didn't already get the guy who pulled the trigger on Kessler, they'll get 'em for sure too. And I know a few of 'em. Good bunch of guys."

Tyler figured Santana was right, as usual. They continued to ruck through the late evening.

The platoons returned to East Tampa just before midnight. They ate, washed themselves in baths of lukewarm water, and most of them crawled into their bunks.

Tyler laid on his mattress, its springs digging into his shoulder, partly wishing he was back in his own house he had spent the last four years sleeping in. He wished he could roll over on his side to see if Anthony was awake in the next bed over. Alas, those days were firmly in the past.

The members of the ETM had been allowed to sleep in their homes at first, but that was soon deemed too high of a risk. If there were any attacks, they would need a united response. The engineers of the town modified a police station to suit their needs, and the married members of the ETM were permitted to live in houses on the adjacent street.

Tyler thought the feeling deep in his gut was homesickness, but he did not want to go home. A house without Anthony was just a graveyard.

He stared up at the distorted springs and stains from the vacant bunk above him for an hour or so, playing with the shapes in his mind. One looked like a baby's bottle, another like a grenade.

Tyler's entire body yearned for sleep, but his eyes refused to close — they would barely even blink.

When he realized that any attempt at sleep was a losing battle, Tyler slipped on his flip flops to give his heels a break, and he left the barracks for a walk.

Tyler found Sergeant Santana staring out into some obscure row of houses that were engulfed in darkness. He had built a small, smoldering fire and was drinking from a dented flask. Swaying rhythmically in his drunkenness, Santana was still managing to thumb fresh 5.56 rounds into his magazines.

"Hey, Sergeant."

"I got a drink in my hand, you don't gotta call me that," he said without looking up.

"Uh… alright." Outside of a firefight, foregoing the militaristic formalities felt awkward.

"He's fucking gone, man. Add him to the list." Santana poured a splash of whiskey onto the ground and took another swig, "We're just warm breaths in cold air, kid."

He took another sip and sighed. Tyler put his hands in his pockets and looked out to where Santana was staring. There was nothing but a dark and endless night.

"You did good out there," Santana said. "I was worried at first. You had that deer-in-the-headlights look, but you stepped up." Another gulp, bigger this time. "Some piece of shit from Lakeland killed Kessler. Lakeland. I used to go drink there with my boys. This isn't like the war before the Red. Every poor motherfucker you kill was an American once, that you prolly saw at the gas station or some shit… now… I don't know what the hell is going on. I don't know why they decided to act like animals, but here we are. But you… you did good out there, and that's what counts. That's all that counts."

For a moment, Santana stared into the dirt.

"One day, maybe you and I, one day we're gonna take those animals down. We're gonna show them that East Tampa don't fall to nobody. And Mayor Hatch — you know she's only got one eye, right?"

"I've heard that."

"One eye, like a fuckin' pirate. We're gonna put a bullet in her head, then we're gonna line up the rest of those shitheads and put bullets in them too. They all gotta go, kid. They all gotta go."

Santana was a tired soul, though his body could take another twenty miles in a heartbeat. Maybe even fifty. The rough man shook his head and continued to push rounds into the magazine in his hand.

He offered Tyler some whiskey, but Tyler declined. He couldn't quite stomach the taste of liquor.

3

*"I got me some pre-redness pop right here, brothers. You might roll them eyes at
the sound of synthesizers and syncopated rhythms — God knows I did before
the redness — but you can't deny, boy does it take you back to those days when
them kids were the biggest concern, and we weren't worried about buryin' our
kin in mother earth, we was just worried about kids buryin' them heads in the
sand a lil' too deep.*
*"Get ready for some electric high-hats and some wobble bass, all on 101.7, the
soundtrack to the end of the world."*

AFTER their equipment was checked and double checked, 2nd
Platoon was released the next day to wander the town as they
pleased. Tyler felt pangs of hunger in his gut, but the thought of
more standard ETM rations did not sit well — there was only so
much dry bread, squeezable cheese, and Florida oranges he could
take. Only on a couple occasions in the previous three weeks had
he found the time to seek out some canned fruit or beans from his
old stash.

The market was centrally located on Hillsborough Road, starting at an intersection just three blocks south of his first house as a child. It tapered off several blocks toward the center of Tampa. The street was lined with stalls, mostly stocked with equipment or food scavenged by locals and traveling merchants. An attempt had initially been made to re-institute some kind of currency, but it never stuck. Tyler figured money only seemed important when you could strategize on how to spend it. These days, most people were trying to survive the week — valuable paper wouldn't help with that nearly as much as a box of ammunition or a car battery.

Anthony had stumbled upon a pallet of canned pinto beans three months back; they spent an entire night carrying the beans back to their house. Tyler had used those beans to trade for just about everything he needed that entire month.

The East Tampa Marketplace was buzzing, as usual. The sun was high, and humidity shrouded them like a warm, wet blanket. The crowd lurched here and there as a formless chaos, teeming with patched clothing and bags full of tradable items.

A woman with a wide, toothless smile stood behind several cans of soup and knives strewn across an empty burlap sack.

"What can I do for ya, honey?"

"How about some of that soup?" Tyler said.

"What've you got in that there bag of yours?"

"Pinto beans." He had five cans in his backpack.

"I'll do a one-for-one with ya. How does that sound?"

"Sounds perfect." They traded, three cans of beans for three cans of soup.

"Young boy like you might need a knife. These are bitter days, sweetie. Ya never know who 'yer gonna have to get to pokin'."

"I'm alright, thanks." He meandered to the next stall, and then the next.

The Motel Royale had been converted to a brothel about two years back. It was the second major brothel that had opened in the area since the Red, and patrons were often spilling out into the street, even in mid-day. They embraced the "post-apocalypse" theme with clever signs that read, *"Fuck like it's the end of the world (oh wait, it is)"* and *"It was an apocalyptic disease, not an apoca-limp-dick one."* Women sat out front in scant leather and lingerie, enticing men to use their last precious resources on the one desire that had remained constant before and after the Red. A brunette woman caught his eye, and before he could look to the ground, she gestured a seductive finger his way and licked her lips. Her dress rode up to her thighs, her low-cut shirt — he ignored her and concentrated on walking forward.

Anthony always told him to stay away from those places, that they were like most places after the Red — they sought only to take, and the worst of them will take from you and make you think that you wanted to give in the first place. Tyler always felt that he had some sort of powerful moral drive, but he was never certain of it. He always felt a deep need for guidance from someone older, more confident, and wiser — he needed Anthony. Still, Tyler knew his parents would have agreed with his older brother, so he kept his eyes locked on the stalls and their vendors.

At least you can just do what you think they would have wanted, he said to himself. He hoped one day he would have some semblance of moral confidence, but until then he would have to use the memory of their compasses.

And as he passed, he glanced one last time at the women of the Motel Royale. Something about them seemed tired. He had noticed that look before, but only now — only after the firefight that took Kessler's life — did he recognize it in himself, though he didn't have a word for it.

Tyler veered further into the street, hiding from the entire dilemma in a mass of people. The further he meandered west, the less food and more weapons and ammunition he would encounter. They would be strewn across plastic tables and warped wooden stalls, guarded by leathery-faced vendors whose eyes only cared for business. In the early years, they would look down on Tyler and scoff if he tried to purchase a weapon or ammunition, which he had on occasion though he never found a use for them, nor did he really understand how they were used. Still, as the years went by, they didn't scoff anymore. They just sold.

It became apparent to Tyler that he was surrounded by malnourished faces who almost seemed to have forsaken life itself, and Tyler often wondered if he looked as miserable. Death had undone many.

And yet among the sea of skeletons, he spotted a living man. He was of average height, well-built, and his t-shirt was relatively clean. Frayed strips of cloth were wrapped around his neck and arms to shield him from the sun, and a pair of dark sunglasses hid his eyes. Tyler considered him for a moment — he recognized most faces in East Tampa at this point, and certainly would remember anyone who looked like that.

The man picked a rifle off a table to inspect it. He handled it like it was an extension of his own body, checking the chamber, disassembling the main pieces —

If he was in the ETM, I would have definitely seen him by now. Maybe he's in Gray Platoon.

But there was some undefined quality within this man that even Gray Platoon didn't seem to possess, though he admittedly knew very little about Gray Platoon. Was it confidence? Expertise? Tyler's curiosity overpowered his sheepishness, and he approached the stall, pretending to inspect a box of 7.62 ammunition that lay on the table. The can was spray-painted black, but most of the paint was scratched or peeling off.

"Are you in the ETM?" He didn't know what else to ask, so he was direct. "I haven't seen you around."

The man paused from reassembling the rifle in his hands. He turned his head toward Tyler.

"You're in the militia?" His voice was low, almost soft spoken but with a distant roughness to it.

"I am." Tyler said.

"What are you, twelve?"

Tyler felt a pang of indignation. "The fighting age is sixteen."

"You don't look sixteen."

Tyler swallowed his next argument — the man had a point. It was another month before he would turn sixteen.

"So you're not in the ETM then," Tyler said.

"Hell no."

Tyler had never heard anyone speak of the ETM in anything but high regard. The way in which this stranger brushed it off like a fly in his ear sent Tyler's head for a spin.

"Ballard, get your ass over here." Tyler recognized Santana's voice behind him, and he turned to see the sergeant standing a couple of stalls over. Tyler glanced back at the mysteriously frustrating man, who went back to his weapon as if the conversation never happened.

"Better find an umbrella in one of these shops," the stranger said out of the corner of his mouth to Tyler as he drifted over to Santana. "Storm's on its way. Just sayin'."

"What the hell are you doing talkin' to him?" Santana demanded, somehow managing to remain hushed and domineering at the same time.

"I was just wondering who he was," Tyler said.

"He's one of those fucking dudes who ambushes caravans and shit. Takes what they have for himself." Santana spat at the thought of him. "He steals, rapes, and pillages then comes here for more supplies, acting like he's hot shit."

"I think I've heard of them before. Aren't they called Marauders or something?"

"They might used to call themselves that," Santana said. "Probably thought it was cool or somethin', I guess it sounds better than 'highwaymen' or some shit. Most of them are dead now — you dedicate your life to fuckin' people down, eventually they're gonna fuck you back."

"Why do we let him in here?"

"Probably brings in a lotta trade. He wouldn't come to trade alongside people he's stolen from. Best case scenario he's stealin' from those Lakeland assholes. Either way, he's bad news, kid."

"Lakeland. Yeah, hopefully." Tyler had heard these "Marauders" described as common criminals. He glanced back at the man, who strode away from the stall and melted back into the crowd, glancing up at the cloudless sky. If he was a criminal, he certainly didn't look common.

Major Kessler's funeral was the next day. There were over a hundred attendees; several people spoke and then they erected a headstone in a cemetery Mayor Whitley himself had recently opened, commemorating those who had served East Tampa in a remarkable capacity. The Mayor had approved Kessler's burial there, though they had no body to bury.

4

*"I was up shovelin' through the piles of records in the attic, and ya know what
I found? I think you'll recognize him — he's the heart n' soul of rock n' roll,
brother. This man did so many drugs, slept with so many unsavory women…
he's put out some albums I think we could've all done without, but hoo momma,
did he put out some classics too. For every mistake he barreled out, my friends,
he barreled out some real doozies too.
"Just remember where you heard all those beautiful mistakes: 101.7, the
soundtrack to the end of the world."*

TYLER wasn't sure if he should focus on his feet — the terrain was
uneven and it took immense focus to keep from stumbling over
roots and vines — or if he should focus on his surroundings. There
were reports of defensive Lakeland militia patrolling the area, and
as far as Tyler was concerned, every tree was a possible piece of
cover for a scout, and every half-collapsed structure was a hideout
for nefarious activity.

Gray Platoon had provided the ETM with intelligence suggesting that Lakeland was gearing up for a head-on offensive, which, as far as Tyler had heard, was unusual — East Tampa had far superior numbers and training. Mayor Whitley had described the Lakeland Militia as "civilians playing at soldiers who don't seem to be able to organize, let alone civilize" — Major Kessler had called them a "a group of country boys who aren't as familiar with effective strategy and tactics as they think." Santana just called them "pussies."

"You're not my first pick, but you've got potential, kid. You're gonna roll with my top twelve guys, see how recon works firsthand. Don't you dare leave my side," Santana had said in his hallmark calloused tone. Hours later, Tyler found himself among the dozen men creeping out of a clump of Floridian jungle and toward the back end of a strip mall. They moved under the cover of darkness, and the buzz of the cicadas was replaced with the chirping of the crickets.

This strip mall had not fared so well from the weather over the years. The roof on the right side had caved in, leaving the interior exposed to Florida's constant barrage of wind and rain in the autumn months. Any trace of sign or lettering had fallen and smashed through the windows — vegetation now claimed both the exterior walls and the interior offices and stores.

The point man in Tyler's formation was a country boy in his early twenties whom everyone called Dusky; he hailed from Brooksville, Florida, and he was one of the few who knew those woods better than Sergeant Santana himself.

Dusky crept up to peek inside the first dilapidated store of the strip mall. Through the thick darkness, Tyler could make out slabs of cement wall that had half-collapsed and formed a precarious ramp from the back of the strip mall to the roof, though the climb would prove tedious. Rebar protruded from awkward angles and vines wrapped their way up the improvised ramp, creating a slick, dewy surface.

There was no telling what would shift under the weight of any of them, if it could support the entire recon element, or if the whole thing would give way at the first press of a boot.

"Ballard, Dusky, Nat, we're gonna check out this roof. Climb carefully, don't make a bunch of fuckin' noise," Santana whispered. "The rest of you set up security, stay out of sight. Roger?"

"Roger, Sergeant," they whispered.

The four crept toward the deteriorating structure while the rest of 2nd Platoon's reconnaissance team evaporated into the woods behind them. They stepped out into the moonlight as it poured its light onto the strip mall and the surrounding pavement. While the increased visibility made the climb easier, Tyler realized that the moon was not partial to one faction or the other — it would reveal Lakeland and East Tampa militiamen alike.

Tyler felt another cold drop of sweat swim down his neck. He struggled to suppress his labored breathing while watching his every step. A simple slip and fall near an enemy position could give away their position and get him killed. Get them all killed.

They were looking for major troop movements, but, so far, every clearing, building, and patch of jungle proved empty. The Red had brought death, and death brought a great emptiness in its wake. A terrible, unnerving silence that Tyler would have replaced with a hundred enemies if he had the choice. But there was nothing.

The first two climbed up the makeshift ramp to the roof of the building so slowly that it felt like minutes before they crested the top and crept onward. Santana and Tyler pulled security at the base with one eye and watched their route up the rubble with the other. When the ramp was clear, Santana and Tyler began to inch up themselves. Tyler grabbed every piece of rebar and stepped in every crevice Dusky had grabbed. If it was stable enough for Dusky, it would probably be stable enough for him too.

As they slipped onto the roof, Dusky shot his fist in the air and froze — the others froze with him. Tyler held his breath, his eyes and ears burning for movement or noise. First there was nothing. In the moonlight, he could make out a street riddled with cracks and overgrowth, and a second, more devastated strip mall on the opposite side of a four-lane road. On their side of the road, there were immense, almost ancient trees in the median between their position and the neighboring strip malls on either side.

Then Tyler's ears caught what must have caught Dusky's attention; it sounded like a human voice. As he leaned his head forward, Tyler could discern the sounds of murmuring in the dark, tired voices speaking quietly to one another.

Santana silently directed everyone into a single line parallel to the strip mall's front, and they began to crawl forward on their hands and toes. As Tyler crested the edge of the building, his eyes first made out two trash cans spewing out a lot of smoke and a little light from a handful of dying embers.

A truck sat between the trash cans, and a couple sat side-by-side on the tailgate, speaking in hushed voices to another man leaning on a streetlight nearby, an amber dot glistening at his face as he smoked a cigarette.

Tyler's eyes grew wide. The truck was red. The two men. The woman.

Memories flooded his mind. He thought of that night, of how they pulled up in front of his house, of how they opened fire into his parent's old bedroom, and of how he watched as Anthony's body was ripped apart. How Lacey had tucked her tail and bolted out the door Tyler forgot to lock and was met with the sounds of a set of roaring rifles.

Tyler gripped his rifle so tight it began to shake, and he aimed it directly at the group of murderers. He knew he couldn't shoot them without cause, but if shooting started, he would be the first of the ETM to pull the trigger. Of that he was sure.

He glanced over at Santana, who kept a careful eye on those below, but was also scanning both ways down the road. Tyler waved at him, but the sergeant was too focused to notice.

"Sergeant…" Tyler whispered.

Santana whipped his head in Tyler's direction. *What the fuck*, he mouthed as he shushed Tyler with a finger. He crawled back behind cover and over to Tyler's position.

"That's them," Tyler said, quieter than a whisper.

"What?"

"The guys who killed my brother."

In that moment, a light beamed across them. The four of them ducked back out of view from those below, and the light extended beyond them as it appeared to light up the entire area. In the same moment, the light turned to the red truck below. As the light turned away, the sounds of engines arrived.

Trucks.

Tyler lifted his head slightly to spot four trucks as they arrived from the north end of the street. The vehicles were loaded with armed men and women, and the front and rear vehicles were equipped with large, police spotlights that swiveled in every direction. The lead vehicle shot the light toward the roof again, and Tyler snapped his head back down. After a couple seconds of silence, the light retracted and continued its search elsewhere, hunting for movement in the night.

Again, Tyler was the first to raise his head. He felt compelled to keep that truck in view, lest it drive away and be lost to another night.

The inbound trucks came to a squealing stop; its occupants mumbled a few unintelligible words to the man smoking near the red truck, and then they drove on. Their lights turned to the road ahead and the trees on either side of it and disappeared around the next corner.

Santana backed off the edge of the roof, put one arm in the air, and rotated it. He was rallying them to leave the roof — Tyler figured they would follow the newly discovered convoy. He glanced at the red truck and back to Santana. Dusky and Nat were already beginning to climb down.

Santana stared at Tyler, bewildered at his hesitation. He threw his arms up in the air. Tyler slid back toward Santana. "I can stay. I can watch them while you guys go."

"What the fuck are you talking about?" Santana whispered back. "Get your ass down there. We'll find them later, kid."

"We can't just leave them —"

"You hear that?" The woman's voice pierced the silence from below. Santana grabbed Tyler by the back of the collar and forced his face to the ground. Tyler lay as flat to the rooftop as possible; Santana unslung his rifle.

"Hear what?" one of the men below asked.

"I don't know, voices or somethin'."

"You wanna call it in?"

"Uh…" Tyler could not discern their words anymore.

Santana began to raise his head to peek over the side when another flashlight blazed over the rooftops. He ducked just in time and put his mouth right next to Tyler's ear. He spoke with a level of gravity that put a lump in Tyler's throat. "If you don't get off this roof right now, I'm going to beat the shit out of you. I don't care if they catch us and shoot us, I am going to fuck you up."

Tyler didn't look back. He clutched his rifle and crept down the back of the building.

A million thoughts raced through his head all at once: he didn't understand how Santana didn't care about his brother's murderers. Isn't that why they were there? To bring justice to Lakeland's door? He also didn't understand how he could be so stupid, how he could jeopardize a mission because of his personal vendettas. He didn't understand why Santana stopped him, and he didn't understand why Santana didn't stop him sooner. His thoughts were a violent, silent ocean, crashing among one another.

At the bottom of the building's backside, Santana grabbed Tyler's collar again and threw him into the tree line. Just as they took cover behind a mess of leaves and vines, a flashlight crested the side of the building and shot across the cement slab. Tyler could see that it was the woman, and her eyes followed the flashlight like a hawk's across an empty desert.

Tyler scurried behind the trunk of a southern magnolia next to Dusky. The rest of the recon element crouched silently in the brush, watching the woman's every move. Dusky raised his rifle, as did two others. Tyler shuffled to a knee and raised his rifle as well — Santana's hand grabbed his muzzle and pointed it to the ground. He gave no explanation and simply shook his head. Tyler wanted to melt into the dark, and his eyes followed his muzzle to the dirt.

The woman took a few steps into the vacant lot behind the strip mall. She shone the light onto the fallen portion of the building and onto the sides of the roof, then she scaled the ramp just high enough to peer over the rooftop.

As she hopped back down, her flashlight dashed across the tree line, dancing through the leaves. For a split second, the light illuminated Santana and Dusky's faces and shirts. Dusky put his palm on his safety, dampening the sound as he switched from safe to semi.

After an eternally long minute, the woman clicked off her light and they could hear the crunching of leaves as she left.

Dusky let out a sigh of relief. Santana whispered in his ear, rallied the rest, and counted them as they moved out. He grabbed

Tyler's shoulder, almost lifting the boy off his feet, and shoved him in their direction of movement.

"You risked every one of our lives out there." After a mile into the woods, Santana had begun to verbalize those rooftop expressions. "You think we haven't all lost something to those motherfuckers? You think I don't wanna pull the goddamn trigger on all of 'em? Except I'm not a dumbass who's willing to let my own people die just because I'm pissed. Did you see the radios on their hips? Did you see that entire convoy that passed through? One shot. ONE. SHOT. And we've bit off more than we can chew. We're taking heavy casualties and hoping we get out alive."

Tyler wished Santana would just punch him. He wished he would throw him to the ground and beat him into a bloody mass of flesh and bone, but instead the words just kept on coming.

"What do you think Kessler would say? What do you think your brother would say? Gettin' us killed because you wanted to shoot some people. I wanna shoot 'em too! But if you don't got no common sense, then you don't got a place in this platoon. I brought you on this mission, I put you on the fucking point team because I thought you were hot shit after that last contact. And that was my bad, I'll take the blame for not seeing you for what you really are. I should be better at identifying assholes who don't have the simple ability to control themselves around people they don't like."

With a heavy smack that reverberated through Tyler's head, Santana stormed off to the front of the formation. His mission had been accomplished: Tyler felt a crushing sense of worthlessness that was entirely foreign to him. Through his younger teenage years, his day-to-day youthful angst and loneliness, even the helplessness as his parents slowly died in front of him — he realized that this was the first time that he really felt that he had no value at all. He didn't have it in him to stand up and take revenge, and he didn't have it in him to do what he was told and complete the mission successfully. As a result, no one alive loved him and no one nearby liked him.

Tyler wished he could crawl into a hole and wither away, but he marched on. They were plowing through some of the thickest vegetation that Florida had to offer, its vines and weeds reaching out, grasping for his weapon and gear like fingers with ill intent. Tyler yanked away from them in frustration, and he hated them almost as much as he hated himself.

His mind reeled at the thought of getting back to the barracks and hearing more from Sergeant Santana. For all its deadly snakes and unforgiving rains, the jungle was at least simple — no reprimand, no honor or shame, just plain hardship and indifference.

As the reconnaissance element continued to advance, Tyler felt a steady breeze against his face. Clouds were forming in front of the moon, and the well-lit forest floor began to darken. Before long, he could hardly make out the next soldier ahead. The formation grew close together, careful not to lose sight of each other as they plodded through miles of swampland.

The man in front of him abruptly halted, holding up his right hand in a fist. Tyler repeated the signal, and those behind him did the same. They all fell to a knee and faced out, searching the darkened trees for a shot at some wandering Lakeland militia.

The soldier ahead leaned forward to listen to the whispers of the next man in line. He offered a thumbs up, turned, and leaned toward Tyler.

"Road crossing coming up," he muttered. "Get ready to move."

Tyler repeated it to the soldier behind him.

Soon the line was up and moving again. Each soldier followed the next like lemmings, circling around trees half-sunken in mud and shoots of bamboo. Leaves scraped across Tyler's face and his legs scraped against rocks that cut through the mud and toward the sky. Another vine caught the front sight post of his rifle, reminding himself that they were still in enemy territory, Tyler suppressed his urge to yank through the vine. He filled his lungs with air and let out a long but silent exhale then carefully pushed the vine aside and continued onward.

It wasn't long before Tyler could make out the road ahead. It was a paved street, two lanes wide, and it curved sharply through the woods. The trees were too dense to see what was down the next bend, not fifty feet in either direction.

Two ETM soldiers were posted behind cover, facing in opposite directions down the road. Tyler took a knee next to one, waiting as each person dashed to the other side, one at a time. When it was Tyler's turn, he kept his head low and rifle ready as he flew across the street. He felt naked on that road, exposed for the whole world to see and open fire.

But there was no gunfire, and Tyler slid next to the rest of the recon element where Sergeant Santana kept a close count of everyone. Without his close attention, Tyler knew how easy it would be to lose track of someone in that kind of all-encompassing darkness.

Just as Tyler watched the next ETM militiaman cross the street, headlights shot down the road. Night blasted into day as trucks veering around the corner illuminated both lanes and their surrounding trees with their headlights. The first pickup truck was outfitted with a mounted M249 light machine gun, swiveling to the cockroaches it spotted in the open.

The automatic weapon roared to life in the same instant, spewing out lead across the pavement. One ETM man was caught halfway across — he dropped to the ground and scrambled to the far side of the road, where the others had already begun to return fire.

Tyler wasn't sure how many were stuck on the other side of the road. He crawled behind a hefty red cedar, shoved his barrel in the direction of the muzzle flashes, and jerked the trigger.

The machine gun turned in response, cutting away at the cedar and pushing him down into the dirt. Splinters, dirt, and rock fragmented past him — Tyler rolled down to lower ground to escape the flurry of lead and fire to seek better cover.

Several feet away, Sergeant Santana rose to a knee and opened fire, but he too found his face in the dirt, scrambling away from the heavy rain of 5.56.

"We got four more guys on the other side, see if you can see 'em. I'll cover you!" Santana said, all of his disappointment and rage lost to the throes of necessity.

Santana crawled to a berm and swung his M4 over its crest. He managed to spit a few rounds out toward the trucks, drawing their fire and giving Tyler a precious second to poke his head out and snatch a glimpse of the other side of the road. He could make out all four figures, two of them lit up by their own muzzle flashes as they returned fire, two of them bobbing their heads with every lull in machine gun fire, desperately searching for a moment to dash across.

Just as he was about to duck back behind cover, Tyler spotted one of the figures stand up and sprint over the pavement. He ran wildly with his hands over his head, like they could possibly shield him. The mounted gun was not forgiving. It raged across the open road and slammed into the poor man — one round of 5.56 sheared off a chunk of his lower leg, and another ripped through his stomach. He fell face first onto the pavement, screaming in agony.

"Shit!" Santana had seen it too.

"Sergeant, if you can draw their fire, I can grab him. I can make it." Tyler's heart threatened to pound out of his chest, but he couldn't watch the man die in the street.

Santana nodded. He slid deeper into the woods, increasing the distance from himself and Tyler. When he found a clump of trees that served as suitable cover, the sergeant nestled behind it and started shooting. By now, the rest of the truck had dismounted and the entire group shifted their fire toward Santana, mowing down limbs and leaves between them. The men of the ETM fired back where they could, though most were still scrambling for cover or blindly returning fire only to have their bullets flutter harmlessly into the trees and the sky.

Santana struck one of the dismounted soldiers in the chest before the machine gun swiveled toward him and forced him to hunker back down.

Tyler dug his foot into a root, pushing off it and thrusting himself into the road. His whole body clenched, bracing for impact — every second that ticked by without a 5.56 tearing through his flesh was a miracle.

He flew into the road and shoved his arms under the wounded man's armpits, who cried out in agony — not a clear scream but a dazed moan that would follow Tyler into the quiet moments of the rest of his life. Tyler grit his teeth as he heaved the ETM militiaman off the pavement and into the safety of the wilderness. He could feel the man's warm blood soaking into his clothes and he noticed that, as he dragged him away, the man's foot stayed behind.

Just as he dropped the man behind cover off the road, Tyler caught a glimpse of the truck's position, now illuminated by the muzzle flashes of the M249 and its accompanying, dismounted gunmen. There was a short stone wall running parallel to the Lakeland truck's position, off to their side in a dark, inconspicuous cluster of trees — Tyler didn't know much, but he knew that someone shooting from behind that wall would be able to riddle that truck with holes, no problem.

The M249 ceased fire with heavy *ca-chunk*, and its gunner snapped open its feed tray in a frantic effort to clear a malfunction. It wasn't long before they were up and firing again, but it gave Tyler and the wounded man just enough time to reach solid cover. In that same moment, the truck's machine gun was back on the road, its attention shifting like a demon from a nightmare when the dreamer steps on a twig or bumps into a wall.

But the 5.56 rained around and above Tyler and his injured compatriot, now relatively safe in a divot in the earth.

Tyler glanced down at the man, his amputated leg spitting out blood as he writhed in pain and cried out in indiscernible moans. Tyler almost didn't recognize him, pale and contorted as his face was. But he did recognize him — Sean Ford. The twenty-something-year-old was borderline hyperventilating and had started shivering violently. Tyler's first thought was how Sean had ever qualified to be on that mission in the first place.

The medic slid next to Sean and Tyler to take over. "Get back in the fight," he said.

Tyler snatched his rifle and dashed toward Santana.

"You get him?" Santana asked.

"Yeah!"

"Good. Listen, we gotta get those other guys across the road so we can get the fuck outta here." He turned to the group of men huddled under a blanket of machine gun fire. "Dusky, make sure that guy gets stable enough so we can move!"

Tyler thought for a moment. "Cover me."

"What?"

But Tyler didn't wait to explain. He darted through the jungle, keeping himself oriented by the muzzle flashes spewing out of the top of the truck. When the M249 clicked empty, the shooter slammed a belt of fresh rounds into the open bolt weapon faster than Tyler could reload his M16.

Tyler was now almost directly at the gun position's side, gliding through the dark toward that stone wall. It was constructed out of varying stones and, like many structures deeper into the woods, had mostly disintegrated at the whims of nature. It may have once been a storage shed or the cosmetic boundary to a driveway — he hadn't the time nor the inclination to discern its origin. He simply slid behind it and stayed as low to the ground as possible.

When the shooting did not shift in his direction, he was confident that his movement had gone undetected.

Tyler lifted his head over the low wall, just enough to see the crowd of muzzle flashes barreling out a waterfall of hatred. Pushing the nose of his weapon over the wall, he eased it into the pocket of his shoulder and lined up the front and rear sight post with the gunner. Tyler's body screamed at him to yank the trigger as soon as the man was in his sights, but he wrestled down the urge and breathed — he breathed in. He breathed out.

And he eased back on the trigger.

The weapon lurched in his arms. A cloud of dust and blood exploded out of the machine gunner's side and he stumbled and tripped out of the truck bed and slammed onto the ground. In a moment of confusion, the shooting faltered to a stop.

Tyler knew the moment of silence would end on someone's terms, so he started pulling the trigger over and over, blazing indiscriminately at the trucks. It was everything he could to keep the rifle from leaping out of his hands.

Two more shooters fell; the rest found cover before they started to return fire. Tyler hunkered down behind the stone wall — the machine gun was down, but every rifle and eye behind it was fixed on him. He could feel a river of lead crashing on the other side of his meager wall, which was disintegrating by the second as shards of stone were flung over his head.

There was nothing he could do now except lay in the fetal position, pressed so low into the ground he may as well have already been buried in it. As he lay in wait for a bullet to career through the weakening stone, he noticed movement — Sergeant Santana and three others were bounding between the trees, almost entirely invisible.

The trio in the woods opened fire and, in the same breath, the barrage of rifle fire was lifted away from Tyler and the handful of stones he was left behind. Tyler didn't wait for a signal or a command from Sergeant Santana. Every fiber in his body urged him to lurch for a new piece of cover, and this time he listened. With his weapon dangling awkwardly around his neck, Tyler scrambled to a mound fifteen feet further away from the trucks, littered with dead logs.

He turned back toward the trucks just in time to spot another Lakeland militiaman crawling up toward the machine gun. The new gunner spat a burst of 5.56 toward Sergeant Santana and the others, but with another deafening *click*, the gun malfunctioned.

The militiaman fumbled with the weapon — he was not as proficient as his predecessor. He spent a moment of panicked confusion with his fingers tracing the M249, struggling to open the feed tray. It was more than enough time for Sergeant Santana to take steady aim and put three deadly rounds into the man's chest.

Another Lakeland Militiaman, cradling a bloody arm, clambered into the driver's seat of the rear truck. He reversed, jerking the wheel and turning the vehicle so erratically that Tyler thought it might tip over. The remaining few dove into the truck bed and they sped off in a cloud of dust.

Santana and his three approached the pickup, now riddled with bullet holes, and put a round in every dead Lakeland Militiaman, just to be safe. Major Kessler had once mentioned a tendency for Lakeland soldiers to play dead simply for an opportunity to put one last bullet into an ETM soldier.

Tyler hurried over to Santana and the others to begin dismounting the machine gun and collecting Lakeland weapons and ammunition.

As the sound of the retreating truck bled away into the night, Tyler became acutely aware of the noises that remained — the rustling of men scrounging bodies for ammunition, his labored breathing, the agonizing moans of Sean Ford, and the singing crickets.

After darkness fell, East Tampa was lit by a handful of flickering lights. They were watchtowers, for the most part solar powered lights that lined the sparse perimeter of what had been settled. They were little more than sparks against the black sky, but they inspired another breath of energy in Tyler's chest as the reconnaissance element of 2nd Platoon plodded through the swamplands that seemed to stretch on without end. The flickering white shone from three- or four-story buildings on slightly higher ground, signaling the city's location for miles around. City lights meant nothing before the Red; they were a rare sight to see now. To outsiders it meant strength, resilience, and coordinated efforts toward security. To East Tampa's residents, it meant warmth, rest, and safety.

And yet the lights were deceiving, as they promised a rest for weary feet but made no hint at the true remaining distance. Light carries far in the dark — it can radiate for miles — but they were on foot, and Tyler had to remind himself that the journey was far from over.

Every time he wrestled his foot up from the mud of a swamp or heaved himself over a boulder, he thought his body would finally collapse into a heap on the ground. He could only stare in amazement as Santana slogged effortlessly through the muck and the water, not only lumbering up and down the formation, but ensuring each member of his troop was on their toes.

"Keep your head up, pussy. We're not even close yet. Those lights are like eight miles away."

Tyler wondered if he would ever have such energy, should he one day work his way into a leadership position in the ETM.

A leader in the ETM. It was the first time the thought wandered into his mind. It seemed like such a fantasy, an idea so far out of

reach, but the dream crept in anyway. He didn't know if he would
be as brash as Sergeant Santana, but he respected the man's sense
of responsibility out there in the wilderness when no one was
watching.

"You good, kid?" Santana hopped a log next to him,
splashing his soaking boots into another deep puddle of swamp
water.

"I'm good, Sergeant."

Just behind him, four others carried the litter hoisting Sean
Ford home. The group had taken turns carrying the heavier boy,
and Tyler's blistered hands had just been given a break. Sean was
delusional after hours of pain, in and out of consciousness and
constantly moaning through his teeth.

With every moan and every step forward, a single question
burned deeper into the back of Tyler's head.

"Sergeant…"

"What?"

"Was that my fault?"

"Was what your fault?" Sergeant Santana kept his eyes on his
surroundings.

"Did we get ambushed because of what I did at the strip
mall? Maybe they followed us after I gave away our position or
something."

Santana glanced at Tyler. "What you did at the mall was
fucking stupid. You could've gotten people killed, I already told you
all that." He held a couple branches up to keep them from sliding
across the litter bearers' faces. "But it had nothing to do the
ambush. I saw that truck come around the corner. The machine

gun was tilted up, and the only person paying attention was the driver. They weren't lookin' for us in particular, they were just patrolling around. We got unlucky. Ain't gonna fault you for bad luck, kid."

They dropped the branches and Santana continued down the line.

5

*"Ya know, one-a the great philosophizers of our nation once said somethin'
along the lines of: 'ya can't get what you're lookin' for, but if ya look…' aw
hell, I think I got it here somewhere, lemme throw it on.
"101.7, the soundtrack to the end of the world."*

SANTANA'S eleven healthy men from his reconnaissance element stood shoulder-to-shoulder in a large office. Sunlight beamed through colossal, double-paned windows facing the town square, looking down on the bustle of everyday life in East Tampa. The town residents were the size of ants from that height, scurrying from one unknown task at the queen's behest to the next.

The office's hardwood floors had been freshly mopped, and every surface in the room shone with treated wood. Books lined the shelves, and a great desk spanned almost the entire width of the room, housing several stacks of organized papers.

The eleven were nodding off to the gentle embrace of unconsciousness as they stood; they had only hobbled into East

Tampa several hours earlier. Just as they had refit and thought about resting their eyes, Santana had thundered into the barracks and called them to attention. "Mayor Whitley wants to see us," he said. No one knew why it couldn't wait until they had recharged their own batteries, but when the mayor called, he was always answered without question.

They stood in a gradient of experience, Tyler on the freshest-faced side to the left and Santana standing like a statue on the right.

A man with an elderly hunch to his back, white hair, and thin glasses stood before them.

"The Mayor will be here any second now," he said. Tyler knew him as Magistrate Brown, and Tyler knew he had some role in the judicial system they were trying to develop. However, his position had slowly evolved into an advisory role, though Tyler was never quite sure what sort of advice he was there to provide.

The side door opened and Mayor Whitley strode in, his chest swelling with pride at the sight of his hometown heroes.

"You boys really did it last night. Sergeant Santana gave me the full report, and I can tell you that you prevailed against all odds. Not only did you knock out an enemy gun position, but you acquired that weapon for us to use against our enemies. And use it we will.

"As you all know, I was previously speaking to the late Major Kessler regarding the implementation of medals. Since then, I have been personally recording every act of bravery, and once our system of medals is refined, be assured you twelve will be receiving a unit citation of bravery in dire circumstances. I realize that a bit of colored ribbon probably doesn't mean much to you, but you ought to be recognized. It's the least I can do."

He paced the room, sure to look each man in the eye. "Rest assured, Sean Ford will be receiving top-of-the-line medical care. We recently acquired a top-notch surgeon who will be taking better care of him than you'll find in any other town or city... well, that we know exists anymore.

"Thank you for your courage, I know you all want me to stop jabbering so you can get some sleep. You are dismissed."

They began to file out of the office, but the Magistrate placed a gentle hand on Tyler's shoulder. "Stay for a moment, boy." His voice crackled wet, like he needed to cough but chose not to.

Mayor Whitley ran a hand through his jet-black hair as he admired the busy town below. Tyler watched as Santana left the room and his mind began to race. He was alone here, and he hoped his actions at the strip mall weren't about to get him fired.

Wouldn't Santana be the one to fire me? What if the mayor asks me to say something that incriminates Santana for something? Why just me?

Questions both reasonable and otherwise began to whirl about in his mind like a hurricane. But he waited in silence, making his greatest effort to look as stoic and unwavering as possible. As Mayor Whitley swiveled on one heel to face him, Tyler made sure he did not break eye contact.

"Sergeant Santana told me about what you did last night."

Great.

The mayor sat down behind his desk. "Have a seat," he said, and Tyler sat across from him. "Sergeant Santana told me that you proved yourself more than once last night. That you braved enemy fire and dragged Private Ford to cover before single-handedly taking out the mounted machine gun on a…" He turned to the Magistrate. "What was it called again? A technical?"

"That's right, sir."

Tyler didn't know what to say. The art of receiving a compliment had been lost somewhere during his training with the ETM, but still, he managed to cough up a response.

"Uh, thank… thank you, sir."

Mayor Whitley smiled wide, like a camera was about to flash. "You could make a great candidate for Gray Platoon one day. You know what they are?"

"I know a little bit."

"They work directly for me. Like the Secret Service used to work for the government, you know, from before the Red."

Tyler knew he was fifteen. He knew he was young and that sometimes meant explaining things a little more carefully than adults could explain to other adults. But from the moment Kessler's brains were splattered on that school wall in front of him, he felt that he had taken a dive headfirst into adulthood, in some form or another. Whitley had a way of explaining things to him like he was a child again, and it was unsettling.

"I remember, sir."

"Well, one day, when this whole thing is over and you're a little taller and a little wiser, maybe we can work something out. I've got a burning need for young men like you who don't think twice when jumping into the action."

"That's me," Tyler said, his voice flat.

"Perfect! I knew I could count on you. Like I said, we're working on releasing a set of medals for you militia men and women, and rest assured you'll get specific recognition for your actions last night, no doubt about it."

"Thank you, sir."

"That'll be all. Magistrate Brown will see you out."

Tyler sat up on the edge of his bed. He laid back down. He turned to one side, then lay on his back again.

It had been two uneventful days since the ambush. Sean Ford was alive and recovering, and Major Whitley swore to the public that Sean would never want for anything again. That his service and sacrifice to East Tampa would be repaid to the best of his ability.

Tyler knew that the mayor had used the same framework of words when he "paid respects" to Major Kessler at the man's funeral. Something about it didn't sit right with Tyler, like a small nail resting upward in his pillow, preventing him from drifting off into sleep's embrace.

Tyler's uncle was a military man. He was an officer in the Marine Corps and had served a full twenty years. He was a moderate, kind, and intelligent man. Tyler wondered if Uncle Percy had ever questioned his loyalty to those under whom he served. If he looked at them and was simply not impressed. After all, as far as Tyler was concerned, few men were as impressive as Uncle Percy, especially the politicians on TV.

But Uncle Percy had served under a single country. The residents of that country had bickered and argued, but they didn't really realize how their goals were ultimately the same until the Red came along and cracked the whole thing open.

That's when people started to steal to survive. At first, it was a simple scramble to stay alive week-by-week, but after a while "survival" wasn't so simple. Instead of simply accruing weapons, it meant controlling the access to food and weapons. It meant giving one son or daughter the equipment and training to protect another son or daughter.

When Mayor Whitley had taken control of the ship that was East Tampa, Tyler thought he was calming the storm. He thought the charming hero was taking the chaos from the Red and breaking it like one would break a horse — now Tyler wondered if it was a bit more complicated than that.

He wished he could ask Uncle Percy what he thought, but there was no Uncle Percy. No mother or father for parental advice, no Anthony to at least join him in bemoaning the complexity of it all. It was just him and his thoughts, rattling around like marbles in his skull as he tossed and turned on his mattress.

Stop thinking like that. No one cares what you think about the mayor, and if they did it would make no difference.

Long, early morning shadows were cast across the barracks floor. Tyler's bunk was in the middle of a sea of randomly scattered bunkbeds, and he wasn't the only one alert and restless.

Finally, he laid on his stomach, his head tilted to one side, ready to drool on the faded sheets that smelled of the same leftover, powdered laundry soap that his clothes were hand-washed in. His eyes began to flutter closed —

A terribly loud sound roared through the room. It was louder than anything he had heard before, and the very ground beneath them shook with the sound. It thundered with an intensity far greater than any rifle or machine gun he had heard so far, and it rattled through his bones.

Tyler shot up in his bunk, and the others around him did the same. There was an instant where the lot of them sat in shock, like they were waiting for someone to kick down the door and tell them all to grab their weapons.

Instead they received the command in another form — the *rat-tat-tat* of gunfire reverberating down the street.

Each man scrambled for the closest pair of pants and shirt before grabbing their gear and sprinting out of the barracks. Tyler was not the fastest, nor was he the slowest, and he kept an eye out for any type of leadership as they grabbed what they could on their way out the front door to see what was happening.

It was earlier than Tyler realized. Though it was light out, the sun had not yet risen. The air was crisp and cold and the sounds of war cut through it like some kind of terrible alarm.

They couldn't find Sergeant Santana because he was already outside. He had just started drinking, and now instead of drinking liquor he was spewing lead, not two buildings down the street.

A large fire enveloped a building halfway down the road and to the left, bellowing out a pillar of black smoke. Muzzle flashes flickered just past it, the sounds of gunfire catching up a split second later.

"Shoot those dickheads!" Santana fired more rounds as he yelled to the unorganized mess of ETM soldiers as they gained their bearings.

A truck with heavy steel welded to either side came screeching around the corner. Tyler ducked behind a neighboring wall and fired several shots at the vehicle, just to watch them plink harmlessly to the side.

A crude skylight had been cut through the truck's top, and Tyler barley caught a glimpse of an arm poking out of it, tossing a satchel out. It bounced off the ground and landed near the barracks wall. A 2nd Platoon man bent over to pick it up as Tyler started to move that way.

Santana turned and screamed, "WAIT —"

His ears didn't register the sound of the explosion, but Tyler felt the heat on his face. It passed through him like the wave of an ocean, and he felt his feet leave the ground.

By the time his brain switched back on, he had pivoted, dropped to a knee, and was shooting at the tires of the escaping truck. There was no time to think about the lost moment of consciousness; it didn't matter now. The truck swerved away and Tyler turned his head to the source of the explosion.

There was a gaping, smoking hole in the side of the barracks wall. Part of the old police station roof had fallen and lay wedged against the ground. It was still too dark to see most of the blood spattered on the walls and in the dirt, but he could make out body parts scattered across the ground. He bent over and picked up… he wasn't sure what part of the body it was. Fabric was steaming off it, infused into the flesh. But it was the warmth that made him want to vomit — not the searing heat of an iron in the fire, and not the cold dead hand of a lost loved one, but the steaming warmth from a cooked meal, a feeling bound in unholy unison with the sight of human flesh in his own hands.

Tyler gagged and dropped it, unsure why he had picked it up in the first place. He could make out the torso of a dead man under the collapsed roof. His head drifted over to a severed piece of —

Santana grabbed his shoulder. "We're still in the fight, kid. Let's go!"

And like a switch had been flipped, Tyler was running at Santana's side toward the nearest firefight just down the street. He knew there would be no digging through that rubble while bullets were still shrieking over their heads.

The further they ran, the more chaotic things became. Several buildings had been set ablaze now, and Tyler could hear more explosions echoing through East Tampa. Muzzle flashes seemed to be materializing from dark places around every corner. Unarmed men, women, and children were scrambling about in a panic with little discernible intent — Tyler could feel an electric kind of chaos to it all.

Near the town square, he and Santana took cover in an abandoned café. They slid behind a half-corroded bar where they could clearly see the roundabout and its surrounding buildings. The shadows began to shrink as the sun peered over the horizon and illuminated all.

A muzzle flash erupted from a dark spot under a fallen oak tree that leaned against a storefront and a slew of bullets slammed into the café's storefront. "There!" Tyler said. The two of them opened fire and the enemy muzzle flashes ceased. The two of them changed magazines one at a time.

"On the right!" Santana said, and they snatched the life from a Lakeland man trying to roll over a heavy table for cover.

A volley of gunfire tore through the café, originating from a rooftop on the other side of the square. Bullets smashed through the countertops and shattered the glass shelves behind them. Santana and Tyler dove in either direction, Tyler blindly firing back at the roof as they split. A trail of rounds followed Tyler into the next room until he slid behind a solid cement wall. He frantically shot his hands across his body, searching for a gunshot or shrapnel — he found none.

Sergeant Santana opened fire, resulting in silence on the rooftop. Tyler could see the stocky man at the other end of the café, peering through the town square for more Lakeland militia.

"How many mags you got —" Santana was interrupted by the crack of another rifle. Tyler poked his head around the corner and could see another shooter on the rooftop.

Tyler crawled over to a blown out window further down the café, and he dug his M16's handguard into the corner of the window. He didn't know if Santana would have yelled at him for poking his muzzle out of the window, but he needed the stability to make the shot. He aimed just above the figure on the roof, little more than a dark shape silhouetted by the morning light. Tyler breathed in, and he exhaled until the air had all left his lungs and he was at the natural bottom of his breath. His finger gently moved backward until the rifle jolted back into his shoulder.

By the time Tyler reacquired his sights on the shooter's location, the space was vacant. There was no way of knowing if his shot had landed on its target, but all that mattered was that the Lakeland soldier was no longer firing his weapon at Santana.

Tyler swiveled his rifle around to clear the rest of the rooftops — he found no one.

Keeping low to the ground, he carried his weapon by its slip ring and darted through the next room to Santana. The sergeant had pressed himself against a wall, and he was drenched in sweat and just about out of breath.

"Shit, man." He was stuffing a bandage into his shin.

"Sergeant! You alright?"

"Bullet went right through this pussy-ass wall. Right in my f —" He cried out in pain as he packed the wound full of white gauze. "Right in my shin. Wrap this up."

He handed Tyler more gauze, and Tyler carefully wrapped the man's leg several times, holding the packed bandage tightly in place as he had been taught.

"Can you walk?"

"Of course I can fucking walk." Santana used Tyler's shoulder and hobbled upright, keeping the weight on his good leg.

"ETM?!" A coarse voice was emanating from the front room.

"ETM! Don't shoot," Tyler echoed.

A large woman toting a hefty shotgun lumbered in. She spoke with a borderline unintelligible southern accent. "We got 'em on the run, they's all spread out over town, ain't gonna be but a minute 'fore we got their pretty lil' heads on spikes."

"Jesus." Santana smiled at the sight of her.

"You need some help, honey? Saw yer boy fightin', but he barely looks a buck fifty, can't be carryin' you around."

"Sure thing, baby. Just don't break my heart."

She rolled her eyes and threw his arm over her shoulder, supporting him as they staggered out of the café. Tyler kept a sharp eye on the rooftops to cover their exit.

"Put me over there." Santana pointed at the oak tree from which the first muzzle flashes had erupted. Tyler kept his head on a swivel while they moved, though shooting sounded fainter than it had before. The sun was well over the heads of the buildings by now, and it illuminated all the dark corners and fighting positions, now vacant and empty as before.

They arrived at the tree, which was cracked at the base, resting tediously on a nearby brick building. Another satchel bomb had gone off earlier in the night, forcing the oak into submission. They approached the impromptu fighting position to find a dead girl, no older than twenty, lying with part of her face in pieces on the ground behind her.

Tyler stared at her for a moment and his heart couldn't help but feel the bite of pity. Mayor Whitley, Sergeant Santana, and even Major Kessler all spoke of the monsters of Lakeland, but here was a girl not five years older than himself. Anthony's age. She didn't seem to fit the descriptions given to him.

They hunkered down in her fighting position — she had made a good choice in location, just ventured too far out from cover in the name of getting a clear shot. No one else was there, no Sergeant Santana to tell her to keep her head down, no Major Kessler to train her in the art of properly utilizing cover.

What a small thing, moving your head two inches too far to the right, Tyler thought. *What a small thing to die over.*

"Ballard," Santana interrupted non-stop internal monologue. "Check it out." Tyler followed his finger down the street.

A red truck.

Like Santana, the truck had taken a hit in a wheel and was barely hanging on. Smoke bellowed from the hood and it was moving so slow, Tyler wondered why they didn't just ditch it and start running.

The sight of the truck sucked the air out of his lungs, like it had on the roof of that strip mall — the icon of his brother's murder. He turned his head toward Santana to ask a question, though he could not find the words.

"Go get those motherfuckers." Santana's words lit a fire within him. Tyler grabbed his rifle and barreled toward the truck as it struggled down an overgrown road away from East Tampa.

He had never run so fast in his life. The truck hobbled down a side street into the jungle with trees so thick one could hardly see twenty feet through. They were limping east where they would presumably find safety in the arms of Lakeland defenses, provided they could make the journey. Tyler bolted across the forest floor parallel to the road, ducking limbs and hopping logs, keeping a careful distance from the truck — he needed to be just far enough to stay out of sight, but just close enough that he wouldn't lose them.

One of the men was driving. Tyler could see him better than ever now: he was well into his thirties, scrawny, with a trucker's hat on his head and an AKM at his side. Tyler couldn't quite see the other two just yet — they weren't in the cab.

In that moment, it occurred to him that he had just sprinted into a fight that he couldn't win. After all, three against one weren't great odds.

You've been lucky enough to spot this truck twice already, this is number three. No way it happens again, and probably never like this. Turning back wasn't an option, so he doubled down and hoofed it.

The truck swerved down another dirt road and may have even tipped had it been going faster. The road ran alongside some high ground, complete with thick jungle greenery providing adequate concealment along the parallel ridgeline. Tyler scrambled up the side of the mound and followed the truck, glancing down on it as he ran alongside just out of sight. He could see the other man and woman lying in the truck bed, clutching their rifles. He figured they must have dove into the back of the truck last-minute.

The damaged vehicle started making a loud clicking noise, and it began to lurch and heave forward. The man and woman in the back sat up.

"Let's ditch it!" the man said, and the truck skidded to a stop in the dirt. The two hopped out of the back — they were younger than he had thought, now that he could see them in the light. They were both in their late twenties with round cheeks and bright faces. They carried backpacks, and the man had a revolver on his hip.

The man driving slid out of the cab and put his hands on his hips, shaking his head at the smoking truck. "The ol' girl's about done," he said.

Tyler kept low and crawled toward them. He had thrown a new magazine in his rifle, but he would have to be careful and keep his shots precise. They had the numbers and the firepower. All he had was the element of surprise.

He watched from the ridgeline as they checked their weapons and strapped their bags tight to their backs, ready for the long walk home. They were expecting to make the same walk he had just made a couple nights before. They were expecting to have blisters on their heels, but ultimately to return to their fathers, mothers, sisters, and —

Tyler hardened his heart and aimed his rifle. The woman had seemed the most observant the night of the reconnaissance mission, so he assumed she would be the greatest threat. He peered through his sights and placed the front sight post on the upper portion of her chest, just below the neck. Like Major Kessler had taught him.

He took a breath and switched his safety from safe to semi, using the soft part of his palm to suppress the sound, just as Dusky had in the woods the other night. He breathed in and gently placed his finger on the trigger. He breathed out…

A shot rang out. Then another. The younger man's torso was ripped apart by the impact of several rounds, and he slammed into the truck face-first before he hit the ground in pieces.

Except the rounds weren't his.

Someone was firing in bursts down the road, and Tyler eased off the trigger and glanced down it as the two survivors from the truck dove behind its wheels and returned fire. Tyler could make out three shooters hiding in the brush, ripping into the truck with three-round bursts. He spotted three more circling around to the vehicle's flank, unbeknownst to the two remaining Lakeland soldiers.

"Shit! Shit! Shit!" The driver's voice shuddered and his shots were ineffective. The woman was crying, but her hands were steady. She fired a handful of rounds back down the street. Her closest shots sputtered harmlessly in the dust a dozen feet shy of the mysterious shooters.

As the flanking element drew closer, Tyler realized who he was watching.

Gray Platoon.

The entire group simultaneously ceased fire. For a moment, the only sounds were the panicked grunting of the man and the muffled sobs of the woman as she tried to contain herself. They were bracing themselves for an inescapable fate.

"Drop your weapons and step forward!" a voice boomed from the original shooters' position. A familiar voice.

Tyler inched forward to see who was speaking, but they were too far down the road. He kept low, careful not to expose himself.

"Screw you!" the woman responded.

A shooter from the flanking element fired a single shot, striking the older man in his ankle, which was only slightly poking out. He crumpled to the ground like a trembling leaf, crying out in pain. The woman whirled her head to the side, now aware that their chances of escape had just been obliterated along with the poor man's ankle.

"Put your weapons down," the man in the flanking element said. The two Lakeland soldiers tossed their guns into plain view on the dirt road and the woman turned the corner with her hands up. In the morning light, Tyler recognized something in her, like he had known her before the Red but couldn't quite put a finger on where. He may have considered her pretty, but too much dirt and blood were etched into her face to tell.

The older man scraped through the dust across the road, attempting to keep his trembling hands up as he moaned in pain. A trail of blood followed his wounded leg.

The flanking shooters crept from the concealment of the sticks and leaves, revealing themselves with their weapons raised and fingers on their triggers. One secured the rifles on the ground. The other two simply watched as more Gray Platoon personnel from the end of the road began their approach.

Tyler noticed one man, not so tactically dressed, walking amidst the safety of their defensive posture. He recognized the jet-black hair and unmistakable magnetism. *Mayor Whitley.*

Whitley studied the woman, who had since stopped crying. She stared at Whitley with a disconcerting, profound level of rage that even made Tyler uneasy at that distance.

The mayor grabbed the hair of the man, who was writhing on the ground in pain. He yanked it back and studied his face. Unsatisfied, he did the same with the dead man wedged against the truck.

"This isn't them. Are you sure it was this truck?" Mayor Whitley asked of Gray Platoon.

A lieutenant in the center of the group spoke up. "Reports said she was in a red truck."

The woman forced a defiant smile.

"Have something to say?" Mayor Whitley drew uncomfortably close to her.

"I know who you are —"

"Good for you. Where's the vehicle we're looking for?"

"There are a lot of trucks out there, Mayor."

"Don't play dumb, you know who I'm after."

"Mayor Hatch."

"That's right. If you've got any answers, we'll make this easy on you."

"Back in Lakeland, took a blue truck if I remember right. Or maybe it was a gray sedan? I'm just so awful when it comes to cars and trucks —"

The Mayor backhanded the woman with the force of an actual punch. Tyler wasn't sure why he didn't just punch her, but he figured the mayor wasn't used to using his fists, just the back of his hand.

The act only made the woman's defiant smile wider. She was no stranger to pain.

Tyler was careful not to move. Gray Platoon had not cleared the high ground, but he was looking directly down at them and his concealment wasn't perfect. The smallest crackle of a broken leaf could be received by a hail of bullets.

"If you were trying to get the mayor out here, your plan obviously failed," the woman said. "What else do you want from me?"

"From you? Everything you've got. I want your ammunition, I want your people, I want your food and medicine stores. I want your copper caches —"

"You know damn well we barely have any copper," the woman spat back. "What are you really after?"

"I just want to find Hatch," Whitley said. "To have a friendly conversation. There's been a lot of violence, you know. A lot of big booms. I wouldn't want her to get hurt."

"I'll be dead before I give up any information about anything or anyone."

Mayor Whitley smiled at her like a pretentious man looks upon an uneducated child. "Well, this is a useless conversation anyway. Why? Because you're useless to me." He pulled a pearl handled pistol out from the back of his waistband and pointed it at the man writhing in pain on the ground.

"Nothing to say?"

"I — I've got information!" the man said desperately.

"Oh, do you? Have information?" Whitley shot two rounds into his other leg without hesitation, his eyes growing wide in pleasure at the sound of the man's agony. Whitley's bullets followed the man's leg up and smashed his hip into pieces. He was not crying out anymore, just shaking. Seizing.

The woman leapt forward, unsheathing a hidden knife from the small of her back. She slashed recklessly at Mayor Whitley, gashing his upper arm. One Gray Platoon soldier punched her in the face, and another held her back, disarming her once again.

The Lakeland woman looked helplessly at her fallen friends. This was over for them and she knew it.

Looking her in the eye, Whitley put a bullet in the man's head. His skull caved as the shot ripped through his face, and his violent shaking came to an abrupt end. Tyler's heart shook in its cage.

"Sir, should we take her back and see what she knows? We can probably get something out of her." The Lieutenant of Gray Platoon would not look the woman in the face.

Whitley babied the wound on his arm; it was mostly superficial. "Nah. She cut my fucking arm. Do what you want with her then kill her. I'm headed back. We have to plan our next search and seizure." Mayor Whitley began to walk down the road. "Oh, and Lieutenant," he said without looking back. "Don't just shoot her right away. I know you savages can come up with something... a bit more interesting."

The mayor gathered half the soldiers of Gray Platoon and started back to East Tampa. A handful of men and women stayed, swarming the poor woman after forcing her into the bed of the truck.

Tyler couldn't bear to watch any more. He crept backward and carefully slid down a berm to level ground. He walked a straight path through the woods. Her screams grew quieter and quieter as he continued on.

Trudging out of the forest took an eternity compared to sprinting in. The sun was beginning to heat up the humidity in the air; his mouth was dry and his skin was soaked in sweat. In the burning heat of the day, a dark cloud had fallen over his mind.

I wanted this. I wanted this, he said to himself over and over.

After around twenty minutes he heard a single, distant gunshot behind him.

This was the justice he had so ferociously sought after. His brother Anthony was avenged, and not by a merciful, painless bullet. Murder must be answered for, the pain they brought upon him must be answered with —

He shook his head.

Something deep within him had been twisted, warped out of shape. Where was the overwhelming feeling of relief, now that justice had been served? Now that his vengeance had been fulfilled? There was nothing. There was less than nothing.

He wanted to puke. He wanted to cry. He just walked instead.

"Sergeant. I'm telling you, something about it was just wrong. He was saying that he wanted everything. I thought this whole war was about defending ourselves? And he said something about copper. I don't understand, I thought copper was just a resource we needed that Lakeland was hoarding? After the National Guard stripped it, year one. But that woman… she said they hardly had any, and the mayor didn't say anything about it. I don't know, something was wrong. Everything was wrong."

Sergeant Santana was switching out the bandages on his leg. The round had ricocheted before it struck flesh, so it was barely lodged in his shin. Still, the doctor wasn't quite sure when he would be making twenty-mile movements again.

Santana's tattooed arms moved carefully, directing his bloody fingers to muscle through the pain and pack a fresh bandage.

"Kid, just be glad they killed those shit-heads."

"I don't feel any better. I don't... I don't know." The words were piling up because there were no coherent thoughts behind them. His heart was a flurry of contorted thoughts and damaged feelings.

"I know. It don't change anything, that's why. They're just dead now. You still lost a brother. That ain't gonna change no matter what."

"Mayor Whitley isn't telling the truth. He's not telling us something."

Santana raised a skeptical eyebrow. "You one of those conspiracy nuts? Man, just chill. You got yours, and you prolly just heard the mayor wrong. You said you were far enough out that they didn't know you were there. Everyone knows that Lakeland's been hoarding plenty of copper for themselves. We want to share, they want it all. Plain and simple. Wouldn't make sense for Mayor Whitley to say shit like that, you prolly heard him wrong. Must have."

"I could hear him."

"I could hear him, *Sergeant*," Santana corrected him.

"Sergeant, I... I don't know what to do."

"Don't do a fuckin' thing. I knew I shouldn't have let you out after that truck." He paused and looked directly at Tyler. "Look, kid. You've got a lotta potential. You've fucked up, but everybody does. It's fine. You've learned from your mistakes and gotten better because of 'em. You could do some solid stuff here, but you can't go around askin' stupid questions about conspiracies and shit. Makes you look weird."

As Santana went back to tending his wound, he began to look physically different to Tyler. He wasn't quite as built and his posture wasn't quite as rigid as he remembered. He realized the man had traces of acne along his jawline, and that he must have chewed his fingernails short instead of cutting them. He waited for some kernel of wisdom that would put all those words into context. It never came.

The soldiers of 2nd Platoon were temporarily staying in 3rd Platoon's barracks, but most were outside scraping up body parts and rubble. Tyler stormed out as fast as he could. By the time the door swung closed again he was already halfway down the block.

He hadn't yet brought his things to 3rd Platoon's barracks; they were still among the smoldering rubble of the old police station. He went back there and packed his bag as heavy as his shoulders could bear. He made sure to grab enough food and iodine tablets for a month, and he grabbed the ammunition allotted for him. If it belonged to anyone else, he didn't take it.

He didn't know exactly what he was doing, and he wasn't sure exactly why he was doing it. Still, Tyler wandered into the woods and did not intend to return.

6

"You got music to fire you up and you got music to soothe the soul... sometimes it doesn't matter what tunes grace the airwaves around you, sometimes it just matters who yer sittin' around listenin' to it with.
"Everybody needs somebody; find someone and listen along to 101.7, the soundtrack to the end of the world."

I'M a deserter. The word burned in his mind, a word spoken only with disdain and shame in every book of war he had read in the past. From the stories of the ETM's first skirmishes with Lakeland to the bandits from Orlando, the worst and most shameful were always of the deserters. Those stories were burned into his mind, and now he was one of them. He left those whom he had specifically promised to stay and fight alongside. He gave Major Kessler and the ETM his word, and now that word was broken.

Tyler's head reeled with these things as he walked aimlessly along the forest floor. He had no direction, no destination. He was an insect wandering among the trees, his limbs at the mercy of the whims of Mother Nature.

This wasn't the America, Florida, or Tampa his uncle had fought for, though if he was honest with himself, he wasn't paying enough attention in the days before the Red to know what exactly that was either. Still, this felt like something else, something new. It was as if the Red had killed most and driven the rest to insanity. No matter how shameful the brand of desertion, he could not stand among them for another second. He was deceived, and his attempts at pointing out that deception only led to more lies and deceit. Or worse, in the case of Sergeant Santana, willful ignorance.

Perhaps it was inevitable, he thought, that his brother would die. Could good men survive under such deceitful leadership? Would it have only been a matter of time until Tyler met the same fate? He couldn't say, but he knew that he had to go.

So he walked. And he walked some more, and he wasn't sure where he was going or what he was going to do when he got there.

He crossed several streams, passed through several neighborhoods on the abandoned outer sections of town, and trudged over a crumbling bridge above a dried-up river.

The sun was a few hours from setting, beginning to fall behind him. He figured that meant he was generally heading east, which could be right into Lakeland territory. Maybe he'd get in a fight with some.

Maybe he'd run. Maybe he'd die. He didn't know. Didn't care.

He wandered into the shadow of a great building and peered up at a deteriorating sign in front of it. It read: BARLEYTON MALL. Some of the mall's windows were blown out, and the entire thing was in desperate need of a pressure washing and some landscaping, but it was still standing.

It's as good a place as any.

He strolled in, his weapon slung casually on his back. The interior was filthy; the stores had long been cleared out of any and all valuables, and a tree in the center grew wildly upward, struggling to drink any sunlight from the shattered skylights. Tyler put a hand gently on the tree, an ancient living thing that simply endured.

Voices suddenly rumbled around the corner. Tyler dove into a deserted jewelry store, keeping low behind a counter, careful not to step on the shards of glass scattered across the floor. Of all the stores, this had not been ransacked — the glass had been broken by weather and time, not by human hands.

Tyler spied four men and two women, all Lakeland Militia. They were armed with either hunting rifles or shotguns, and one had a handgun on her side. Tyler pressed the buttstock of his rifle into his shoulder, but he didn't have a round in the chamber. If they saw him, he would have to charge his weapon before he could fire. He could almost hear Santana's voice in his head: *Come on, kid, cut it out with that rookie shit.*

The Lakeland Militiamen laughed among themselves, lighting up cigarettes under the tree, flicking ashes onto its roots.

"Yeah, man, I can't believe they missed me. I've almost gotten smoked more times by some little ETM shit than I can count. But that business at the bank — too close for me."

"I don't know if that's good luck or bad…"

"Well, maybe the ETM is runnin' around here and they can *almost* kill you again."

"Dude, if I see any ETM here, I ain't takin' prisoners. Hatch can get her intel from somewhere else, I ain't takin' that chance."

"Me neither. That's how Harrison from Unit Three got clipped. Whoever he was taking into custody put down their rifle, then pulled out a pistol and put three in his chest."

"Damn. Yeah, fuck that noise."

"Where are we going after we clear this mall?"

"Nowhere, this place is way too big. It's almost night, we're done after this."

"Well, what're we waiting for?"

"Don't know about you, but I'm gonna finish my smoke."

"Yep, sounds about right. You just sit here and smoke while we do the actual work…"

A hand swept out in front of Tyler's face and grabbed his mouth. He felt the cool barrel of a pistol against his neck as strong hands pulled him quietly back, further into the jewelry store.

"Don't make a sound." The whisper from the unknown man was barely even a whisper. "I'm not going to hurt you. There's a backdoor to this place that leads to an exit. I know you're not from Lakeland. They'll kill you if they find you. We need to go — *now*."

Tyler backed away from the militiamen with the stranger, careful not to bump into the counters as they moved. With a firm hand, the man pressed Tyler into the door, opening it carefully. There was something about this stranger's grip, about the way the pistol was tight against his neck — he was completely at the mercy of this man.

After they passed through the doorway, the man shut it softly behind them and they crept through an office rife with cobwebs reaching from cubicle to cubicle. The stranger used Tyler as a human shield, breaking through the cobwebs.

"Seriously?" Tyler whispered as he squinted through the spiderwebs, trying to spit them out of his mouth.

"Quiet."

They passed under an exterior exit sign and reached a desolate parking lot. The sun was low in the sky. Tyler felt the hand release and he turned, immediately recognizing the man from the marketplace in East Tampa. He wore the same frayed strips of cloth around his neck and arms, though his sunglasses rested on his head to reveal eyes that seemed a little too old for a man of his athletic build.

"You're that Marauder."

"You're welcome." He did not holster his pistol.

"Who the hell are you?"

"I'm that Marauder."

"Where are you headed?"

"Home."

"Can I come?"

"Sure."

Tyler wasn't sure how to respond. He wasn't expecting an easy yes from a man like him, the epitome of roughness. Without another word, the stranger headed for the jungle, his body moving with confidence and speed, but his head and eyes keeping account of his surroundings. Tyler scrambled to keep up with him.

"I don't care what you do," the Marauder said. "But you can't have any of my things. That includes food."

"Okay."

The man spoke very little after that, and they plodded through the ends of the town and headed deep into the under-brush. He navigated down animal trails, rugged remnants of a path only visible to a well-trained eye, moving effortlessly across the forest floor. Tyler often had to break into a jog to keep up. He was allowed to follow the mysterious man for now, but he was sure there would be no waiting up for him.

"How did you find me?" Tyler broke the eternal silence.

"Saw you head into the mall, recognized you. Saw the Lakeland Militia go in there too. Didn't seem like an ideal situation."

"Thank you."

"Don't worry about it." His insincerity was apparent.

They reached his camp after a few hours of trekking without speaking or stopping. A humble, single-bedroom cabin stood in a small clearing in the woods, with a well-kept garden nearby walled off by an impromptu fence and an outhouse just twenty feet downhill.

"You've really got it made out here," Tyler mused. The man paid him no mind. "So… what's your name?"

"You first." The man carefully leaned his rifle on the wall near his front door. He had built a makeshift sink — a PVC pipe running from a rainwater reservoir built out of an old bathtub, propped up on a stand facing the break in the trees with mosquito netting stretched across the top. He splashed his face with water and sat down on a lawn chair.

"Tyler," the boy said. "Tyler Ballard."

"Miles."

"Miles… got a last name?"

"Yep."

Tyler didn't press him.

"Sit down, man." Miles gestured toward another camping chair, its floral pattern almost entirely faded to a brown-gray.

Tyler sat. He had not considered that this might be some kind of trap, and he realized now that it was probably a bad idea to follow a stranger deep into the woods, so he kept his M16 close. Miles smirked.

"I'm not gonna pull anything on you." He leaned forward. "But I would like to know a couple things, if you're willing to talk."

"What kind of things?"

"You're in the ETM, right?"

"I was. Don't think I am anymore."

Miles paused, some kind of internal wheels turning in his head, though his face remained expressionless. "East Tampa is going to take over Lakeland, one way or the other. That's highly likely, from where I stand anyway. I'd like to know what they plan on doing after that. If they're trying to start some kind of empire or something. And if they're gonna start expanding north."

Tyler didn't know how to respond — this was the first he had ever heard of conquest or expansion. "I, uh, I don't know about any of that," he stammered. "I was just a soldier, Lakeland has been attacking us and we were just defending ourselves —"

"Bullshit."

Tyler's knee-jerk reaction was to tell him about the raids Lakeland had pulled, and about how the people there had fallen to inhuman levels since the Red — but he realized that they were Whitley's words and not his own. He knew Lakeland killed his brother, there was no way around that, but he also knew things were far more complicated than was ever indicated.

"Yeah, probably," Tyler said. "But I don't know what their plans are."

Again, Miles took a long pause, studying the boy. He leaned forward and spoke. "Tell me why you left." He seemed genuinely curious.

"Why I left? Ummm... well, I guess..." Tyler didn't quite know where to begin. Each potential starting point required too much background information, so he ultimately decided to tell this strange man everything, and he started from the beginning:

"Men from Lakeland murdered my brother. They came one night and shot him dead in our parents' old room. They killed my dog too, her name was Lacey."

He poured it all out — about Anthony and Lacey, about how he joined the ETM under the command of Major Kessler and Sergeant Santana. He told Miles about his training, first mission, and how the Major was blown away like paper in the wind. His voice trembled as he spoke of how he almost compromised the reconnaissance mission, and it sped up as he described the ambush soon after. The attack on East Tampa, how he followed the red truck and what he saw Mayor Whitley do and say, Santana's indifference to it all… it all tumbled out before he knew it. He didn't know why he told Miles the whole story. He just knew that he had to tell someone, and Miles was the only person around with an ear to listen.

Miles was very quiet for almost an entire minute.

"Man," he said. "That was stupid."

Tyler's eyes widened, "What?"

"Your boy, Santana. When you guys were crossing that road, why the hell would he put his security element right on the road like that?" Miles leaned forward. "Those two guys you had out on the road? Push them further up the road, so you can — you know — mitigate the chances of someone driving down the road and catching you guys unawares. And your other buddy would still have his foot right now. And he goes around telling you after-the-fact that it wasn't your fault… no shit it wasn't your fault. And then he goes and sends you on a one-man mission to take out that truck? One on three? For what — a cool revenge trip? Really?"

Tyler wasn't sure what to say. He had just poured his heart out and this man had tactical improvements on his mind.

"No go…" Miles muttered to himself, while a slight smile.

"Well, I'm here now," Tyler said. "Pretty lucky that I ran into you, huh. Do you believe in coincidences?"

"Yes."

Again, Tyler didn't know how to respond. "I don't understand."

"Don't understand what." Miles said it in a way that Tyler wasn't sure whether or not he was asking a question.

"Why they killed the two men from the red truck, but they kept that woman alive just to kill her later."

Miles's eyes softened for half a moment. "Times like these are rough. Rougher for women."

Tyler sat still for a moment. Miles retrieved a dented flask from what appeared to be thin air, unscrewed it, and took a swig.

"Life is hard," Miles added. "People are going to try and make it easier by getting you on board with their shit. Their agendas. It's their way of getting you to do the heavy lifting while they sit back and 'manage.' But if you take care of yourself, make yourself capable, serve your own agendas... well, then no one can infect you with theirs."

"Sounds like you're trying to convince me of another agenda."

Miles laughed. "That's the kind of thinking I like to hear."

He offered Tyler the flask and Tyler took it. He gently lifted it to his lips, took a fraction of a sip, and almost spat it all out. It was everything he could do to force the half-gulp down his throat. He handed it back.

"It's good," he lied and the other man chuckled.

"So what's your plan?" Miles asked.

"No plan," Tyler admitted. "Can I sleep here tonight?"

"Sure thing, just gotta give me that gun of yours. Can't have you trying to wax me in my sleep."

"I won't."

"Sure. I'll still need your gun, though."

Tyler slept on the couch.

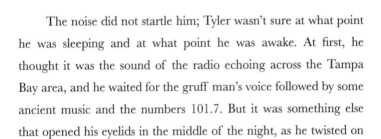

The noise did not startle him; Tyler wasn't sure at what point he was sleeping and at what point he was awake. At first, he thought it was the sound of the radio echoing across the Tampa Bay area, and he waited for the gruff man's voice followed by some ancient music and the numbers 101.7. But it was something else that opened his eyelids in the middle of the night, as he twisted on the lump in the center of Miles's couch.

The beginning sounded like the hammering of nails on wood, but it wasn't from outside. It was emanating through the crackling veneer of a tired speaker in the darkness of Miles's cabin. Tyler rolled to his side and listened, wondering why a speaker would be playing the hammering of nails.

He figured it was coming from Miles's room, just around the corner and walled off with a hanging blanket. Sitting up on the worn cushions, Tyler tried to discern what type of device was playing the recording. Was it a television or some kind of phone or tablet? But there was no light peeking around the corner, and his eyes had completely adjusted to the night. Was it a record player or a stereo of some kind? Perhaps, but the sound quality seemed too poor.

The hammering soon turned to the laughter of a child.

"Be careful!" Tyler recognized Miles's voice. *"We gotta build this thing, but how about we build it without falling to the earth and breaking all of our bones?"*

"Daddy, you're too big to fit up there! I'm the only one," said the voice of the laughing child.

"Listen —"

As the cobwebs in his sleepy mind dissipated, Tyler realized that perhaps, whatever this was, it was best left to Miles's ears. He lay back down on the couch, put a musty smelling pillow over his ear, and went back to sleep.

7

*"I don't play many of these tunes, 'cause honest to God they used to make me
wanna cringe up in a ball so hard I might just implode like a submarine gettin'
hit by a torpeda' in the ocean. But hot damn, brother, young love is somethin' I
ain't seen or heard in a long time, so let's chill a bit and listen to the teenagers
of the past spew poorly written lyrics from purely honest hearts.
"Hear 'em on 101.7, the soundtrack to the end of the world."*

TYLER crept across the jungle floor. His eyes scanned the swamp's
murky surface — Miles said the gator here was around nine feet
long. As he yanked one foot out of the mud and pushed it forward,
he wondered why a man like Miles would take him in. He was a
loner, and by the looks of his well-kept home nestled in the heart of
the most untamed corner of the jungle, he had lived that way for a
while.

Maybe if he dragged back a nine-foot gator — a dinosaur, as
far as Tyler was concerned — he wouldn't win any affection or
admiration, but maybe he could earn a sliver of respect. He hadn't

met anyone like Miles before, but he was familiar with the expression permanently plastered on the man's face. When everything fell into catastrophe, Miles had lost respect for the entire world. It wasn't because of the Red itself, but the peoples' reaction to it. To gain an ounce of that respect through an act of violence would surely be proof of his own strength, Tyler thought.

He peered upward through the dense canopy at the large clouds hanging above. The tops of the leaves had begun to blow with a strange consistency to the north. He thought nothing of it and continued on.

The water was up to his shins, and with every labored step it grew deeper, first to his knees and then to his crotch. It was not cool and it was not refreshing. The water was thick with muck and mire, and it clung to his skin as he waded deeper in.

Miles told him the gator usually hung out on the furthest end of that swamp. A small gap in the trees fashioned a kind of pathway as the swamp weaved its way through a narrow valley between shallow hills and large rocks.

"She'll be somewhere down that swamp in the valley," Miles told him. "Stay away from the valley and stay away from her. Nature's brutal when you don't have mommy civilization taking care of you."

What Tyler hadn't expected was the inaccessible terrain surrounding him. The hills were unusually steep for Florida's typically flat swamps and fields, and so he was left with no choice but to be funneled down right into the water. If he took the high ground, there was a chance that he would skirt too far away and miss the beast. In addition, the woods played with his sense of direction, and if he strayed too far from this narrow swamp, he may stumble across another and confuse it for this one.

Instead, he thought it would be best to tread right into the mouth of the beast.

Every time the swamp forked off, he kept to the larger, wetter path, as he assumed that's where the alligator would be lurking. His elbows were high as he endeavored to keep his M16 above the water. In the brief moments where his attention drifted, his muzzle would dip into the water and he would yank it back up.

Every log looked like an alligator to him; every configuration of sticks and rocks looked like the rugged back of an ancient dinosaur whose home he was wading through.

The water was at his waist now and he could feel his heart pounding faster. He wasn't sure how alligators swam, if they preferred to float above the water like in pictures and movies, or if they ever submerged themselves completely and snatched their prey by the legs. Still, he relied on his stubbornness to keep his legs trudging forward.

Just as he was considering a trek out of the slop and crawling up the steep incline, a log moved. The log lay half in the water and half in the dirt, glistening a little shinier than most pieces of driftwood. It was about twenty feet away, just where the creek began to dwindle into the trees and trickle to a larger body of water beyond the thick vegetation.

The mosquitos that nabbed at his neck, the nameless bugs that scurried across the water around him, the cloudy water and the relentless heat — it all disappeared at the sight of that movement.

The nine-foot alligator turned, moving with the muscle memory and confidence of any predator at the top of its food chain. Tyler lifted the rifle to his eye and aimed to slay the ancient thing. He could see its jagged teeth protruding from its long snout, its rough scales and light underbelly. He could see her eyes — the eyes of a snake on the body of a monster.

He was supposed to fix his front sight post on the body of the alligator, but his focus remained on the beast. It breathed and blinked. And he hesitated.

After killing the man in the black windbreaker, he had gone back to East Tampa and wondered if he wouldn't be able to pull the trigger on an animal. Could he gun down an innocent deer with its large, dark eyes? There were wild dogs that roamed the city, but there was no way he could kill one of them unless it directly threatened his life, not after Lacey. But this monster? This demon of the swamps held just as much malice as the deer or the dog, he knew that now. Was it any different from them?

His thoughts were interrupted by a voice to his side.

"Lower your rifle." It was a young woman's voice. He lowered it.

"Turn around," she said, and he obeyed.

Tyler found himself staring up the edge of the ravine and down the business end of a barrel. A girl, maybe sixteen, clutched a .243 bolt action rifle that was probably twice her age. Her dark hair was done up in a ponytail, and she was thin like him. She wore a tank top and tattered jeans that had seen their fair share of jungle use.

"Hi." The word stumbled out of his mouth. He wasn't expecting to run into a pretty girl in the lair of a beast in the jungle.

"What're you doing out here?" Her aim was unwavering and her finger was on the trigger.

He glanced back at the gator — she hadn't moved. "Looking for that big gator over there. I was planning on shooting it."

"In the water? Better hope she doesn't come after you, one bullet probably isn't going to cut it."

He said nothing.

"Sling your rifle," she said, and then she cleared her throat. "And uh, climb up here."

He slung his rifle and crawled his way up and out of the ravine. He slipped several times, and, had they been friends, he was sure she would have laughed at him. She did not.

"Give me your rifle," she said when he reached her, so he handed it to her. She took it and struggled to sling it on her back while keeping her own weapon trained on him. He waited patiently, and it occurred to him that he should probably be more uncomfortable with a gun in his face.

"Who are you?" she asked, her soft voice feigning a level of authority. He had no doubt she would shoot him if he tried anything, but her presence suddenly made him realize how un-intimidating he had been all these months he had played at being a soldier.

"My name's Tyler —"

"You from Tampa?"

"I used to be. Are you gonna shoot me?"

"Maybe."

"I don't work for East Tampa anymore," he said. "I left."

"I've seen a few of the wanderers out here. I've never seen you."

"I just left yesterday."

She smirked. "And I'm supposed to believe you're what, a deserter? That takes more dedication than one day."

"I'm not going back."

She studied him for a long moment, then lowered her rifle slightly. "You can't shoot her, I like her," she said.

"The gator?"

"I named her Ivy."

"You named her?"

"Ivy."

"Is she your pet or something?"

"Something like that. I used to have a cat, but he got killed. By some of your friends."

"I'm sorry to hear that. And they're not my friends."

"She's still an alligator, so I can't exactly go up to her. But I watch her from up here sometimes, and I don't have to worry about her like I have to worry about a cat. Well, I didn't think I did anyway."

"I won't shoot her. I didn't know she was yours," Tyler said. "So, her name is Ivy… what's yours?"

She eyed him head to toe, unsure what to make of him. "Allie. You're Tyler, right?"

"Yeah. What're you gonna do with me, Allie?" He made sure to use her name. He remembered something about how captors and captives having first name familiarity was only helpful. He thought maybe he had seen that on TV before the Red.

"I don't know yet. You really left Tampa for good?"

"East Tampa. And yeah, I'm not going back."

"Why not?"

That's a loaded question. He was tired of pouring out his soul from the day before. "They lied to me. About everything."

"That's what they are. They're liars."

He didn't argue with that.

She shifted her weight, staring at him intently. Her finger was still on the trigger and the safety was off.

Their gaze was interrupted by the sound of distant gunfire, and Allie turned her head in their general direction. "I think that's me," she said.

"I'd hate to keep you." Tyler thought he spotted a smile, but she started backing away from him.

"Don't shoot Ivy," Allie said, and she tossed his weapon halfway down the ravine. She turned and ran toward the gunfire.

"I won't!" He watched her curiously as she left. When he was once again alone, he climbed down the edge of the ravine and grabbed his weapon, keeping an eye on the nine-foot dinosaur lurking at the base of the swamp.

"Sorry I was gonna shoot you, Ivy. I didn't know you had a name."

"Come on, you must have seen her around. You know everything about these woods — I bet you know where every mine, booby-trap, and ambush site is on top of the hill with the radio tower."

"Every mine, booby-trap, and ambush site." Miles smirked as he cooked a roasted a pigeon over a fire and boiled several potatoes in a cast iron pot. It didn't smell like anything Tyler could remember in recent years — fresh food was a thing long forgotten. "But I have no desire to mess with the only source of music in this part of the state."

"I know you've seen her around."

"Okay, fine. You win. I've seen her there. She hangs out there all the time, I think she likes exploring or something. She would probably do well to pick another hobby in this day and age."

"You ever talk to her?" Tyler asked.

"No," he said. "I don't talk to most people."

"You talked to me."

He scooped up some potatoes, put them in a bowl, and handed it to Tyler. "Tell me if these are done yet. And I didn't talk to you, I saved your ass from a bullet to the dome. The talking came later, don't make me regret it."

"Think she'd ever need help like that?" His mind was already wandering to the scenario: she's captured by ugly, nameless figures with rotting teeth and he careens in, guns blazing to save the day.

"Sure, I don't know," Miles said. "There are groups of bandits that patrol around the woods there. Lakeland is fighting them off all the time. They just beat down like ten of them last week."

"Have you come across bandits like that?"

"I don't stumble across all this stuff by accident, man."

Tyler thought back to Santana's words in the marketplace; Marauders like Miles were known for stealing and taking what they could. He had always assumed that meant from East Tampa or Lakeland civilians, though Miles never quite measured up to the heinous image Santana had built in Tyler's mind. There were a lot of things Santana had told him that didn't quite measure up.

"So you're like Robin Hood."

"I think a key part of Robin Hood was giving to the poor — me? Not so much. But yeah, I only take from assholes. They're not hard to find these days."

"And who decides who is and isn't an 'asshole'?" Tyler's dad used to talk about the dangers of dictators overseas who considered themselves judge, jury, and executioner, and Tyler thought parroting a smarter man than he would make him sound intelligent.

"I do. Is there an asshole police? Any police? Not out here. Out here it's just me, you, and your little girlfriend."

"She's not my girlfriend."

"Isn't she a little young for you?" He thought for a moment as he tore off a piece of pigeon and tasted it. "I guess not, you're both just kids."

"I'm not a kid."

Miles took a nibble of one of the potatoes and savored the taste. "People are so damn stupid for not farming these days," he said to himself. "Sustainable, for one, and the taste..." He closed his eyes and relished the moment.

"I was a soldier," Tyler said, defending his adulthood.

"A child soldier. Add it to the list of reasons why East Tampa sucks. And Lakeland, too." He eyed Tyler for a moment. "But I guess you wouldn't see it that way, would you."

It didn't sound like a question, but Tyler answered anyway. "I volunteered," he said. "I was useful too. I could have done a lot more if I would've stayed."

Miles gazed at him, and Tyler caught a glimpse of what he might have described as sadness, but it was gone just as quickly as it came. "I believe that," Miles said. "I don't know, man, just try that potato and tell me what you think."

8

"I've got one today that folks might turn their nose up at, but damnit I was a metalhead so I'm gonna subject y'all to the musical love of my past, pre-redness. Listen here, brothers, despite all the kickin' and screamin', this is actually a love song. No shit, a love song. Honestly, it sounds a lot more like my first ex-wife than any other song I've got in the inventory.
"Hear the screamin' sounds of love on 101.7, the soundtrack to the end of the world."

TYLER had been "hunting" in those woods for a few days straight. He swore to Miles that it had nothing to do with the chance of running into Allie. He told the man that he was looking for rabbits, and he saw plenty of rabbits to hunt — he just didn't bring any back for Miles's stew.

In the past, Tyler had always felt a purpose that he could sink his teeth into — finish school, survive the Red, scrounge for food, avenge his brother's death. Now he was faced with an existence devoid of meaning. The emptiness so prevalent in the abandoned houses had found its way into his heart and it threatened to hollow him out entirely. But a chance encounter with this girl gave him something. It gave him a reason to continue to scrape forward in the dirt. So, he wandered. "Hunting."

One such day Tyler roamed fields of sawgrass, imagining a scenario in which he ran into Allie out there in the wild. He meandered into a patch of woods and gazed up at the canopy, watching as the leaves blew harder under the constant wind that had been building for days. His eyes followed the rays of light down onto the Florida forest floor. Lizards scampered from bush to bush, and a snake lay in a clearing, basking in the sun. The gnats and mosquitos were out in full force, reminding Tyler that even a simple stroll in the woods would be met with some sort of nuisance.

Still, he appreciated the quiet. He relished the chance to walk without the need to navigate conversation or concern himself with his own disposition. Tyler had never considered himself the stereotypical outdoorsman, but there was something about the jungle that called to him.

It's just like a firefight, he thought. *Simple. Dangerous, sometimes awful, but simple.*

The connection his mind made troubled him, but he wasn't sure if it was wrong.

Then, out of the corner of his eye: *movement*. Tyler lifted his rifle and turned toward it, cautiously ducking behind a nearby cluster of bushes. Peering around them, he could make her out — it was Allie, wandering through the woods just like him. Her rifle was slung over a white t-shirt and the same jeans from before.

She squatted down to inspect a bushel of berries, turning them in her fingers and studying each individually.

Tyler felt that he had handled himself quite well in her presence the first time and had dreamt up all sorts of scenarios should this reunion actually occur. He imagined saving her from the clutches of bloodthirsty bandits, taking her in after she defected from the Lakeland militia, or even pulling her away from Ivy's gnashing teeth if she ventured too close.

This was not quite any of those, but it was safe. That was something, he supposed.

Her back was turned to him, so he strode out from behind the tree, weapon raised.

"Now *I've* caught you with your back turned," he said. He wasn't sure if that sounded good, and he knew he would replay that single line over and over in his head later.

Startled, she whirled around and put a hand on her weapon.

"Don't do that!" he blurted out. "Don't do that, please."

She froze in place; her eyes were wide, and she was tensed up like invisible ratchet straps were torquing down on every muscle and tendon in her body.

Tyler realized his safety was off and his finger was begging to pull slack from the trigger. He eased the tension, unaware that his reflexes were even remotely that adept.

"It's me, Tyler," he said. "We met over there with Ivy, your alligator friend."

Her shoulders relaxed, and she let her hand slide away from her rifle. "Oh yeah. Hi."

"I'm gonna lower my gun," he said. "Can we just be, like, normal people for a second?"

"Sure."

For all of his vivid and heroic daydreams of saving the girl, he realized that he had not considered what he would say if they met under completely undramatic circumstances. He stood in front of her, his mouth unwilling to form words of any significance.

"You gonna lower that thing?" she asked, eyeing his rifle.

"Oh, yeah — of course." He politely pointed the muzzle toward the dirt but kept it ready in his arms.

Birds chirped in the morning sunlight. A few distant shots rang out, miles and miles away. They both turned their heads in that direction.

"Isn't that East Tampa?" Allie asked.

"It's west from here, so maybe," he said. "I don't know. Could be a lot of things."

"You really ditched them?"

Tyler fidgeted with the pistol grip on his M16. "Yeah." He felt that his palms were sweaty. *Are they always this sweaty? Must be from the heat.*

"Lakeland isn't so bad, you know. We're all just trying to get by."

He nodded. A part of him wanted to tell her about Anthony, about Lacey — "I think most people are just trying to get by," he said.

She smiled. "Yeah, I think so."

He had never seen a smile like that before. It was like every other pretty smile he had ever seen, but this one pierced his heart and clouded it with a haze of wonder. He didn't know what to say, so he smiled back. He knew it was an awkward, unnatural smile, but it was the best he could manage.

"So what, you live out here now?" she asked.

"I guess so. I'm not sure where I'm gonna end up next." He liked the idea of sounding unpredictable and independent, like Miles.

"Dangerous out in the woods. There are bandits here all the time."

"You're out here."

"I know my way around."

"You ever run into any bandits? Why not just stay in Lakeland?"

"Yeah I've seen 'em. And I don't like the idea of being tied down to one place so I sorta bounce here and there when I'm not working —"

"But then why enlist in their militia?"

"I didn't. Well, I got drafted — everyone over fifteen got drafted. Not sure if I would've joined otherwise… maybe." She paused for a moment. "Wait, are you saying all the soldiers in the East Tampa Militia are volunteering —"

"Allie!" A voice resounded through the woods. "Who the hell are you talking to?!"

Tyler spun around to find two men approaching fast. Their hunting rifles, bound with burlap strips and dirt-stained medical tape, were pointed directly at his chest.

Allie swore under her breath. "Uh… he's my friend!"

The two men stopped only feet away from Tyler and Allie. One was a large, muscular man around six feet tall; the other was wiry looking, with graying hair. They looked at Tyler the way Santana used to look when he talked about the Lakeland militia.

"Keep your hands off that rifle, boy," the big man said.

"Yessir."

"Where are you from?" The wiry man's southern accent might have had a hint of charm to it, if it wasn't accompanied by the rifle pointed at Tyler's chest.

"He's just a wanderer," Allie said, before Tyler could speak for himself. "Came down this way lookin' for food. I came up on him, he didn't pull a gun on me or anything."

Tyler glanced back at her — who was this girl that she would already lie for him? Was she smacked in the gut with the same haze and wonder? Or was she just being a charitable human being to a lost puppy in the woods? The men lowered their rifles less than an inch.

But Tyler had read too many books and watched too many movies to think that trying to navigate his way through a lie could work.

"That's not true. I was in the East Tampa Militia… then I left. For good." He hung his head. The rifles swung back to full alert.

"What the fuck?! Allie…" The large man struggled to understand her lie. "What is going on here?"

The color drained from Allie's face and it dawned upon Tyler that he may have just incriminated her along with himself. He turned to her. "Sorry to lie to you too, I shouldn't have told you I was a wanderer," he lied. And then he told the truth: "I was just trying to make you like me. Nobody likes a deserter."

Tyler could almost make out a blush beneath Allie's feigned anger.

"You're one of them?" she said, glancing back at the two and hoping they wouldn't catch on. "Well, I didn't know that. But he seems like he's really out here on his own. I haven't seen anyone else around here for a while."

"I don't much like liars, or deserters," the wiry man said, and his rifle tilted upward just a hair further, directly between Tyler's eyes. *Shots to the chest are practical,* he thought. *Shots to the head are personal.*

These men could shoot him dead at any moment, and that reality was beginning to settle in his gut. They might get a rise out of Allie if they killed him, but realistically he and Allie barely knew one another. At a maximum, she might be upset and not speak to the men for a few days — but he'd still be dead, and ultimately she would need them just as they would need her in the war with East Tampa.

Tyler kept his hands in plain view.

"Look, please don't shoot me, I'm just trying to figure out what I need —"

Tyler heard the sound of a gunshot and his entire body clenched. He felt the disconcerting force of bullets cut through the air he breathed.

When he peeked through his tightly shut eyelids seconds later, Allie and the two men were nowhere to be seen. He spun his head around as if it were on a swivel — nothing. They were all gone.

"Don't think I don't see you all!" A deep, boisterous voice echoed through the trees. It was almost theatrical. Tyler whirled around again, but no one was to be seen.

"Those were warning shots, my friends. You are all surrounded, and the next shots will find a home in your chests. Even the little girl."

Tyler heard a scraping in the leaves. A rumbling in the wind.

He realized quite suddenly that there was nothing between him and a bullet, so he leapt to the nearest large tree he could find. Rounds cracked off into the air. Several slammed into the dirt near Tyler, sending it flying upward in tiny particles.

"The next person that moves without our say-so gets a bullet!" the voice commanded.

Tyler thought that he ought to be afraid; after all, he was afraid every other time someone had fired at him. While that fear still thrashed about in his chest, another feeling was stronger now — he felt profoundly irritated at the man's voice. Not the shooting, not the Lakeland soldiers who may have executed him, but this strange, melodramatic voice. If he would have stopped to think about it, he would have known it was a silly thing to get so upset about, but whenever that faceless person called out to them, it irked Tyler like a thorn was stuck right under his ribs.

He carefully moved his hands to grip his M16. He felt confident in his grasp around its small pistol grip; he felt powerful as he pushed the buttstock into his shoulder. Of all the places he had been in the last month, the battlefield — though it presented itself in many different circumstances — was the most familiar.

"Tyler…" It was Allie's voice. He turned his head and saw hers, poking out from behind a smaller tree approximately thirty feet to his right. "I think we found those bandits," she said.

The voice boomed from nowhere once again: "Place your guns on the ground, kick them away from yourselves, and walk forward with your hands up. We have you surrounded. Try and escape and you'll see nothin' but black real quick."

Every syllable prodded and poked at Tyler's soul, infuriating him more. He noticed Allie's head bob once again out from behind her chosen position of cover. Their eyes met for a split second, and she turned her gaze past him.

Tyler whipped his head around, following her line of sight. He noticed a slight decline just beyond his tree. The gradual slope might just be enough to get out of the line of fire of the bandit, that is, assuming the bandit was alone. Tyler scanned the trees in every direction, still unable to discern any signs of life. If he started crawling along that low ground and there was a shooter anywhere on his left, he might find himself in pieces.

He glanced back at Allie, unable to read her wide eyes. He decided not to think anymore, and he dove onto his stomach, sliding down into the defilade.

More shots smacked into the tree behind him as he crawled away. They comforted him, as their fire remained on the tree and not on his body wriggling away from it.

"STAND UP!" the voice screamed. "You leave them, they'll pay the price!"

But the shooting stopped. *They can say Allie will pay all day, but if they don't have a clear shot, they don't have a clear shot.*

The defilade continued downward until it hit a clump of trees and a small hill that took him entirely away from Allie and her friends. He glanced back again at her. She stared at him. Tyler realized that she probably thought he was fixing to leave them to fend for themselves.

Is that what I'm doing? He hadn't even thought about it. His instincts were to find the threat and figure out how to make the situation safe again, whatever that took. But who was she to him, really? Miles was alive because he separated himself from everyone and everything. She was not only liable to get him attached to civilization once again, but she was trying to get him attached to Lakeland of all places. Besides, she seemed like a capable person, as did the men that came to find her. They would surely take care of her. She would surely take care of herself.

He didn't look at her again; he just began to crawl away. Keeping low and out of sight, he maneuvered through the trees until he was confident that he could stand and run and without catching a bullet.

And right then that same feeling came scraping through his heart. The disgust, the despair, the familiar guilt that had crawled into him the day he walked away from his brother's murderers. The profound loathing — not of himself, not of fate or God, just a directionless, faceless loathing of the way that things were. He felt the brokenness of the world and realized it only felt this way when he walked away.

He remembered that Miles lived and survived alone, but if it weren't for Miles then he would likely not be living.

So, he gripped his rifle, scanned the horizon, and cautiously rose to his feet. Over the slowly rising breeze, the heavy air drowned them all in humidity. Sweat poured down his arm and onto his rifle, which was beginning to rust along the barrel.

His mind raced back to Major Kessler's advice, about flanking an enemy by using a "terrain feature." He wasn't exactly sure what that meant, but he could tell that the hill between him and the bandit — though he realized there may be more than one — ran as far as he could see into the woods. It could provide cover enough for him to sneak behind the shooter, if he kept his head down and eyes up.

Now that he was in the woods with guns firing and lives on the line, he wished someone would have explained all of that better, or that he had asked more questions. When revenge was on his mind, the practical nature of the battlefield was secondary to him. Now it was all that mattered, and he hoped that he knew enough.

Too late for that now anyway. Tyler crept forward, as smooth and silent as he could. Still, his head bobbed up and down as he checked his surroundings and then checked his path for changes in terrain or rocks that might trip him up. He had no idea how people like Miles or Santana could move so effortlessly with their eyes straight, without tripping over a thing.

"ALRIGHT! Come on out with your hands up. You first, missy." The voice echoed through the trees; Tyler found it difficult to ascertain the origin of the voice, so kept on forward.

"Weapons on the ground — WEAPONS ON THE GROUND!"

Right then Tyler realized he had just passed the voice — it was behind him now, on the other side of the tiny hill. He lifted his rifle up to his eyes and inched up the slope where he found a tree on the hill's crest and kept close to it, using it for cover.

A gray streak of movement rustled near a thicket on the other side of the tree, about thirty feet away. A burly woman drenched in sweat crouched there awkwardly, holding a large revolver that was covered in rust and would have surprised Tyler if it fired at all. Her gray t-shirt was stained with years of mud and her pale skin was blotched red from bug bites and rashes.

He continued to examine the dense brush around her until he could make out what looked like a pant leg and a boot, indicating someone laying prone.

That must be the man yelling at them, he thought, *though there could be others.*

Tyler searched the woods for other signs of movement or odd shapes or colors, but he saw none. Just the two of them. If he was wrong and he opened fire, his position would be given away and whoever was left would get a moment to take aim and put one right through his head.

He decided to give the woods one more scan before handling the two in front of him. But then what would he do? Should he start shooting indiscriminately? Call them out and take them prisoner? Would Allie's friends just shoot them anyway? Options began to pour into his mind, pulling at every last choice he might decide to make — until the woman on the ground made it for him.

Click! Tyler snapped his attention back to her, realizing that she was desperately clawing at her revolver, trying to get it to fire.

She yanked the hammer back, locked eyes with him, and raised her weapon —

Tyler opened fire and the rounds split her chest open, painting the thicket behind her with blood and bone fragments.

Gunfire erupted through the same thicket from the man's hiding place, cracking and cutting through branches safely above Tyler. Pieces of bark and leaves fluttered down onto his head as he shot back. He couldn't see whether or not his rounds were hitting the man, so he kept firing as he consciously made an effort to keep his aim on the thicket.

Movement. Tyler could make out the man disappearing behind a cluster of vines and bushes. Tyler fired another two rounds — *click.*

Tyler fumbled as he changed his magazines, cursing under his breath that he wasn't as quick as he could be. He put the old magazine in his back pocket and shoved the new one in, releasing the bolt forward. With a fresh round in the chamber, Tyler rose to his feet and bounded forward to get a better angle on the retreating man.

Shots from Allie's position rang out, and Tyler saw the scrambling body fall from behind a tree. The man, skinny enough to be considered starving, crawled away from the tree — he was too far for Tyler to see where he was shot, but Tyler recognized the face of anguish as the bandit rapidly approached the end of his life.

Another bullet went through the back of his head, exploding out of his jaw, and every muscle in the bandit's body went limp. The wiry Lakeland man stepped forward, whirling his weapon toward Tyler, who let his weapon hang from his sling and threw up his hands. Tyler tried to keep his surrender somewhat casual-looking, as Allie stepped out from another tree nearby, but in truth his heart was pounding so fast in his chest he thought it might sprout legs and run off into the woods.

The wiry man dropped the muzzle of his rifle. When the larger one approached, they scanned the rest of the forest together.

"I thought you were gone," Allie said to him.

"Nah. I wouldn't do that," he said, and would later think of a hundred wittier responses.

"Hey, bud," the wiry man spoke. "You didn't have to do that."

"I didn't?"

The man chuckled. "Well, thank you."

"You're welcome. You guys aren't gonna shoot me now, are you?" Tyler asked.

Another chuckle. "No, actually I was thinking —"

BOOM! BOOM! BOOM!

More gunshots screamed past them, this time from two different directions. Blood spattered from Allie's side as she took cover; the larger man took a round directly in the thigh. He dropped to the ground and his unslung rifle fell several feet away.

Firing back blindly into the wilderness, Tyler, Allie, and the wiry man found whatever cover they could scramble to first. Tyler realized he had chosen a rotting log that would take a bullet about as well as a wet piece of paper. Allie had her back to a tree nearby, and the other man had scurried to another further off.

Tyler thought he could identify three muzzle flashes. Though they weren't entirely overwhelming, they were effortlessly keeping Tyler's group's heads down. The intent wasn't to rob them anymore, the intent now was to kill — if they were flanked the way that Tyler had flanked the others, there would be nothing he could do about it.

"Did they get 'em?!" the voices communicated with one another.

"I think so! Johnny! Faye! Can you hear me?! You there?!"

Tyler responded with some rounds in their direction. He glanced back at Allie, also hammering at the trigger. Her eyes were filled with fire as she shot wildly toward the forest voices — the streak of blood on her left side must not have registered, or perhaps she just didn't care.

Despite their frenzied response, the mysterious shooters did not seem deterred. A hail of bullets rained down upon them, and soon Tyler had his rifle pressed up above his log, firing as his head cringed below. Shards of wood slapped past him — Allie managed to roll behind a larger tree, but before long she too was stuck with her head down.

The enemy's fire was not as focused on the tall, wounded Lakeland man, who was desperately trying to stay lower to the ground than the leaves on the forest floor, all while applying pressure to the gushing wound on his leg. He grimaced and grunted, his eyes began to water, and he started to shake, but he kept low.

Tyler glanced to his right. If he could make it back up the hill, he would possibly draw their fire and at least Allie and the wiry man would get away. Maybe they would even be able to drag the wounded man off too — but it was a long shot. The bandits already had a clear view of Tyler and the others, and they were probably just waiting for him to lift his head.

But his choices were limited and his time was dwindling away with the log that only covered his exact location but did nothing for him in the way of effective cover. His heart was tired of racing and slowing and racing and slowing, and he knew this was going to end soon one way or the other. Tyler took a deep breath, then another, dug his foot into the dirt and —

Two shots rang out, different from the rest. Not only were they a different caliber and pitch, but they were fired so closely together that they almost overlapped. Had more than two shots been fired, Tyler would have assumed it was coming from an automatic weapon.

But there was no time to think about that — the firing from the bandits had momentarily ceased, and Tyler seized the opportunity to bolt from his cover.

Two of the bandits fired at him, but their shots were sporadic and they were split between firing in another direction. The second of reprieve had given Tyler just enough time to dash out of sight behind a small berm where he kept low and maneuvered to a better vantage point, just behind a boulder jutting out of the earth.

Muzzle first, he peeked over the boulder to gain his bearings and figure out where the other bandits were. Tyler identified one figure in a bright red shirt, moving straight toward him.

Before he could even aim, three unbelievably quick shots tore through the red shirt and spattered red on the leaves behind it. Out of the corner of his eye, Tyler detected movement. A man was gliding through the trees, quick but controlled.

"John!" The third bandit's voice was panicked. "Talk to me, John!"

Tyler recognized the fast, powerful frame moving through the woods: Miles. He moved directly toward the shaking enemy voice, without faltering — every step held more confidence than any step Tyler had taken in his life. He wasn't a tank like Santana; he was fluid, like an unrelenting and unstoppable flood of precision and determination. He moved with the rising wind above the jungle canopy.

Miles slowed to a walk where he crested each tree individually. Tyler watched as he moved through the trees, keeping a few feet from each but strategically moving from one to the next. The moment a shot was clear, Miles put three more rounds into the last bandit's upper chest.

Like it was entirely routine, Miles put another round in each bandit's body, took the weapons and ammunition that were most easily accessible, and dissolved back into the woods like he was never there.

For a moment, Tyler stood behind his rifle, pressed against the boulder, staring at the peaceful woods before him. What the hell had just happened? Miles had come and gone so quickly, a part of him wondered if he had really been there at all.

"Who was that?" Allie was standing just behind him, whispering over his shoulder.

"What?" Tyler turned, shaking it off. "No one. I mean, I don't know. We'd better get out of here."

They headed back to the large man with a bullet hole in his thigh.

"Let's go, quickly and quietly. Not making the same mistake of standing around bullshitting again," said the wiry man. "We'd better head back before any more show up. Hey, bud, can you help me carry him?"

The taller man already had a tourniquet wrapped tightly around his leg above the wound, and a bandage was secured to the bleeding mess. He was unconscious, and his chest rose and fell lightly.

Tyler was already squatting down to help lift the man. "Let's do it."

9

"So as y'all know, my stash is limited, and when it comes to classical music I don't got much. However: I know I talk a lot about the 'soundtrack to the end of the world' and what-not, but I got some real soundtracks from some old movies for ya today. Now, I will warn y'all, unlike some of my classical music, soundtracks are first and foremost tailored for the silver screen. That means they're not usually built for listenin' casually and sometimes they have moments of silence followed by moments of brass and horns, fixin' to have you jumpin' out of yer seat, then quiet piano liable to rip yer heart out. But, brother, lemme tell you, if you just close yer eyes and let it take you over, you'll have one hell of a time.

"I got soundtracks on soundtracks on 101.7, the soundtrack to the end of the world."

HE was not an overweight man, but where he lacked in fat and muscle, he made up in sheer height. Tyler never really noticed the difference between men of medium and large statures until he had to carry one.

The three of them — Allie, Tyler, and the wiry man whose name he discovered to be Lane — grabbed what limbs they could and awkwardly lugged the tall man back to Lakeland. They were closer than Tyler thought, but even a few feet is backbreaking work when carrying 220 pounds of dead weight.

By the time they had already passed Lakeland's outer perimeter defenses, Tyler realized he hadn't been paying much attention to the world passing by. His mind was narrowly focused on keeping a grip on the tall man's legs. When four medics came rushing out to relieve them, he finally straightened his aching spine and took a look around.

Lakeland was nothing like East Tampa. Most of the buildings were little more than piles of rubble, and slabs of tin were propped up alongside canvas and plastic tarps, making for a shanty town floored with slops of trampled mud.

He didn't know what to make of it — his mind's eye had pictured a group of people in a situation more or less similar to Tampa. After all, they weren't all that far away.

"Hey." Allie stepped in front of him, just as out of breath as he was. "Thanks, that was really cool what you did back there."

"Who's this?" Two burly guards toting battered AKMs inserted themselves into the conversation, keeping a close, uneasy eye on the boy. They kept their shoulders squared off toward him.

"Piss off. You saw him help us carry Wagner in," Lane said. "He saved our asses out there. Got hit by some bandits. If it wasn't for that kid we'd probably be goners."

"Well, we're gonna need his gun."

Lane turned to Tyler with an extended hand. Tyler didn't see much use in resisting, and at this point running was out of the question. He handed his ETM M16 over to the Lakeland soldier.

Lane passed it to the guards, who retreated into a nearby shed, and then steadied one shaking hand with the other. "Thanks again, kid. Despite uh…" He glanced around at pedestrians roaming the streets, none of whom seemed to give them much attention. "…despite where you came from, you really proved yourself. Maybe we can get you in a meeting with the boss."

Mayor Hatch. Tyler had only heard the words "terrorist" or "animal" when describing her, and the only physical description he was aware of was her infamous eyepatch. Just as he knew all the glorious stories of the ETM, he knew all the horrors and terror of Mayor Hatch — but then again, Tyler had heard a good deal of things from East Tampa that never quite lined up.

"Sure," he said.

"Stick with Allie for a bit. We'll get you fixed up."

Tyler felt naked without his weapon, but something about Allie told him to trust her, and she was armed so he felt a little better. Not much, but it was something.

The pair sat patiently in a building whose four walls had crumbled to three. Allie's side hadn't taken a bullet; the round had smashed into a nearby tree and sent splinters across her side, just under her arm. She had a few bandages wrapped around her torso under her shirt, but the bleeding had stopped before they even made it to Lakeland.

A tarp had been tied up to protect the building's exposed side from wind and rain, but the flimsy rope had unraveled and the whole thing had collapsed, opening the small, one-room building to the elements. A jumble of zip ties, rope, and plywood lay on top of the tarp, which had begun to flap on the ground like Lacey's ears when she would stick her head out the car window.

Lacey. Riding in the car to school. His mother's hands on the steering wheel. His brother staring out the window and listening to music from his phone. *Was that this same life? Maybe those memories are from someone else.* He put them out of his mind.

Tyler stared at the tarp and wondered if the wind was picking up or if he was just imagining it.

Allie and Tyler sat on two opposing cots in the decaying building, their eyes wandering in every direction about the camp except toward each other. Tyler spied an antique radio that would have been considered ancient even before the Red. It sat lonely in the corner, with its wood finish and bronze-colored, chipped plastic knobs.

"You ever thought about going up to the radio station?" he asked her.

"No way."

"Why not? I bet there's a way past the mines and booby-traps. I mean, the guy up there has to come and go to find food, right?"

"I'm not worried about those. There's some group of insane people up there. Like, after the Red they climbed up there and surrounded the tower. They scalp anyone they take alive — not something I'm all that interested in. I heard the guy on the radio say he can barely ever leave because of those psychos."

"Ah. Yeah, I heard about them. That doesn't sound so great…"

Another painfully long silence passed between them.

"So, uh," Tyler tried his best to sound natural, entering the ring for round two at breaking the ice. "What happened to this place?"

"What do you mean?"

"Everything seems… broken, in one way or another. No offense."

"That's just how the world is now."

"It's not like that in Tampa."

"It's not? What's it like?"

"You've never been?"

"Nope. Not since the Red."

"It's like… I mean, it's not like it was before the Red or anything. But we have generators and electricity sometimes, we've got… you know…"

"What?"

"Walls."

Allie cracked a smile. "We've got a wall! We've got at least three!" She pointed to the crumbling walls, each one on the verge of total collapse. They laughed.

"Look, we've even got buildings." She pointed out the opening at a small building with a stark blue door and a lamppost just outside. "You guys over there with your fancy walls." She smiled slyly and looked him right in the eye — his heart melted like butter on a stovetop.

"I, uh, I didn't see any farms coming in," Tyler said, desperate to keep the conversation going. "You guys not do that?"

"No time for that these days. What about Tampa?"

"No time," he said. "Oh, you didn't answer my question. About what happened here."

"Mortars." A hoarse voice spoke from the door behind him. It commanded their attention, and Tyler froze and listened. "When the National Guard went northeast with all the usable copper in Tampa Bay, they wound up getting dissolved near Orlando. A group got a hold of some of their mortars right after that. Not sure how they got so many rounds. They tried to take Lakeland for themselves — we didn't let them. It hurt, but we held our ground."

Allie shot to her feet and put her hands behind her back out of respect. Tyler turned to find an athletic, rigid woman standing in the makeshift door. Her clothes were stained with months of mud and wear, her hands were clean but calloused, and her hair was cut practically short. A leather patch covered her left eye and ancient scars peeked out from behind it.

"Mayor Hatch." Tyler stood to greet her.

"Yes, and I'm sure you've heard all about me." Despite its raspiness, her voice was strong and unwavering. "There are a lot of rumors over there in East Tampa, but this is the only one that's real." She pointed at her eyepatch. She spoke with a level of certainty and poise, like every word out of her mouth had always been crafted and delivered just as intended.

"My name is Tyler, ma'am. Tyler Ballard."

"And you're from East Tampa."

"Yes ma'am." Tyler's mind was beginning to race. He was in the presence of a woman who could order his untimely death — she could pick up a gun and shoot him in the head without repercussions. He was in the belly of the beast and had forgotten to bring a piece of meat to bribe his way out.

"Thank you for helping my men, and Allie here. She's a good kid, and it seems like you are too." Hatch turned to the girl. "Allie, would you mind taking a step outside? I'd like to speak to Mister Ballard in private, if that's alright."

"Yes, ma'am." Allie hurried out the door without a second thought. Tyler, in his ever-wandering mind, wondered why everyone was using the door when an entire wall was missing — *focus, Tyler.*

Hatch was staring at the fallen tarp in a heap on the ground. "Can you help me with this?"

Tyler rose and they moved to the rubble. She grabbed the frayed rope and began to twist it back into some semblance of what it used to be. It would never function quite as well, but it would serve to tie the tarp back up for a period of time.

"I'm not known for mincing my words," she said. "Sometimes I can come off as a little crass, sometimes I don't take other people's feelings into account." She clamped the rope in her armpit, pulled out a small pistol from the small of her back, and casually waved it in her hand.

"I probably shouldn't bring this to friendly conversations, huh?" With a smirk she tossed it safely onto the cot.

Mayor Hatch took her time as she twisted the rope with her rough hands; Tyler unwrapped the tangled mess of tarp, wood, and broken ties. Dribbles of murky, stagnant water spilled onto the ground.

"What are your intentions here?" the mayor asked.

"My intentions?"

"You're from East Tampa."

"Yeah…"

"I'm not accusing you of anything, and I'm not insinuating anything. I just want to know what your intentions are, in the context of this war we've all found ourselves in. Hand me that corner, please."

"I left the war. I'm a, uh… a deserter, I guess." The words in his mouth tasted like dry vomit.

He passed her the corner of the tarp, and she threaded the rope through a grommet, stretching the tarp out toward a piece of wood standing strapped to the slab of concrete.

"Listen, I understand," she said. "You're not a deserter. Maybe you are, I don't know. I don't care for broad labels like that." She began to secure the corner to the wood. "I was in the military before and during the Red, and I understand things like honor and dedication. I would not have abandoned my post then, but had I found myself in the employment of Mayor Whitley, I would certainly have taken the same path as you. Have you heard of the Nazis?"

"From World War Two." Tyler grabbed the other corner and got it ready to pin up on the opposite side.

"Would you have blamed a Nazi for leaving their post to fight with the Allies?"

"I don't think so. But… how do you know who the Nazis are and who the Allies are?"

"That's a good question." She paused in thought. "I suppose you have to answer it for yourself. Everyone just does their best. We don't ask any more than that from anyone here."

Tyler rubbed his brow. "I… I don't know if I'm interested in switching sides, I just want to… I don't know, get away."

She tightened the last knot and smiled as warmly as a woman like her could manage. "Of course, and I didn't mean that you had to. I'm just saying you shouldn't feel so bad for leaving someone like Whitley behind. He's a bad, bad man."

They stood in silence for a moment. She handed him the rope and he took it. He stood on a stool and began routing it through a center grommet and tying it to the ceiling.

"Are those your intentions?" she asked, examining his handiwork. "Just to 'get away'?"

"Ma'am, I just wanna be left alone in the woods for now."

The tarp began to slip; Hatch swooped in and held it up as Tyler continued to tie.

"And are you staying out there with someone?" she asked.

"No."

"Who was the man that shot those other bandits? I would like to thank him myself. Mister Lane said he was quite proficient with a rifle."

"He's just a guy I met out there a couple of times."

"Do you know his name? Where he stays?"

"All I know is that he's a Marauder." Tyler moved to the far corner and started tying; the mayor held up the remaining portion as he secured it.

"A Marauder," she mused.

"But I don't think he's a bad one —"

"Marauders have only been good news for us, you don't have to worry about them."

"...they have?"

"Well, they were good news. We were under the impression that they were all dead. They weren't saints by any means, but they generally stole from the bandits who came from the northeast, like the ones you ran into today. You might not hear about all that, since most bandits hit Lakeland far before wandering all the way to Tampa. They've been coming from Orlando for about a year now — the place has turned into a breeding ground for bandits.

"The Marauders were the ones who lived in the area but swore no allegiance to Lakeland, Tampa, or anyone else... including each other — the only thing they really had in common was the name. They died off, one by one. Dangerous living, stealing from thieves."

"I wish I could tell you more about him," Tyler lied. "I don't even know his name." He wasn't sure what made him lie, but he knew Miles wasn't the type of person who wanted anything to do with the upper echelons of Lakeland. With a firm tug, Tyler tightened the last knot and they stepped back to admire their work.

"You know," Mayor Hatch said, "if you get tired of living out there, you have a place here. It doesn't have to be now, you're welcome any time. I get that this is not as luxurious as East Tampa, but this isn't exactly our finest structure. And I feel like a boy such as yourself is more interested in doing the right thing over a little comfort. I won't lie to you, there's something in it for me." That was a type of blunt honesty he would never expect from Whitley. "The things you know about the inner workings of East Tampa and the ETM could be very useful to us. And when we show them that we won't be bullied by the strongest kid on the block, then maybe they'll leave us alone."

"I'll... I'll think about it. Is that okay?"

"That's fine. You're free to go, and like I said — you're welcome any time. I'll have one of my men return your rifle to you, and Allie will see you off camp safely."

"Thank you, Mayor."

Mayor Hatch called for a guard and he came in, standing attentively before her. "Let's get this building back up and running with a more permanent solution than this tarp here. Tell Mister Owen that repairs and resources must be annotated, you know how I am about that kind of thing."

"Yes, Mayor," the guard said, and he left.

Tyler started to follow him out.

"One more question," Mayor Hatch started, and Tyler paused in the doorway. "What did they tell you happened? Between us and them."

"That you wanted our excess of canned food, and that you would seize any copper anyone found for yourselves. That you all have been hoarding a whole bunch, taking as much as you can for yourselves. That your greed made you attack our people. That's what Mayor Whitley said. That's what they all say."

She smirked. "Ask Allie what really happened on your way out."

"I will."

Tyler wasn't sure how long he had been sitting and staring at the side of Miles's house. Allie's words were bouncing around in his head like ping pong balls, and the rest of his body wouldn't move.

Two things had happened: Allie told him why Lakeland was fighting East Tampa, and then she kissed him on the cheek.

Both sides had been skirmishing with Plant City just after the Red; with the chaos and confusion Allie admitted that they all had done regrettable things, but the residents of Plant City had been quite aggressive. Most bandits allegedly came from there, eventually dispersing into the woods to the northeast.

Mayor Whitley teamed up with Mayor Hatch to make sure Plant City's residents stayed contained at the very least. While Hatch's newly formed militia was keeping a tight hold on the eastern side of town, Whitley had Gray Platoon swing down south and intercept one of Lakeland's caravans full of ammunition and a few weapons. Lakeland had a unique trade agreement with Fort Meyer and Mayor Whitley wanted in.

Lakeland was forced to pull back, abandoning an ETM platoon in Plant City — the ETM platoon wound up taking serious casualties. Whitley would tell everyone that Lakeland turned on them in their greed and lust for power. Allie didn't say exactly why Lakeland was forced to pull back.

Tyler had once learned that Lakeland was hoarding all the copper necessary for them to one day rebuild the electrical grid, but Allie told him they barely had any copper at all — just enough to fill a couple sheds up north. The National Guard had gone through and stripped most of it after the Red, and whatever stores that still existed had been seized by the East Tampa Militia.

After that, the stories he had heard and memorized over the years were true, Allie confirmed that. Lakeland stole a meager stash of remaining copper after the conflict began, an East Tampa woman was raped in a fire station, though Allie did claim her Lakeland attacker was exiled upon his return and likely killed by bandits.

Tyler told her about his brother but made sure she knew he held no animosity toward her. He kept the details vague and she didn't press for more.

Mayor Whitley is a conqueror and a politician, nothing more. That description fit Tyler's perception of the man quite perfectly. It did not seem to fit Mayor Hatch. He didn't know if she could be trusted, but he knew she wasn't Mayor Whitley, and that was something.

There were rumors, Allie told him, that Whitley had orchestrated the intense mortar attacks that destroyed a good portion of their city, embedding elements from Gray Platoon in the bandit force from Orlando, though proof of that was shaky at best. "Everyone knows it," Allie told him.

Allie would have walked him home, but the others were hanging new power lines to a broken-down bank, with the intent of turning it into a barracks. He didn't think they had the power to supply a place like that, but everyone was out digging holes into which they could drop the new posts for the wiring they did have. She didn't want to leave all the labor to someone else, so while he set out for the jungle, she headed back to Lakeland.

Before they parted, she kissed him on the cheek.

He didn't quite know what to make of all that, so he just stared at the wall instead.

The wall hadn't moved and neither had Tyler. He heard thunder in the distance.

"You gonna help me with this or what?"

Miles was behind him, dragging in a dead deer, shot three times in the side and once in the neck. He was hauling it on a plastic litter, and the animal's corpse was crudely strapped in with nylon tubular webbing. Tyler hopped to his feet and helped the panting man drag it the final stretch. Together they untied the beast and heaved it off the litter.

Tyler tried to think of the right thing to say to thank Miles for saving his life from those roving bandits — he hadn't seen Miles since. They heaved the deer onto Miles's outdoor table for cleaning, just outside smelling range from the cabin itself.

"Pass me that blade." Miles pointed at a medium-sized, freshly sharpened knife behind him. Tyler gave it to him.

Miles flipped the deer over and shoved the knife into its flesh, cutting straight up the underside of its belly. It seemed to cut easier than Tyler would have imagined.

"Uhhh… thanks. For helping us out there."

"No problem, man." He cut deeper into the animal until he was able to shove his hands in. "Can you un-fuck that plastic, please?" Miles nodded down to the plastic sheeting that lay tangled at his feet under the deer. Leaving a mess on the ground would only encourage other wildlife to enter into Miles's area of operations. Tyler did as instructed.

The thank-you went easier than Tyler expected. *Should I be more grateful? What do I say?*

"Can I ask you something?"

Miles was still cutting. "You always ask me shit, I always answer. I don't have secrets."

"Why did you save me? That's twice now. And why did you take me in in the first place? You're a loner out here, and you're not a pervert —"

Miles snorted a half laugh and kept cutting.

"— I just don't get why you let me hang around here."

Placing the tip of his blade in the beast's fur, Miles made another incision, cutting with the blade toward the sky. He spoke, a little softer this time. "You told me earlier that you didn't know anyone whose family survived the Red. I lost my wife and six-year-old son, but my daughter survived. She was twelve and she watched them both die." Miles began cutting shorter, more violent notches through the deer's soft fur. "She made it to thirteen."

He yanked out the heart, lungs, and other organs and tossed them to the plastic on the ground. "Two months after her thirteenth birthday, she wandered out onto a dirt road and got hit by a car." Miles's voice shook with sorrow and rage. He started to pull out the animal's lower guts and drop them on the same sheeting. "They weren't bandits. They weren't from any of the militias. They were just travelers who weren't paying attention. Just a stupid accident. Doesn't make any sense, man." He picked up the knife and carefully cut the deer's backside. "Doesn't make sense."

Tyler picked up other pieces of plastic and wrapped the heart and liver in them.

"I was eleven when the Red hit. She was just a year older than me."

"You remind me of her," he said. "That's why I did what I did."

"And Allie? She's a girl. You said you saw her wandering around a few times."

"She never needed any saving. Not until today."

"Well, I'm glad you helped. I've never seen anyone fight like that."

"You have the same dumb-ass bleeding heart as my daughter. The world's over, man. Go back to East Tampa and look around. Everyone's a fuckin' zombie. The Red came through and everything died." The gravity in his voice made Tyler's heart sink.

"The world's not over," Tyler gently protested. He didn't know what to say after all that, a trend he was noticing in himself — but he knew the world couldn't be over. He was still living in it, it didn't make sense.

"It is for me. I'm just not much good at dying." His voice shook a little. "Throw those in the smaller salt jars, like how I showed you before."

Tyler trudged back to the cabin, heart and liver in hand.

10

"It's about time we brought some gospel music to these heathen lands. The truth is fixin' to set you free my brothers, my gramma always said it. It's too bad the cancer got her just two months shy of the redness... well, maybe that ain't so bad, come to think of it.

"But if she was alive today, she'd be speakin' truth on 101.7, the soundtrack to the end of the world."

"YOU ready?"

They had been training non-stop for the last six days — Miles said that the one rule for living in his cabin would be to train with him. He said it was for both their sakes, since tactical skills are "more perishable than milk."

There was something about practicing the same drills over and over again that seemed to give Miles energy, not expend it. It was everything Tyler could do to keep up. The callouses on his hands were constantly threatening to rip off, and every small muscle and tendon in his body screamed at him to take just one day off. But there were no days off, not out there, and it gave him something to put his mind to. He felt there was inherent value in mastering a skill — the fact that that skill was killing troubled him, but he knew it was necessary. Every day under Miles's tutelage made him feel a thousand times more capable.

Tyler inspected the rifle in his hands. An M4 with a red-dot optic mounted on the top rail and a bag of batteries to keep the optic running for the foreseeable future, with iron sights as a backup.

"I don't have to… earn this or anything? At the ETM I had to earn my keep, all you've done is save my butt over and over."

"What?" That familiar incredulous look fell on Miles's face. "Why the hell would I not want you to have the best weapon possible when we're about to get into a gunfight? That's stupid, don't say stupid shit like that. Besides, you already zeroed it and I don't feel like re-zeroing it. So are you ready?"

"I'm ready."

"Alright then."

Tyler was squinting through his red-dot optic, holding the dot dead center on the chest of a man with a pistol he did not recognize in his hands. The man in his sights, tall, hunched over with a crooked nose, was the only one holding his weapon in hand — the other three men carried revolvers on their hips. The four of them were meandering down a road that had almost entirely been reclaimed by grass and weeds. The edges sunk into the ground and potholes were more common than smooth pavement.

Tyler was hidden among a cluster of sticks and leaves just off the road, looking down its long axis. He was immersed in foliage so thick that he imagined someone would have to step on him before they noticed him.

Miles was just off the edge of the road ahead of them. He was pressed up against the backside of an oak that he had meticulously selected, and he carefully aimed at the group as they approached — only a sliver of the man was exposed, the rest firmly camouflaged among the trees.

The four froze when they saw him.

"Don't move." Miles's voice was stern and unforgiving. Tyler kept his eye on the man with the pistol ready in his hand, as he had been instructed. Any quick moves and he would be the first to go.

"Where'd you get those rucks?" He indicated the heavy bags on their backs.

"None of your business. You're outnumbered, back off."

"I wouldn't be so sure about that. Why don't you just leave your loot on the ground and carry on. I know what you did."

The four cautiously put their packs on the ground as their eyes darted around the forest, searching for any sign of Miles's accomplices. None of their gazes landed on Tyler.

"Guns. Put 'em on the ground," Miles instructed.

Before a word was spoken, the group of bandits dove off the opposite side of road. Tyler couldn't accurately shoot fast enough, so he eased off the trigger to keep himself concealed, hoping they would dash away and never return.

Just a few feet into the woods lay the years-old wreckage of a yellow sedan. It was consumed by rust and vines, and the four men dove behind it. They were behind ideal cover if Miles were to start shooting, but Tyler could see the entire group of them as clearly as the car itself.

They all had pistols in hand now, and one peered through the blown-out car windows, taking aim at Miles.

Tyler opened fire. The man fell to the ground, struggled for a moment, and then fell still.

The remaining three whirled around to the car's opposite corner, taking wild potshots in Tyler's direction, though none of their rounds were even close to hitting him. Still, Tyler flinched with every shot but forced himself to fix his gaze down his sights at the men.

"Toss your pistols out onto the road!" Miles called out.

"Fuck you! Toss your gun out!"

Miles fired a shot over their heads. The fourth man, who hadn't said a word thus far, scrambled to his feet and barreled out into the woods and Tyler could see the pack bouncing across his shoulders until he disappeared into the leaves.

"Just do it, we'll let you go, just like your buddy. That shit you stole isn't even yours, don't die over it."

"You're stealin' just like me!" one of the men screamed.

"Didn't say I wasn't —"

"I'm gonna rip your eyes out of your goddamn skull!"

That seemed to satisfy Miles, as he left his cover and began to move laterally down the road so he could peek around the side of the hollowed-out sedan. As he slowly crested the corner from a distance, with a steady eye on his optic and a steady pair of hands on his weapon, Tyler once again mused at the sight of a slow, unstoppable force.

The man who had screamed at Miles leapt out behind his cover to move to a more advantageous position in the trees, not realizing that Miles was already on the move. —

Miles put him in the dirt — again, he pulled the trigger so fast Tyler could have sworn it was automatic fire. The last bandit recklessly shot as he bounded away from the car. Miles drove his barrel in the man's direction and — *CLICK!*

Without pausing, Miles dropped his rifle so it hung by its sling, pushed it to the side and with lightning speed drew his pistol, firing from the hip as he brought it to his chest and extended it out with both hands.

The last man fell with a thud.

They hadn't said much since they left the ambush site. Miles was carrying two packs, one on the front and one on the back. Tyler shouldered the third. They were heavy with untold treasures; Miles had told him not to check until they were a safe distance away.

After about thirty minutes, Miles rummaged through the bag on his front.

"This ammunition sucks. Guns are a dime a dozen, but good ammo? Nope. That's one of the few benefits of having structure over with the ETM. You guys can make your own ammo and develop a system to make it reliable. Lakeland is especially good at that. Out here you're gettin' the scraps." He glanced at Tyler. "Also, when you find a pistol you decide to carry with you, make sure you practice transitioning from your rifle to your sidearm. Practice that shit every day, might save your ass like it did mine today. Just sayin'."

"Will do," Tyler said. For Miles's generally quiet demeanor, he was always uncharacteristically talkative when it came to tactical advice.

Miles fished out a flask, caked in mud and dirt. He shook it to hear the glorious whirling of liquid contents inside.

"You really think what we did was okay?" Tyler asked.

"Yup."

"What makes you say that?"

He scraped off a few hunks of dirt, unscrewed the cap, and took a swig. "They hit a caravan that was headed to East Tampa last week. They walk this road, swing west, and then straight up kill people trying to trade down there. They just fill up their bags and leave the rest to rot in the sun. They killed two kids about a month ago. I came a bit too late last time."

"And you care about East Tampa civilians?"

"Not really." Another drink.

Tyler shook his head; he wasn't going to get a straight answer. "Like, Robin Hood minus the whole good guy part. You're the asshole version of Robin Hood."

"Sure," Miles chuckled. "I guess so. I like 'Marauder' better, thanks, but you can call me asshole Robin Hood."

He extended the drink to Tyler.

"You think I'm old enough?"

"Shit man, you shoot people — you're old enough."

Tyler took it and managed a gulp without immediately spitting it back up. He coughed a bit to his chagrin and passed it back to Miles.

"You know," Miles said, "I was thinking about it, and I take back what I said before."

"About what?"

"You being a child soldier. There's no such thing."

"What do you mean?"

His eyes glazed to that brooding solemnity that came over him from time to time. "A child in combat is not a child at all, that's why it's so messed up to put a kid in that position in the first place. A bullet doesn't care what age you are, it just hits you and you die.

"East Tampa sucks, but for a while it was the last place any kid could be a kid anymore. Now the food's running out and no one's doing anything about it, so soon East Tampa is going to be just like everywhere else. And in that 'everywhere else,' if you can't fight, you're going to die. I've seen it a million times. So, like it or not, you've been flung into adulthood and there's no going back. Tampa lost their shot at retaining the childhood of whatever children they had left when they started enlisting kids. People used to bitch about the evils of 'modern' society... well one of the benefits was not having goddamn child soldiers.

"But you're here now, and the least I can do is teach you how to survive. A little drink to take the edge off doesn't hurt. Just don't drink your face off."

He passed Tyler the flask and Tyler took a fraction of a gulp, barely stomaching the small mouthful.

"I don't think I'm in any danger of that," he said between coughs.

Miles laughed. He took the flask back, glanced at Tyler and the surrounding forest. "The asshole version of Robin Hood..." he said with a chuckle.

Tyler sat on a throne made of books.

They had been stacked by someone in the early months of the Red, reading one and placing it aside when complete. One book turned into five which turned into a dozen, and eventually this person was too engrossed in those pages to keep count, and the piles continued to grow.

That was the only story Tyler could conjure out of the piles of books scattered about the wood laminate flooring, which was bubbling and cracking with years of weather trespassing through the windows and doors.

Something about the stacks of books reminded him of the stacks of bodies in the streets of East Tampa during the Red. Anthony hadn't let him linger around the putrid mountains of rotting flesh, but he caught a glimpse or two and the memory of the smell made him want to vomit. A mass of stories, vibrant individual things with words and feelings all imprinted inside, formed together into a lifeless, unholy mass, left to decay in the rains of time, left to be eaten by mold and forgotten by the minds who remained behind.

"You know what this place is?" Miles asked. He was sitting on another stack across from him.

Tyler scanned the rows of shelves laden with books that surrounded them, unsure if this was a trick question. "It used to be a library, I think."

"Used to be?"

"I mean, half of these books are wet, moldy. Are *you* gonna try and pick those pages apart?"

"There are plenty that are just fine, man. This place isn't dead yet."

"Alright then, fine — it's a library."

Miles was staring at him intently — gone were the nonchalant gazes and the mumbles through the side of the mouth. It felt like every word was important to Miles now, in this place filled with decaying books.

Miles's M4 was slung across his back, and he carried something else wrapped up in a tattered blanket. His best guess was that it was some other kind of weapon. What kind or why Miles carried it remained a mystery.

"What's that?" Tyler asked.

"I'll show you in a minute," the older man replied. "What do you think all these books are for, exactly?"

"Umm… reading?"

"That's right. And why do you read?"

"To get smarter?"

"And why do you want to get smarter?"

"So you can figure stuff out, I guess. I dunno."

"That's right." Miles paused, letting his eyes linger on the sea of books around them. "The first year after the Red, my daughter and I were on our own up near Dade City. We ran into these two groups fighting over a pharmacy full of penicillin, painkillers, other useful things that folks were running out of quick. One group was led by a guy named De Silva, and the other group pushed him too far. They killed a couple people from his crew, and they got him cornered and on the run.

"So, De Silva started to do his research. He tracked their moments when he could, learned as much about them as possible — where they kept and prepared their food, how they cleaned their water, where they slept, where they stored their weapons, all of it. He was looking for weaknesses.

"But eventually they came to a boiling point. They had to bail entirely and risk the wilderness or they could stand and fight. They picked option two, obviously, but instead of holing up just anywhere, De Silva and his people barricaded themselves inside the same pharmacy everyone was up in arms about.

"The other group had twice the manpower and twice the weaponry. De Silva knew it, but they were dug in at that point. Surrounded. And let me tell you man, this guy turned the place into a fortress. There was no getting in without an absolute bloodbath for both parties involved. Neither of them could afford that. Nobody had any explosives back then, ammo was scarce… so the other group decided to starve them out. They locked the place down, muzzles pointed at any and all breach-points, and they waited for the food to run out.

"De Silva figured those other guys would lay siege to the pharmacy, he saw it coming. It was their MO. Now, this pharmacy was attached to a grocery store, and one wall led into an office which was collapsed completely shut, and that office shared a wall with a toy store which he had chained shut from the inside days ago. That toy store was on the edge of a shed, which was basically surrounded by trees and unguarded. De Silva and his guys dug a tunnel into the office, totally out of sight, and they dug into the toy store, and then into the shed.

"But he didn't just evac his guys and flank the group who laid siege to him. That would have been easy, and it may have even been successful, but it wasn't a sure thing, and De Silva wanted a sure thing. Instead, he left three of his own in the store, he kept them moving around in there. The boys outside would hear muffled voices, they'd see the occasional flashlight — they'd assume that De Silva and company were still very much indoors, and in full force.

"De Silva took two others and they got outside under the cover of darkness. You see, he knew where they were storing a lot of their food, so he had his guys inject rat poison right into their food supply. Wasn't a day later, the other group was all stumbling around deathly ill. That's when he finally pulled out the guns, and at that point, he was just cleaning them up."

Tyler felt heavy on those books as the story came to life in his mind. What may have sounded like a series of genius tactics whispered among the boys of East Tampa didn't light that same spark of adventure in him. He could picture the second group writhing on the cracked pavement in anguish, foaming out of their mouths and clutching at the sky before De Silva and his followers put a bullet in each of their heads. It felt like a well of gravity in Tyler's stomach.

He hated every part of it, but more than anything he hated that such things waited for him in his future. What side he would find himself on, he was unsure.

"I asked him how he came up with that," Miles continued. "He said he read it in a history book in this library. I still haven't found the book he was talking about. Found a lot of other cool stuff though."

Miles reached behind him and retrieved the blanket, unwrapping it and revealing its contents. An M4A1 lay among its tattered threads.

"Those guys we hit the other day on the road, you know they killed three people a few miles from here, right?"

"Yeah."

"Well, I went back to the camp they hit and they had picked it pretty clean. Everything except for this. I want you to have it."

Tyler's eyes grew wide as it fixed on the weapon. It didn't have a spot of rust on it; the optic seated on its top rail was a reflex sight similar to Miles's, if a little heftier. It bore backup iron sights and a forward grip with a civilian-made, extendable stock and a sling actually built for rifles. This was not the rust-laden stick of metal Santana had given him; this was a weapon made for war.

Tyler extended his hand, but Miles retracted the rifle just out of reach.

"Listen. I know you understand that this isn't a toy, I know you understand what it does. But you need to know what it is."

Tyler just wanted to wrap his hands around it, but he knew that what Miles had to say must be important. He put his hands on his knees and awaited an explanation, putting on as patient a face as he could manage.

"This is a tool," Miles said. "It's a means to an end, that's it. And with it comes a lot of responsibility that, in my opinion, is ignored by most people. You've seen it—guys running around shooting each other and they don't even know why. You've done it yourself."

"I know." Tyler felt a pang of guilt, but something in Miles's voice was elevating him, not beating him down. He was being taught, not berated. "I understand."

Miles cleared the weapon and admired it in his grasp. "Your rifle is an extension of your hands. In order to use it, you need to be as comfortable with it as you are with a pencil or your shoelaces. But your hands, they're just an extension of your body, and you need to master that too. You need to take care of it, whether you're in hard times or not. But it doesn't end there. Your body is an extension of your mind."

Miles considered the endless rows of bookshelves around them. "This is where you feed that. This is where you exercise the muscles of your mind. You need to teach your hands what to do, but this is where you learn why you're clearing that room. Why you're taking that hill. And sometimes, like in the case of De Silva, being a smart little shit will help you outsmart your enemy. Or whatever adversity you find yourself up against."

Miles put the weapon across his knees and picked up a book within arm's reach. Its spine was cracked, and Tyler could see the pages through it. "I'd recommend staying out of other peoples' fights, but inevitably you're gonna get sucked in. And if you get sucked in, you need to win.

"If you sit around and ask me how you can get better at tactical shit, I'm gonna tell you — you gotta train. Train, train, train," he said. "And if you sit around and ask me dumb-ass questions all day, life-type things, I'm gonna say the same thing. You gotta train. And that training is done right here, in these pages. This is not a forgiving world. It doesn't matter if you're inclined toward it, if you're a book nerd or whatever. God knows I'm not. But I'm a practical guy. Above all else, I'm practical. And this…" He pointed at the book in his hands. "This is practical. Does that make sense?"

"It makes sense."

Miles was silent for a moment, satisfied that he had been heard. He handed Tyler the rifle.

"Look man, all I'm really trying to say is that if you have an army of dumbasses, they're going to do some dumbass shit. That's the main reason why both Lakeland and the ETM are ticking time bombs."

Tyler nodded in understanding. He took the M4A1 in his hands, but his excitement at the thing had been stamped out by Miles's words. It felt heavy in his hands now, though he wanted nothing more than for it to feel light.

"Thank you," Tyler said. "I think I need to think about what you said, but I get it. I think."

"That's literally all I'm asking for, man," Miles said, and he scooted off his pile of books like a child. "Let's roll, I thought I saw some beer a couple blocks back. Hard to beat warm beer on a hot-ass day."

Tyler strapped his M16 to his back and slung his new M4 across his chest. He scurried to Miles's side.

"Hey, what happened to De Silva?"

"Caught an unlucky bullet to the gut a couple years back. Didn't make it. There's only so much you can do."

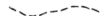

Tyler lay in the dark, staring at Miles's ceiling. He remained flat on the uneven, weathered couch that had been beat up, rained on, flipped over, rained on again, and Tyler was pretty sure the two holes in its side were bullet holes. Still, compared to most couches in the area it was quite comfortable. He was something of a connoisseur of broken couches at this point.

The cabin was even smaller on the inside than it looked on the outside. There was a sink that drew its water from the barrels mounted on the roof. They ran through a basic, non-potable filtration system and gave Miles large but not infinite amounts of running water.

A wall of blankets separated the living area from Miles's bed, though Miles could see the front door and only window from where he slept. Bolts secured each entrance, and he slept with a pistol at his side. A picture of his wife and children was tacked next to the door, and another lay next to his bed. He never seemed to pay them much mind.

Miles had secured tripwires approximately 150 feet away from the cabin. The wires were taut, constructed from sections of galvanized steel taped together; a rabbit wouldn't trip it, but any size of human certainly would. Two years prior, Miles raided several arts and crafts stores scattered about the Tampa Bay area, and he scrounged several bags of tiny bells, among other things he used to patch his living situation together. The bells were poured into bags — plastic bags, laundry bags, drawstring bags — if someone tripped the wire, their arrival would be announced by the crashing of a thousand tiny bells. He walked Tyler through the alert system, along with its unmistakable crash of bells and bags.

But none of that was on Tyler's mind that night. He stared at the ceiling, too far off to make out in the dark, and for a while his mind reflected upon itself. Fragments of what had happened, what was happening, and what might happen played over and over in his head with no real coherence to them.

He thought of his mother's smile, as she reached for a glass of water in the warm sunlight peeking through their house's blinds. He thought of his brother, wrench in hand, knees in the mud, fixing the water filtration system just down the street — he didn't care that it was raining. He thought of Santana, and what he might be doing at this very moment. Maybe he was recovering from the gunshot wound to his shin, maybe he was back on his feet. He thought of Allie, and even though he was alone his heart fluttered in his chest. The world had turned cold after the Red, but she was a spot of warmth. He thought of what might happen next, how he might return to the ETM with stories of getting inside information from Lakeland's defenses. He thought of what would happen if he bought Allie's story and realized that Lakeland was not inhabited by evil savages like he had been taught. He pictured a life in the woods with Miles, robbing robbers and killing killers.

And he thought of these things again and again and again and again....

Tyler rolled to his side and reached for the pocket radio on a nightstand near his head. The device was probably less than ten years old, but something about any piece of technology before the Red seemed archaic to Tyler — they belonged to a time that was now flashes in memory, tidbits of blurred faces, and moments of laughter and light. The technology that was born in those days were covered in cobwebs now, and though they may have been manufactured and distributed four and a half years ago, they may as well have been a hundred years old.

He extended the radio's antennae and eased the volume knob up, heeding the ancient thing as it crackled to life.

"And now that we got the gospel outta the way, lemme tell ya that truth comes in all forms... in the angels and in the demons too." The man's haggard voice turned to a whisper. *"I've got rock, I've got roll... I've got all those things that make you tingle way down low. Just remember, you heard it first on —"*

"Turn that shit off." Miles's voice groaned through the cabin.

Tyler twisted the knob to the off position and said nothing. He placed the radio back on the end table. His eyes were closed and his body lay still, but sleep still eluded him.

Eventually, Tyler heard that same mysterious speaker sputter to life from the other room.

"Be careful!" Miles's voice laughed. *"We gotta build this thing, but how about we build it without falling to the earth and breaking all of our bones?"*

"Daddy, you're too big to fit up there! I'm the only one." It was the voice of a little girl.

"Listen —"

"Miles, just stand under. You're a good catch, right?" Tyler figured that must be his wife and the sound of the little girl must be his daughter. His heart felt heavy for the man in the next room.

CRASH!

His eavesdropping was interrupted by the sound of the bells clattering to the ground, and the speaker from Miles's room went silent with a *click*.

By the time Tyler had leapt out of bed, Miles already had a rifle in his hand and was donning a chest rack filled with fresh magazines. Tyler grabbed his new M4A1 and shoved an extra magazine in his pocket. He left the rest behind in order to keep up with Miles.

Both barefoot, they crept out into the night with their rifles at the ready. The tripwires were all just out of the cabin's line of sight — an advantage Miles gave himself to ensure that no one would be watching the front door when they tripped his defenses. Still, he kept an eye out as he exited the cabin. "People are always inventing some new method of assholery, you can't entirely rely on much," Miles told him a few days earlier during one of their training sessions.

Tyler felt a kind of unfamiliar confidence. Under Santana he felt safe — he knew the sergeant would look out for him, and maybe he could even contribute to the fight and impress the man. But under Miles's supervision he felt capable. Like they were both forces to be reckoned with.

They split into the darkness, positioning themselves to have two angles of fire toward the bells, but not so wide an angle that the there was any risk of pointing at each other.

Tyler could see Miles out of the corner of his eye, and the two of them crept through the woods like panthers. But, like always, the sleek, ninja-like image of himself dissolved as he felt the sticks and rocks on the forest floor driving themselves into his bare feet. If he yanked his foot up in pain, he would step back down louder than the last time.

"What was that?" A man's voice shook in the darkness. Though Tyler's heart softened at the sound of human fear, his mind hardened at the advantage it gave him.

"I don't know," a woman's voice whispered. "Let's turn back and find another route."

"We can't just keep turning back. We stayed too long, we need to b-line it, whatever it takes."

"Don't be stupid, Charlie," the woman said. "We're leaving, alright? But we have to do it smart. We'll talk about this later, we definitely just woke someone up."

"You got that right," Miles said, appearing from a darker shadow.

Tyler made out three figures in the moonlight: a man, woman, and a girl of maybe seven or eight years old. They all shot their hands in the air. Tyler stepped into view, though he kept himself partially obscured behind a tree and with his finger on the trigger.

"Please!" the woman said. "Don't hurt us."

"Is there anyone else with you?" Miles asked.

"Just us. We're unarmed."

"Unarmed? Out here? Bad idea."

Her face twisted in desperation and pain. "I know… we just… we didn't have a choice."

"What are you doing here?"

"We're trying to leave," the man said. "Head north, go anywhere. We just have to get away."

"Get away from where?"

"Plant City. Everyone's leaving…"

"Everyone already left," Miles said.

"No, not everyone. There are still people out there — we tried to stay, it's our home."

"Where are you going?"

"We don't know…"

Miles shook his head —

"It's that bad," the woman said. "If you're out here all the time, you don't know."

"Well, you've got two cities using your home as a battlefield —"

"What?" the man asked.

"Lakeland and East Tampa," Tyler spoke up, curious as to the man's apparent lack of knowledge of the fight he was in the middle of. "They're fighting each other, and you guys are caught in the crossfire. It's awful."

"Caught in the crossfire?" The sound of righteous indignation bubbled up in the man's voice, and Tyler could see him straightening up and stepping forward. "We're the targets. Neither of them have let up on us since the beginning…"

"What are you talking about?"

"You guys really don't venture into town, do you?" the woman said. She started to lower her hands as she began to explain.

"Keep them up," Miles said, and she did.

"Copper. It's all about copper. When the Red hit, the National Guard came in and confiscated most of it in Tampa, Lakeland, Fort Meyer, Naples… all over. They needed it for something up north."

"Yeah, I know. Everyone knows that. That's why it's all gone."

"Before they went up to Orlando, there was a logistical error, some kind of oversight, and they left some pretty big stashes in Plant City —"

"The military wouldn't make a mistake like that," Tyler said.

"You'd be surprised," Miles interjected and then let the man continue.

"A few of our own gathered the stashes and hid them all over town. They're all dead now, killed over the last few months of raids… now nobody really knows where the copper is. So, the ETM and Lakeland come after us day and night — they hit a school recently. A school, just to lock down some blocks for their hit squads or death squads or whatever you call them, to come through house-to-house looking for the reserves. And for what? What are they going to do with it? Everyone's scrambling for something that doesn't... I don't know." The man's voice trailed off. "They're treating it like gold, like it has some value except currency doesn't exist anymore. I don't understand it, and quite frankly I've had enough of it."

"You got proof of any of this?" Tyler asked.

He could see their eyes grow wide in the moonlight. "Proof?" the man said. "There's no proof, just the blood of my friends all over that fucking town. I can't stay there a minute longer." His voice was quivering with fear and grief.

"She your daughter?" Miles pointed at the little girl with one of the fingers on the front of his weapon. The girl kept her hands higher than everyone else's; of the group, she seemed the most familiar with the drill.

"Yes. We all found each other after the Red, but we're a family now. We're just trying to start over. Please don't hurt us..."

Miles studied them for a while. "Head straight back until you hit that road you crossed to get here. Follow it east until you hit a stream, then follow the stream north. Stay west of Orlando, you don't want to wind up there. I heard there's some decent people south of Gainesville, but I wouldn't trust anyone if I were you. Got it?"

They nodded fervently.

"Get outta here."

They began to leave the way they had come.

"Hey," Miles said. "Plant City isn't your home. You take that with you."

Tyler wasn't sure if they heard him. The three disintegrated into the formless darkness; Tyler and Miles grabbed the tripwire and bag of bells to string it back up.

"You know…" Tyler said. "You're not very good at pretending like you don't care about stuff."

"Make sure that other end is taught." Miles tossed the bells back up and over its original limb.

"What do you think they meant by all that? About the copper."

"East Tampa, Lakeland… they're a bunch of assholes fighting assholes — that story fits the bill. But I have no idea, and honestly I really don't give a shit. There are no good guys, there are no bad guys. No one is more or less deserving of copper, antibiotics, guns, or whatever other shit you want or need. People just take and that's it, you gotta use every tool in your toolbox to stay ahead of them. And I know what you're thinking — you're going to ask your girlfriend what she thinks about the copper and Plant City and all that. She won't know shit, I guarantee it. But I'm sure she'll have plenty to say, just like everyone else. Just sayin'."

"She's not my girlfriend," Tyler said, and they pulled the tripwire tight and stepped back into their newly secured perimeter.

Is Miles right? Tyler wondered, turning from one side to the other on the couch as wood under the cushion dug into his back. *Is there no such thing as good guys or bad guys?* Tyler felt as if his eyelids hadn't even blinked once since he got back to the cabin and tried to find the ever-elusive embrace of unconsciousness. He could see the sun's rays peeking in through the blinds, gently nudging him back into the world of the living.

There was a familiar knot in his stomach, and he thought it might weigh through his midsection and down through the wooden floor. He was reminded of that weak, incurable feeling that he felt back when his "justice" was served and his brother's murderers were killed. However, this time he felt that way about the whole world. There seemed to be all these rules, these laws and ideas of what was good and right, but no one followed them. People drew lines and demanded that others fall square into them, and yet in the shadows they themselves lived and danced outside the lines, spitting on those who did exactly what they were asked.

The thought that he was a part of stealing these caches near the school churned his stomach even more. He remembered watching Gray Platoon pass them by just after they lost Major Kessler. And that's when the very uncomfortable thought began to inch its way into his head. It was easy to demonize Gray Platoon as they were faceless agents to him, but they weren't the only ones who knew the truth. Operations like that required coordination from all levels.

Did Major Kessler know about the caches? Did he know about the copper?

His image of the Major — this stoic man of honor and courage — was being torn apart in his mind as the man's flesh was torn apart in Plant City.

You don't know. They could have been lying, they could have been confused. They were scared, and scared people say crazy stuff.

Tyler's mind was twisting over itself to defend the Major against the accusations in his thoughts, spurred by the Plant City refugees' words. At the same time, his mind was finding it increasingly difficult to justify the actions of the Major and his cohorts.

All Tyler wanted was to sleep, but his mind was a hurricane of thoughts, crashing into one another into the morning.

11

"You wanna listen to music of the old world? Love, love, love, baby... that's what it was all about. By the way, any of y'all stepped outside? The world is gettin' windy, my brothers.

"I see a storm a-comin', so y'all best step inside, snuggle up with your lover, and turn yer radios to 101.7, the soundtrack to the end of the world."

TYLER was making sure his face revealed no signs of pain as his thighs were burning up the hill. It was a small hill by anyone's standards, but hills were not common in that part of Florida. Allie was just ahead of him, moving effortlessly as if this were just more flat ground.

"Come on, we're almost there."

After what seemed like an hour — though it was probably more like fifteen minutes — Tyler and Allie made it to the top of what she had told him was the "highest mountain for miles, besides the radio station, obviously." The wind was beginning to pick up with an even more odd consistency — there were no gusts or spurts like usual, just a long, slow build.

Tyler rested his hands on his knees, but straightened up as she turned back to him with a smile on her face.

"See? Look, over there." She pointed. "Lakeland."

Tyler followed her finger and made out the distant town. Buildings peeked over the wild treetops, and several columns of smoke rose from Lakeland chimneys. Still, despite the amount of effort it took to summit the hilltop, it wasn't quite the magnanimous view Allie had promised.

"I thought you said it was a mountain!" he teased. "I can barely see anything up here."

"It is a mountain, by Florida standards anyway," she said. "If you want to go climb up the radio tower mountain and get blown up by a crazy guy and his landmines, be my guest. This is the best mountain you're gonna get."

"Still doesn't count."

"Okay, smart guy. What would you call it?"

"Uh… a hill?"

She smirked. "I'm not sure you want to admit having so much trouble getting up a hill…"

He laughed and shook his head. "Hey, a hill's a hill, I can't call it anything else."

"Well," she said, "it's a mountain to me."

Their smiles faded as they were lulled by the natural grandeur before them, gently bowing before the wind. The untamed wilderness always put a stop to Tyler's wild and chaotic thoughts. *My brain gets crazy a lot these days, I should remember that,* he thought.

Allie sighed at the sight of the ocean of green that stretched endlessly before them, and Tyler just about melted in his shoes at the sound of her. But then a thought drifted in his head, and he wanted to cry when he thought it.

This is what it should feel like. This is what being a teenager should feel like. What a rare thing.

They stood there for a long while, and he did not speak because his words usually stumbled out of his mouth and would surely careen through the moment like a bulldozer.

Eventually they sat down and shared a granola bar and two tomatoes that Miles had grown in his garden. Tyler asked her why Lakeland didn't farm for the future, and she asked him why East Tampa didn't do the same. It wasn't the first time they had discussed the subject, and he expected it wouldn't be the last.

This time, he told her all that had happened the night before: about the noise that woke them up, the family and how they came from Plant City — he told her about their accusations, and her face scrunched up like a bad smell had wafted in.

"You believed them?"

"Why wouldn't I?"

"I mean, you'd believe random people over all of us? Mayor Hatch isn't like that, she's not easy to be around but she's a straight shooter. And what about me? I wouldn't follow someone around if I thought they were just after copper or guns or even food. I know, it sounds exactly like something Whitley would say, but we're just defending ourselves. We want to be left alone. If Mayor Hatch was really lying like that, it would make her and everyone around her like East Tampa."

"And you're sure they're not?"

She shook her head with a parental smile. "We don't have a Gray Platoon, for starters. And we don't kill random people for no reason."

He left the subject to dissipate with the fading daylight. She glanced back at him, as if she were expecting more of a fight out of him; she only got silence.

"Although…" Allie added, "if Mayor Hatch were some evil mastermind —"

"That's not what I'm saying —"

"If she were… she keeps insanely detailed records in her office. Maybe you could ask to see them. I'm sure they're not a secret. They'd tell you about any big surplus of copper or antibiotics or whatever you think they've got hidden away, since she has to write it all down before it can get distributed. She'll show you she's got nothing to hide. She likes you, I think she'd show you all that."

Tyler let this ruminate for a second. "Where's her office?"

"It's the office right past where she brought you, actually. With the big blue door and a lamp post right next to it. You probably saw it coming in… why?"

"Just curious, I don't know. I just like asking you stuff." He smiled and glanced at the ground, dancing from a child to an adult as he often did. She met his gaze and her face softened as a fragment of doubt slipped in.

"You don't…" Allie started, "you don't really think Mayor Hatch is into that kind of bad stuff, do you? I know she's rough around the edges…"

"Nah," he said. "You're probably right."

The rest of the day was filled with small talk, but a corner of his mind was busy trying to remember what the rest of Hatch's office looked like.

"That's a stupid idea."

"Why is it stupid?"

"Because," Miles said as he slammed another nail into the legless wooden table over his window, sealing it off. "You're gonna get a bullet to the face, and if you get caught, they would be stupid not to assume you're an ETM spy or some shit. What did I tell you about playing it smart? Give me another nail."

Tyler handed him a nail; Miles slammed it in and what once was a table was now a wall. Miles stepped off the chair underneath him and yanked it over to the next window. He glanced up at the sky, grabbed a warped piece of plywood, and went to hammering.

"Are you gonna tell me why you're covering these windows up?" Tyler asked.

"You feel that wind?"

"Yeah, I guess. You're hanging up plywood because it's windy?"

"No, dickwad, shut up for a second. And yes, kind of. Just stop and feel the wind. No breaks, no gaps… it just has that feeling."

"What feeling?"

He paused for a second. "Like some 250-pound guy is gently caressing your face before punching you in the mouth and breaking your jaw. It's unnerving."

SLAM! He pounded more nails into the side. "Storm's coming. The wind should break up in the trees pretty good, and as long as none of those trees come crashing through my roof, the windows are all I've got to worry about. Hurricanes are no joke."

"Whoa, wait." Tyler said. "Hurricane? You think this is a hurricane?"

"That's what it feels like, but I'm not a weatherman and we don't exactly have early warning systems like we used to. It's that season though."

They finished fixing scraps of wood to the windows, and then they secured all the objects that could turn into projectiles, either tying them down or moving them inside.

"Go inside, go under my bed, and you'll find a tape recorder," Miles instructed. "Grab it and the tape next to it. Get two freezer bags from the box with the five-fifty cord and bring them out here."

Tyler did as he was told. He pulled out a box from under Miles's bed and picked up a slender tape recorder with a tape inside and one next to it. His father had tapes like that in a dusty corner of his study, though he had never seen one used.

He returned with the tape recorder, tapes, and freezer bags in hand.

"Is this what you listen to at night?" Tyler asked, unsure if even just the question was pushing too far.

Miles sat down in the chair he was standing on; he wiped his brow with a rag. "You heard that?"

"Yes."

"Yeah, that's the one. We were building a treehouse. Never finished, work got in the way. Then one year... well, you know. I've got two tapes, and if something ever happens to me you need to keep them safe. Understand?"

"I understand."

"You're wondering why I'd want something around if I wasn't alive to hear it."

"I didn't say that."

"I don't have a good reason," his voice faltered slightly. "I would just be... I don't like the thought of it disappearing. Even if I'm gone."

Tyler nodded. Miles turned his attention to the tapes and the tape recorder. "I used to have videos of all this, on a tablet. After the Red, something told me that all that high-tech stuff wouldn't last, so I recorded it on these tapes as a backup."

He dropped the recorder and the tape into a freezer bag and sealed it up, except for a small gap on one end. Pressing out all the excess air, he wrapped the bag tight and closed the gap. The first bag went into the second and he sealed that one up too for good measure.

"Tablet got wet two weeks later. Stopped working, just like all the rest of the high maintenance shit from those days. Sucks losing the video, but at least I got the audio. These won't last forever, I know that, but I hope they last for a while."

Miles turned to Tyler and handed him the bundle of tapes and bags. "Put this back under my bed. This is the most precious thing that I have, and now you know where and what it is."

Tyler wasn't sure what to say. "I won't let anything happen to it."

"Alright, thank you. Now grab your rifle. Let's get some training in. For all my talk of books there are always basics you can't forget about either."

After the tapes were returned to their hiding place, Tyler met Miles with his rifle and they once again began to train, this time in the art of urban combat.

They started by clearing rooms — when they had "cleared" his cabin a hundred times, they switched to what Miles called "glass houses." Under the rising wind, they placed sticks and rope on the ground to imitate the layout of a room, and they cleared it over and over, changing the types and sizes and combinations of rooms each time. Just when Tyler thought they were done and Miles would let him rest his head on the couch, he pulled out the tourniquets and gauze and they practiced treating wounds.

Finally, after the sun had long fallen behind the horizon, they ate and retired in the cabin. Tyler's body felt worn and every muscle in his body was sore, but for the first time in several nights he was intent on staying awake.

12

"You think lullabies were made to send babies to sleep? Or were they made to
give mommy and daddy a little time for dirty deeds in the dark..."
"Hush now... it's 101.7, the soundtrack to the end of the world."

THE outer Lakeland sentries were easy to bypass. Under the cover
of darkness, Tyler was beginning to feel at home when uncertainty
and fear were pumping through his veins. His heart pounded so
hard he thought it might echo through the town and wake up its
inhabitants — but the pounding was a familiar one, and for all the
uncertainty he found in combat, it was easier to navigate than the
politics and lessons and social nuances of the outside.

He kept a close eye on patrolling guards, counting them
carefully and searching for a heavy eyelid or a tired yawn.

His mind swam in confidence all throughout his approach,
confidence in the cover of night and in his position as the
aggressor. Confidence all the way up until he realized that he was
well beyond the outer cordon; he was already in the mouth of the

lion, and if the beast woke up — he'd have to be out of there before the jaws of Lakeland closed shut.

There's no turning back now.

No one told him to trudge through those swamps and sneak past that outer cordon. For his whole life, someone had always been guiding him. Even through the chaos and fire of combat, someone, competent or not, had made clear to him their objectives, and they told him what to do and when to do it. Now he was here of his own accord, and the consequences could be fatal. The phrase *"I brought this upon myself"* hung heavy in the back of his throat, as every piece of his psyche braced for the impact of a guard's wandering eyes, followed by a wall of incoming bullets.

There were groups of two or three armed guards along the inner lines of Lakeland's defenses. Like East Tampa, the city hadn't had the time to breathe required to build walls or guard towers, so they relied on these small groups to cover one another with intersecting fields of fire. Miles called them "blocking positions."

East Tampa had the same problem with too much ground and too few personnel, though they were planning on fencing the area soon. A fence may have stopped Tyler, or it may have just angered him enough to dig under it. He couldn't say.

Either way, Lakeland's gaps between the guard positions were significant enough that one person could, with a lot of care and a little luck, move between them without being detected.

Crawling through a field of tall grass and into a stretch of low ground, Tyler immediately felt water under his hands and knees. He continued forward and cringed as the water lapped up at his socks, soaking through and drenching his feet. Tyler wished he would have paid more attention on his previous entry to Lakeland, which was in broad daylight. He wished he would have kept an eye out for points of ingress and egress that were dry. Not only was it profoundly irritating and uncomfortable, squishy boots slogging through a swamp did not make for a quiet infiltration.

Too late for that now.

The decline eventually became an incline again and Tyler crawled back out to dry land. He didn't know if it was a stream running through the grass, a storm drain, a sewer run-off, or some other source of wetness. If there was a stench, it didn't reach his nostrils.

He took the question and stored it away in his mind, as it was not useful to him in the moment. Tyler kept a low profile and remained careful to shy away from any source of light, particularly ones that would appear behind him and silhouette him.

Then there was the plodding of a dark figure only feet away, and Tyler froze. It was a man, who must have just slogged through the same wet spots Tyler had passed through. He was grunting with every movement as if to lament each and every step — all of which brought the man closer and closer. Tyler could only make out the figure's silhouette from the light of a distant trash can fire behind him and the gentle backlight of the moon on his bald scalp.

The man appeared to be paying little attention to where he was going, and he fiddled with something in front of his face, walking without looking. Every one of Tyler's muscles was tense, uneasy. He willed each one to stay completely still — the slightest movement would undoubtedly alert him, and yet moving was the only way to get out of the oblivious man's path.

A spark lit in front of the man's mouth, lighting up a face that looked like it was made of rock and leather, and revealing a rifle strap slung across his chest. The spark faded, then reappeared. He was trying to light a cigarette.

The figure paused, sparking the failing lighter again and again. "Shit," he whispered to the empty night.

Tyler thought he could reach out and touch the man's boot. He had one hand on his rifle, but as he was scraping through the brush he had grabbed it by the slip ring in the center, and he wasn't sure if he was fast enough to pull the rifle forward, shove the buttstock in his shoulder, take aim and fire before the other man did the same. *Hell, if he thinks quick enough he could probably just jump on top of me before I could shoot.* Instead, Tyler waited, awkwardly positioned in a half-squat, half-crawl only feet from the man in the pitch-black dark.

The man took another step forward and Tyler grit his teeth, planning the moves in his head: *swing the rifle around while keeping your balance, move back onto a knee as you do it, aim in his direction and fire five shots, at least. Once you see him go down, start running — the game's up at that point. Just start running.*

Then, for a reason unclear to Tyler, the man turned to his left, swearing to himself and the cigarette lighter and the empty night as he walked away from his probable death at the hands of a fifteen-year-old boy.

For a moment, Tyler remained frozen. After a handful of eternally long seconds willing every fiber in his body to stillness, he was finding it difficult to shift gears back to forward movement.

Keep going. Keep going.

With a deep breath, Tyler switched from a crawl to a low walk, keeping both hands on his rifle.

As he reached the perimeter of the camp itself, he was surprised at the lack of sentries roaming about. He remembered a similar thought regarding East Tampa's security when he and the reconnaissance element from the ETM had returned from the mission where Sean Ford had been wounded.

Does everyone have such awful security?

He didn't know what else he ought to have expected. Everything that had been explained to him operated on the assumption that both towns wielded amounts of power that only adults could really understand, with a spiderweb of defense mechanisms so complicated only someone like Miles could weave their way in. Despite the fact that the whole mission was his idea in the first place, and that it hinged on such deficiencies in security, Tyler was still surprised when he saw it. Lakeland's security was indeed little more than a few armed guards and unfounded rumors of an impenetrable perimeter.

Maybe smoke and mirrors are all anyone can afford these days. Maybe it's all most security ever was, he thought, excluding Miles's defensive perimeter from that assessment.

Tyler kept to the shadows, away from the soft moonlight, moving from crumbling wall to pile of rubble. He glanced into an opening of a canvas lean-to and counted five bodies nestled warmly in sleeping bags, none of them stirring.

How easy it would be for the ETM to come in here and just light the place on fire, he thought. And as he thought it, he remembered that Lakeland had done just the exact same thing to them, starting with the distant explosion that rattled him from his bunk bed. His mind drifted to the explosion that erupted right next to him that night, and the wave of heat brushing through him —

Stay focused.

He turned a corner, keeping his body low and his rifle up. He tried to move how he had seen Miles move through the woods, gliding across the forest floor with a low profile and his eyes calmly scanning his surroundings. But Tyler kept stubbing his toes on a broken cinder block here or stepping on a piece of fallen tin roofing there. With each glance downward at where he ought to put his feet, Tyler imagined someone would round a corner and send him the way of Major Kessler.

On top of his difficulties in stealthy maneuvers, Tyler was running off a very limited memory of how to get to Mayor Hatch's office, and he wasn't entirely sure what he'd do when he got there. *Idiot,* Tyler murmured to himself, *you always dive in without thinking. That's why you wind up places like this. Here in some stupid thing that's gonna get you shot.*

The plans had all been made for him when he worked for Kessler and Santana, and he knew nothing about planning a mission — he barely even knew how to execute one. He was the leader and sole proprietor of this mission, the reinforcements and the tip of the spear all in one.

Nothing. All you know is nothing. Every time you jump your butt into trouble, you find out that you're just an amateur at everything. What are you doing? WHAT ARE YOU DOING?

The thoughts pounded in his head, and he felt his throat grow thick and heavy; his head felt like a block —

STOP. One way or another, you're here. Pay attention.

He realized he had moved carelessly past two buildings while his thoughts had taken over, and only by raw luck did no one see or hear him. The heaviness in his head disappeared suddenly into the dark, humid air. He felt pins and needles across his skin as he became acutely aware of how distracted he was and how vulnerable that made him.

Tyler peered forward and recognized the mayor's blue door about forty yards away. The moonlight struck the wood and illuminated its color, and the crumbling world around it faded to black. The lamppost he had seen from his first trip remained switched off, but it stood strong and steady before the door like a flagpole missing its flag.

Tyler's first instinct was to move directly toward it, but he thought better of himself and squinted toward the sides of Mayor Hatch's office that were immersed in shadow; he began skirting from building to building, searching for any kind of sentry or guard shack. Brushing past the building with the tarp that he and Mayor Hatch had fixed up together, he noticed it had since fallen back down and was covered in wet, muddy footprints.

Now that he had something to move toward, he felt as if he was moving with purpose; his mind was able to push him forward without the need to consciously look down at his feet so often — he didn't know why, but he didn't stop and think about it either. Tyler circled closer and closer to Mayor Hatch's office. There was no sign of a dedicated guard force.

He approached the door, mesmerized by its blue paint, which stood in stark contrast to the colorless town of rubble and ruin. Just as he was about to advance and put a hand on the doorknob, he thought that maybe it would be smarter to go through the window.

Tyler wrapped around the building and found two windows, but both were locked, one from the inside and the other from the outside with a hefty padlock securing it down. However, the padlock was secured to a rickety piece of metal screwed in from the outside. Tyler retrieved a multitool from his pocket and unscrewed the rusty screws, removing the locking mechanism entirely. He let the padlock and the hinged locking mechanism hang to the side as he carefully swung open the window, gritting his teeth as it creaked and groaned. Tyler clamored in through the opening, perhaps not as gracefully as he would have liked, but silent nonetheless. If it weren't for the rising winds and distant thunder outside, he was sure someone would have heard him.

Mayor Hatch's office was in better condition than any building that Tyler had noticed in Lakeland thus far. The office was lined with blankets nailed to the walls, impromptu insulation or soundproofing, he wasn't sure. The place was lit by several windows beyond the first one; some were half-covered with sheets or blankets, and others were left open to stream in ambient moonlight. Several desks were littered about, built out of scrap wood and metal but refined and sturdy. Three maps were pinned to a vertical piece of plywood in the center of the room, one depicting Tampa, one Lakeland with defense diagrams scribbled about, and the third of the entire Tampa Bay area stretching out to Orlando.

The thought flashed through Tyler's mind that if he grabbed these maps and their accompanying documents, he could be welcomed back to the ETM with a pardon. He imagined Santana's assured anger at his desertion, probably shouting obscenities, immediately tempered by the display of enemy papers. He could just lie and say he was tired of nothing really progressing. He could say stealing enemy intelligence was all he ever set out to do.

Tyler shrugged the thought from his mind. Thinking about such things — thinking about anything right now — would only distract him from the task at hand. He had already decided what he was going to do, and if he was going to bring Santana into the mix, he may as well remember the sergeant's own words: "Just figure out all those moral dilemmas before the shooting starts, alright? Because when it does, the moral decision part of your brain ain't gonna be in control. If you don't know what you're doing, you're just gonna freeze up and get your dick shot off."

And he didn't want that. He settled on doing what he had come here to do.

As his eyes scanned the darkened room, Tyler's heart sunk in his chest. He had no idea what to look for and no idea where to start. *Evidence? What kind of evidence? What am I doing here?*

There were drawers everywhere. Maps. Papers strewn on the desks and ledgers shoved into dusty corners.

Did you really think you could just walk in here and find some kind of smoking gun? A map outlining some grand conspiracy that you could simply snatch off the wall?

He shoved those thoughts back down into his revolving gut. This was not what he expected, but it was what had happened and he needed to work with that. Tyler noticed what looked like a partition set apart from the rest of the desks, housing a larger desk, much tidier than the rest. It sat in a place of prominence, over-looking the other desks like Whitley's office over East Tampa.

Tyler crept carefully toward it. It neighbored a makeshift filing cabinet with another large padlock, of the same brand and size as the exterior window, fixed to its front swinging door.

Nothing screams "Important Things Here" like a giant padlock, he thought.

Unlike the window, the door to the filing cabinet was secure. With a set of extra hands he could have probably lifted the entire thing up and out, but even if that was possible Tyler wasn't sure the contents had anything to do with what he was there for. He needed proof that what the Plant City refugees has confided in him was true, and that meant some annotation regarding the caches of copper.

Tyler studied every inch of the filing cabinet. It was a metal box crudely welded together at odd angles, standing approximately three feet high. He carefully heaved it out, away from the desk, and tilted it on its side. It was heavier than he imagined, and he could feel the contents shift within. Careful not to slam it on the floor, he gently laid it down.

On the cabinet's underside were four large screws holding the bottom plate in place. Tyler almost laughed to himself — *are people really this stupid?* He knew that Miles would say yes, and he was beginning to understand why. He also knew that in the same breath, Miles would point out the countless things Tyler had done that were equally as stupid, or worse.

He retrieved his multitool again, swiveled out the flathead screwdriver, and went to work. Unscrewing these proved a little more tedious than the screws on the window outside, as these were tightly rooted into the metal and he feared he would strip the heads.

The monotony of unscrewing gave him a little comfort, there in the middle of Lakeland territory. He had an easy task and he knew what he had to do. It was done soon enough, and the bottom of the filing cabinet was pushed out by the contents bursting forth into the open air. It was an ocean of files, and had he not stuck one hand under them, they would have poured across the floor.

Tyler removed the files with caution — he knew that if Mayor Hatch was as meticulous and organized as Allie had described, she would no doubt have a clear, orderly system in place. Jumbling it all up would only make things more difficult.

The folders were all stacked by date, bland numbers written on the extended tabs poking above the rest.

As he sat on the floor, he stacked them all neatly around him. Picking one off the top of a nearby pile, he opened it and flipped through the contents. He could read well enough from the ambient light and moonlight spilling in through the window: mission reports described the comings and goings of troops and kept close track of their essentials — food, weapons, ammunition, medical supplies, and other miscellaneous equipment. At the end of the folder lay the number of resources scavenged on that day. This particular folder read: *"Fuller Heights private stash: x5 crates of vegetable oil, x10 portable water filters, x1 working generator, x2 inoperable generators, x4 barrels oil, x14 bundles of rope. Note: More rope bundles found two blocks south-east of Fuller Heights location, need to make another trip to gather extra."*

It began to dawn on him that he was swimming in a sea of information, and that it would realistically take him all night to sort through. Tyler wondered if there was some kind of master list or legend he could refer to, but he saw no sign of one.

Then his entire brain clicked, like every winding, mysterious road in his mind immediately aligned, and he was struck with a moment of clarity: *The Flea Market Skirmish, August 9th, 2 PR (Post Red). Four ETM wounded while trying to save Plant City civilians from Lakeland, ETM retreated to cut losses and Major Kessler fought off enemy combatants with his last magazine* — at least, that was the story branded into his mind.

He searched through the piles of folders until he found the stack dating back to 2 PR. There, he found the folder: *"8 - 9 - 02."*

He opened it, surprised at the single sheet of paper inside. He squinted his eyes, but they soon began to grow quite wide as he read.

"Grocery location 46-98, South Central Plant City: x84 crates of assorted canned meats, x31 crates of dog food, x145 boxes of protein bars, x510 boxes of toothpaste, x40 boxes of soap (x5 ea), x92 crates of assorted canned fruit, x45 boxes of uncooked pasta, x15 boxes of assorted cereal, approx. 900 boxes of tomato seeds. Excess NG copper caches.

"Casualty Report: 1 Lakeland KIA: Williams. 0 ETM KIA. 12 Plant City civilians killed; 2 armed Plant City civilians killed."

Tyler put that folder to the side and grabbed the day before. The supplies were scant. He grabbed the day after — not much to show.

His mind raced through the stories of battles and tales of heroism the other boys had recited over and over. *The Episcopal*

Church battle, he thought, *one dead and six wounded — ETM lost ground and almost had to pull out of Plant City entirely. That was… 21 July, 3 PR.*

He had caught a whiff of something sinister and no one had helped him do it. Tyler found the folder labeled *"7 - 21 - 03"* and he almost tore the thing in half opening it.

"Church stash 13-11, previously ETM controlled, east Plant City: x14 barrels of gasoline, x55 crates of ammunition - 5.56, 92,400 rounds; x10 boxes of ammunition - 7.62 loose, 10,000 rounds; 7.62 loose belts, varying length, approx 5,900 rounds. Excess NG copper caches.

"Casualty Report: 2 Lakeland KIA: Garcia, Nance. 1 ETM KIA. 6 Plant City civilians killed."

These numbers were not small. The famous battles that had lived on in whispers from boy to boy throughout East Tampa all happened to coincide with huge resource deposits. Tyler realized that despite the convoluted stories of who had how much, the reality was that both Lakeland and East Tampa had gathered far more copper than either had let on. . The story was being painted before his eyes, each number a brush stroke: East Tampa and Lakeland were throwing their armies at each other for these resources, and the residents of Plant City were suffering for it. For every stash discovered, multiple Plant City civilians were lost.

Tyler confirmed by checking other random days: they had small finds — a few cans of food here, a few magazines of ammunition there. A few of them mentioned Plant City casualties who were killed over a few meager scraps of food or medicine, or simply because unknown patrols were trespassing in their backyard.

Why write all this down? he wondered, because surely Mayor Whitley kept no such record. He didn't know if it was a necessity in the spirit of accounting for resources or if it was a simple oversight in the name of Hatch's painstaking attention to detail.

But there could have been a million reasons. Knowledge is power, and if any of the Plant City residents came out with grudges, Mayor Hatch could easily weave together stories that would fit the narrative of what really happened — Tyler pictured her standing in front of outraged Plant City civilians, the picture of a rough but caring leader: "Die? They didn't just die, they were murdered," she would say. "Six civilians of Plant City, I won't forget that moment until my dying day. We watched as ETM gunned them down, and they have blamed us all along. They always blame us, it's in their nature to lie as it's in their nature to kill. They're from East Tampa, a bunch of city dwellers who graduated from cutthroat business to literally cutting throats."

Tyler thought back to De Silva and Miles's advice on fighting with his mind as much as his rifle. He knew this information could be used as a weapon. Where ETM had superior firepower, Lakeland had information.

He kept searching through the expanse of papers and files. Wherever he remembered a large battle in Plant City that Lakeland won, the gains were significant. If he remembered a victorious return of ETM, the records reflected as such.

And with each win for either side, Plant City lost.

He knew then that no rational person would deny the evidence before him. It was too much of a coincidence for Lakeland to have won these battles and just so happened to stumble upon stashes of a lifetime. Tyler knew he ought not under-estimate Hatch and Whitley's abilities to snake their way out of things with some well-placed words and a show of false patriotism, but with this evidence he wasn't sure it was possible. It would take some serious mental gymnastics for the people to look past this kind of evidence.

And it struck him there, sitting in the dark with the beam of moonlight peering just over his shoulder, peering intently at a couple pieces of paper. Hatch, Whitley — for all their undeniable differences, they were the same. Their chief, shared quality was that they fancied themselves chess players, and each of these numbers on these papers were moves. Each life lost was a wooden piece on the board, and each bullet gained was a square taken.

Tyler organized a stack of papers to take with him: several regular, unremarkable days to show how they ought to be, and several days with significant Lakeland victories and the surge of resources that coincided with them.

I need more to show when the ETM won too… this has to be airtight, he thought, reaching for the stack from January, 03 PR.

Suddenly, he heard the slam of a door from the opposite side of the building as it swung open and smacked into the wall behind it.

"Who's there?!" It was the rough, commanding voice of Mayor Hatch. He whirled his head around to see her, facing just away from him and toward the common area. She gripped a pistol tight and was peering into the dark, wearing what appeared to be the same clothes he had last seen her in, minus the boots. Her eye was not yet adjusted to the dark, and the patch was not on her head; he could see now the lump of mangled scar tissue that replaced her other eye.

Tyler grabbed his stack of folders, shoving them quietly under his arm, and dove out the window with a crash. It wasn't the same one that he had entered through, but it must have been built by the same person — instead of breaking the glass, the whole thing flew off its hinges and awkwardly shattered on the ground near where Tyler landed.

He scrambled to his feet just in time to hear Hatch open fire.

The first shot broke the heavy silence, and he felt an electricity rip through the town alongside the sound. Tyler dashed toward the nearest building.

Two more shots rang out, but he didn't dare look back to see if she was zeroed in on him. He swung around the corner of the first building and kept at a full sprint, weaving around a low wall and keeping his head low as he clutched the papers in his arms.

And as he barreled through the Lakeland buildings, around the piles of trash and over the broken remnants of walls and buildings, Miles's voice rang in his head: "Don't do anything in a room 'till you've cleared the whole place." *Stupid*, he thought. *You're not ready to do this kinda stuff alone —*

More gunfire. There wasn't time to kick himself over it; he kept running.

Hatch's shots were not effective, something he was unaccustomed to after working with Miles. When Miles said others were criminally undertrained, perhaps he was right, or perhaps Miles held a standard so high for himself that few had the time or inclination to meet it. Tyler understood he was part of the "criminally undertrained" demographic, but he was beginning to understand what Miles meant.

As Tyler scrambled further away, he started to hear hurried voices echoing through the shantytown as the Lakeland beast awoke from its slumber. The wind from Miles's alleged hurricane was building with it.

Tyler slid around a corner of a half-constructed cinderblock building and ran head-on into a powerful man that felt more like a brick wall than he did a human being. Tyler's weapon slammed to the mud, but he kept tight hold on the papers.

"Whoa — what's goin' on — " the man stammered.

"Over there!" Tyler pointed behind him. "Two guys are runnin' through the camp, I'm supposed to hit the edge and catch 'em on the way out. I think Hatch is hurt? I don't know —" Tyler scrambled back to his feet, grabbed his rifle, and began to run, nodding back behind him with a sense of urgency.

The man's face twisted into an expression of anger and concern as he stormed off toward the mayor's position. It would probably only be a few seconds until he discovered the truth, but a few seconds was all Tyler needed. He had melted into the dark.

He raced through a field that was moist from the night's humidity and covered entirely in trash bags. A landfill.

Many of the bags had burst open, but there was no time for the smell to reach his nostrils as he rushed toward the tree line. Just as he dove out of the trash and into the trees, flashlights swept the mass of garbage bags and discarded junk. Thick jungle smacked and cut his face, but none of it mattered. He had slung his rifle tight to his back and he clutched the folders close to his chest like they were a cure for the Red itself.

Tyler knew he was either north or northeast of Lakeland, but he wasn't sure where. All he knew was that he just needed to run and run and run, until he felt safe enough to stop behind cover and re-orient himself. "Running" meant awkwardly stumbling over vines and through thickets at this point, but whatever obstacles met him would also meet any forces in pursuit.

Tyler careened through the dark jungle, often closing his eyes and lurching forward through poking branches that tore his clothes and scraped his skin. He counted it as a miracle that his eyes were intact and throat uncut by the time he reached the first major clearing.

From there, he took a quick breath and headed east. He dared not let his mind catch up to him just yet — he knew enough now to leave his pondering mind behind until he found himself deep within the warm blanket of safety.

A paved road ran straight north to south just east of the camp, so wherever he was, he could count on its existence to reorient him to his surroundings. Once he found it, he stayed deep enough in the trees to avoid being seen by any patrols but close enough that he could still make out the road and follow it through the night. From there he began to tread north. He would cut back west at a large boulder next to the road, uncharacteristic of the Florida swamplands and therefore easy to recognize. Several hundred feet in, there would be a path that would lead just over two miles to Miles's cabin.

13

"You know, I talk about metal a lot because I was into it as a teen, and people just don't get it. It wasn't about hurtin' or dying' or sufferin'... When I was just a youngin', I just wanted so hard for one of them stuffy adults to even act like they were on the same planet as me. I knew in my bones that not everything was alright, and I just wanted one of 'em to look at me and agree with me on that. And then these metalheads come outta the woodwork and they're talkin' about all the same things I was feelin'. For once I knew that someone else was angry too, that someone else was able to say 'Hey! The world sucks sometimes.' It was like they tore down the façade of all those adults I grew up 'round. "And that was somethin', just to know that I wasn't alone. I'd like to share that with you today on 101.7, the soundtrack to the end of the world."

THE sun had begun to rise and the wind was coming with it. Clouds hung dark in the sky. By the time Tyler made it back to Miles's cabin, he could feel the wind in even the densest parts of the jungle.

A figure stood in front of the cabin, but it wasn't a man.

He recognized Allie by her silhouette. As he approached her, he noticed she was paler than usual, a cold sweat running down her face and neck, and her knuckles were pale white as she gripped her bolt action rifle. He didn't think how she knew where Miles's cabin was, he didn't realize why she might be there — he was just glad that she was — but something stopped him just shy of her and made him scan the tree line. He shoved the files into the back of his belt under his shirt and unslung his rifle, watching the trees around him.

"I'm alone," she said. "For now. But they'll be here soon. They know it was you."

"What? How?"

"You ran into a guy who described you. Mayor Hatch already had her suspicions." She was beginning to tear up. "I can't believe you did this to me. I told you that she had that stuff in there so you could ask her about it, not steal it!"

Tyler noticed Miles was sitting quietly under the shade of his cabin, watching them carefully. His face was obscured in the shadow of the awakening morning and one hand was not visible.

"Look at me," her voice trembled.

Tyler snapped to attention. He pulled one of the files from his back. "Have you seen these? Allie, Hatch has been lying to you. Look," he said as he flipped through the folder. "This one is from April 20th, 3 PR. They —"

"Stop. They did nothing wrong, you're obviously looking for something to find. And what about Tampa? Why don't you go through their files? Anything you find here is gonna be ten times worse there —"

"What? Allie, I have proof right here, it's in my hand —"

"Just stop." She studied him long and hard. "I can't believe I was so wrong about you. You're East Tampa, through and through. You have no idea what they've done to us, no clue what they've taken from us. What you've taken from us."

He didn't know what to say. His head felt like it might explode in anger; his heart felt like it was about to shatter in heartbreak. He wanted to argue, he wanted to cry, but he just stood there and tried to find the right words to say. None came.

"They're on their way here. I'd give it like thirty minutes or so before they're crawling all over these woods. I don't want to see you again. Ever." She stormed off into the woods and disappeared as quickly as he came.

Tyler watched her go, bewildered. Enraged. Heartsick.

He turned to Miles, who had not moved. "East Tampa through and through? What they've taken? They killed my brother!" Tears were rolling down his cheeks. "They took everything I had left! Then I left East Tampa because I let myself, just for a second, think about what was really happening…"

Images of Anthony were starting to fly through his head, and he realized in that moment how much he missed his brother and his calm and reassuring presence. He realized how much he missed his parents and their umbrella of love and affection. Things obscured to memory now. Imprisoned to a few snippets in his mind.

The papers from the file fell from Tyler's hands.. His body shook and he dropped to his knees, but no tears came. He wanted nothing more than to sob and howl, but it was all stuck behind an invisible wall inside of him. Tyler dropped his head and he thought that if he was no longer capable of crying then at least he could cry out.

"Why does nobody care?! Everyone says they care, but nobody actually cares! About anything!" The words just sort of tumbled out of his soul and through his mouth; he didn't know what he was saying, he was just yelling.

Tyler caught his breath, grunting as he struggled to gain control of himself. The uncontrollable despair in him was transforming into a controllable rage. Not a rage at East Tampa or Lakeland, and not a rage at either mayor or at Santana or Allie — a rage at the way of things. A rage that life was the way that life was.

His grunts dissipated and turned back to regular breaths. For a moment he remained on his knees watching each of a million thoughts stream through his mind.

"We need to leave," Miles said after a few moments of silence. His voice betrayed no sign of emotion.

Tyler nodded and gathered his things. The wind was rattling the cabin's wood, and it looked as if it were going to rain.

Tyler was pretty sure he heard the crashing of bells as they heaved themselves over the second hill away from the cabin. He and Miles strode with a purpose through the woods, and Tyler was confident Lakeland could not catch them, not when he was with Miles. His heart burned and his head boiled, or maybe it was the other way around, but he was no longer concerned about getting caught.

They walked for two hours, neither saying a word to one another beyond Miles's occasional quiet but stern commands.

"Grab my extra water."

"You look down the right side of that road, I'll check the left."

"Keep an eye out for a creek bed. The rains from the last few days probably have it running a little stronger than usual."

As far as Tyler could tell, they were in the heart of the Florida swampland. Besides the occasional overgrown road, there had been no sign of civilization. But Miles seemed to be walking on a map he had memorized a thousand times over.

"When someone's chasing you, or trying to find you, you have to outsmart them," Miles said, adjusting the ruck he had pre-packed in the event they had to run. "If they get hot on our trail, we'll book it down some paths or roads, then b-line straight through a thicket, or some shitty bushes. They'll figure we just kept down the road, it doesn't make sense to randomly tear through a thorn bush when someone's chasing you. But that's what we'll do."

"Alright." They continued on in silence.

Miles stopped, and they unslung their bags. Tyler had packed a bag similar to Miles's, but he was sure it was not as well packed. Miles pulled out two peanut butter flavored protein bars and tossed one to Tyler. Not a word was spoken as they ate; the only sound between them was the crinkling wrappers. They faced each other, each sitting on opposing fallen logs.

Miles stuffed the wrapper in his pocket as he finished his bar, and he watched Tyler do the same. When the wrappers were tucked away, the two were beset by a blanket of all-encompassing silence. Despite the swirling wind and the sound of distant, incoming thunder, a period of stillness passed between them.

Brooding in the calm, Miles eventually spoke. "The mayors meet with each other every month, down at the old abandoned factory where they used to manufacture and repair a bunch of heavy equipment. The commercial welding place. It's out in the boonies, if you go past the community center and those RV parks. If I'm right, they'll be there soon."

Tyler let this soak in for a moment.

"Just north of Plant City… there's a pond there, right?"

"That's right."

"Why didn't you tell me that before?" Tyler asked.

"It wasn't relevant before."

"How do you know they're gonna be there?"

"I watch major troop movements, scouting parties, raiding parties, and I watch when the bigwigs do things worth watching."

"Why didn't you tell me before?"

"I just said —"

"That's bullshit." The words fell out of his mouth — he had never spoken like that before, but he didn't have the energy to apologize or take it back. He just stared at Miles.

"I knew you'd do something about it," Miles said.

"And now?"

He didn't respond for a long time. "Now you do something about it. And I'll back you up."

The fire's flames raged and spat against the light shower of rain crackling upon it from above. Its fiery tongues licked under the rising wind, which built in strength by the minute. Tyler and Miles sat in its dwindling warmth and light, hypnotized by the flames.

"You ready?" Miles asked very seriously of Tyler. The question was not from a teacher to a student, nor was it from a master to an apprentice. It was from one person about to do a hard thing to another.

"I'm ready."

For a moment, a sadness crossed Miles's face as he watched Tyler, but it soon passed and he stoked the fire to keep it alive.

14

"We got the storm ragin' outside... I think this one's gonna be a doozy. To match, I've got some Beethoven for y'all tonight. I'm fixin' to pair the storm outside with a storm of classical tunes that'll rage inside the safety of your chosen location of shelter.

"I'll make connoisseurs outta y'all, just you see. Hear it all on 101.7, the soundtrack to the end of the world."

THE sky was dumping rain onto the earth like a desperate man dumping water from a sinking ship. The wind howled, and one could barely hear the raised voice of the another unless they were standing within a few feet of each other.

The precursors to the storm had been relatively calm, but the new winds and rains swept in swiftly. The light rain had promptly turned into a downpour — Tyler passed one road and noticed little more than a few rising puddles; the next street they crossed had essentially turned into a river.

"Are they really going to meet in the middle of a hurricane?" Tyler asked Miles, shouting over the howling winds and crashing rains.

"Damn straight. The north end of the factory is one of the safest places still standing. The south end is crumbling to oblivion, but the north is a hell of a lot sturdier than anywhere in Tampa or Lakeland right now. They're probably holding hands and singing kumbaya in the most protected location in Florida."

The thought of the mayors holding out through the storm together put a knot in Tyler's stomach, but it wouldn't surprise him if it turned out to be true.

The pair were just a mile out from the factory, and Tyler was getting sick of slogging through the deluge. He longed for a single step on dry ground that didn't threaten to pull off his shoe as it sunk and stuck in the mud.

How Miles knew his way around the woods in the middle of a hurricane, Tyler wasn't sure, but he also wasn't going to ask. Not yet, anyway.

"That shack is our last stop before the factory." Miles pointed through the heavy rainfall. The mist formed by the boatloads of water hitting the ground made it difficult to see anything further than a few feet ahead, but Tyler could make out a solid, brick structure standing firmly in the midst of the storm.

They plodded toward it and readied their rifles on the approach. Tyler opened the front door and Miles pointed his rifle inside, staying out and sidestepping across the entrance just as the two had practiced a thousand times. Miles was able to clear most of the interior from outside the building, and the single-room brick shed proved empty. Inside, they found a relatively dry, empty room with pieces of a salvaged generator strewn about. The shed was built to withstand weather like this, though it had suffered several small, leaking cracks over the years. Puddles were beginning to emerge across the floor.

"Okay, we're going to do this, but we're going to do it the right way. Give me the more damning half of those files," Miles said.

Tyler shrugged off his pack and laid it down on the driest spot in the room. He pulled out a large trash bag that had been twisted several times, unraveled it, and pulled out the files. He sorted through them quickly and handed Miles half, the half with the battles he had so eagerly memorized once.

Those stories seemed dirty now. Tainted.

Miles dropped his bag to the floor and extracted a dry-bag: a thick, waterproof, nylon shell built for outdoor weather. He opened it and retrieved several pairs of dry clothes, putting them in a less secure trash bag of his own. Folding the files in half, he stuffed them in the dry-bag and returned it to his larger pack.

Then Miles fetched a small, sleek backpack and filled it with a trash bag containing two pairs of socks, an aid-kit, and some extra ammunition. He retrieved a cloth chest rig with several magazine pouches and full magazines within; a grenade pouch was strapped to the upper chest, and in it sat a compass, girth hitched to the rack's webbing.

He placed his large pack behind a small pile of discarded ceramic tile in the side of the room.

"Here." Miles handed Tyler a thick canvas belt with empty magazine pouches affixed. It was a little loose on him, but it was comfortable, and it was the first thing he had ever worn that really felt like it was suited perfectly for its purpose. He grabbed his magazines and stuffed the pouches full; he put another extra in his back pocket and left his pack next to Miles's.

"Is the rain gonna affect the guns?"

"I hope not," Miles said with a grin. And then, "Nah, they'll be fine. We just need to make sure they don't rust afterward."

Tyler stuffed the remainder of the files back in his trash bag and into the small of his back, securing them behind his belt so they wouldn't fall out, even if he were running and shooting.

"For this to work, we've gotta bluff, and we've gotta bluff hard," Miles said. "If they figure out that they can actually just kill us and get away with it — they're gonna do it."

"They're gonna try."

Miles grinned again, but it soon faded. "What if your girlfriend's down there?" he asked.

"She's not my girlfriend —"

"I'm serious, Tyler."

"She's not part of their inner circle. She wouldn't be down there."

"Plan for the most likely outcome; expect the worst possible one."

"If we have to fight our way out of there, we'll fight our way out of there. I won't let you down," Tyler said, lifting his chin with a confidence he wasn't sure he felt.

Miles studied him for a moment. "I won't let you down either."

He extended a hand to Tyler, who shook it.

They double checked the half of the files that they were leaving behind — they were out of obvious sight and secured away from the elements. They only required the return of a live human being.

Tyler's jaw clenched as they strode back out into the hurricane and his cold, wet skin was once again subject to the rain.

The factory came into view when the trees started to dissipate. There were no smokestacks or water towers, only a looming, once "modern" building with rectangular shapes, sharp angles, and a sign made from colossal letters that had since crumbled and fallen.

The ground was soft and uneven here, and the factory stood in a prominent position on one hill in the center of many. The low ground between the small hills were rapidly filling with water, and in a matter of hours Tyler guessed they would look more like a moat than parking lots and walkways.

Despite the factory's prominence, it still felt nestled in a jungle that had run rampant, undisturbed for four long years. The trees encroached on the fence that surrounded the property, the grass pushed through the pavement, and vines and weeds crisscrossed all the way up its walls. The whole structure looked like a tired old man, bound to collapse at any moment.

Still, Miles said it was the safest place in the Tampa Bay area — at least, one side of it was. Tyler had his doubts about Miles's bleak outlook on a good many things, but he never doubted the man at his word. He had never met someone so capable who could so casually say that he didn't know a thing, and with such confidence and no further explanation. If Miles said the structure was sturdy, Tyler knew it was sturdy — not an increment weaker, not an increment stronger. Sturdy.

The steadily rising wind and rain didn't bother Tyler — he found it invigorating. It just made him grip his rifle tighter.

With the roar and rumble of the hurricane, Tyler hadn't realized that Miles was calling out to him. He stepped closer and turned an ear toward Miles.

"Heads up for debris in the wind!" Miles said. Tyler jerked his thumb up into the air and they continued forward. *I gotta worry about getting shot, and I gotta worry about getting smacked in the head by flying tree branches?* he thought. *Fantastic.*

There was a final berm before the slope that led down to the factory grounds. As they approached it, the two kept low and pushed their rifles forward, slowly cresting over the top of the berm.

It was easier to see a moderate distance without every raindrop smacking into every branch and bush every foot of the journey. In the clearing surrounding the building, Tyler could make out several figures clumped together just outside two enormous front doors, both boarded up with layers of heavy lumber. Tyler squinted as he scanned the rest of the factory — the front appeared to be standing tall, but the back had been sheared off as

Miles described, perhaps by planted explosives or mortar rounds; it was impossible to tell. There was no doubt that the weather had accelerated the destruction, and more progress in tearing down the structure would surely be made in this new storm.

"I got an eye on Whitley." Miles could barely be heard over the wind.

Tyler peered back through the hurricane at the clump of men and women. He could make out a figure that looked like Whitley who was being escorted by several members of what appeared to be Gray Platoon. Tyler couldn't be certain, but there was no time to doubt Miles.

"Hatch is always early," Miles said. "She has to be in there. Those are Lakeland soldiers just outside on the west there." He pointed at two militiamen poking their heads out of a side door, who quickly disappeared again to the safety from the hurricane. Whitley and his crew slipped inside after them seconds later.

"Tell you what, man, I'm about ready to get out of this storm."

"And into the next," Tyler added, trying to sound serious.

Miles just laughed at him. Tyler kept his mouth shut as they maneuvered onto the safe side of the berm. A fence ran around the compound with few breaks in its perimeter, so they skirted it gradually, out of sight from watchful eyes, making their way to the entrance.

Creeping up to the front door felt effortless. The windows were either boarded up to shield the occupants from the hurricane's wrath, or they were left open and unoccupied. Tyler felt a kind of safety in using the environment to his advantage, in leveraging the natural world instead of fighting against it.

The two of them barreled to the entrance, concerned more about staying on their feet in the raging wind than taking enemy fire.

Out of the corner of his eye, Tyler caught a glimpse of a brown blur spiraling toward Miles.

"Look out!" he cried under the deafening storm.

Miles swung his rifle toward some unknown enemy but saw the debris — a severed branch skipping across the ground toward him. Both leapt in either direction as the branch was flung between them.

They continued forward without a word.

The two of them reached the door and shouldered the wall on either side. The building seemed colossal now that Tyler was leaning right up against it. The wall was solid cement and the door was made of a broad steel. Something about the structure seemed impenetrable, solid to the center — Tyler wondered if two mortals stood a chance at infiltrating the walls of such a place.

Tyler could feel his lungs desperately sucking for air as he rested for a moment, though he couldn't hear himself over the hurricane. It felt good to lean up against something, instead of constantly fighting against the wind, and a distant, irrational part of him thought he might have liked to stay there for a while.

Miles nodded to the door, and those thoughts blew away. Tyler took a step out, once again bracing himself against the wind, and he gripped the door's latch and swung it open.

They rushed in with their weapons raised — Tyler was struck by the sudden clarity in his senses as they left the rain and dove into the silent factory interior. His ears burned at the shock of stillness.

They were in an empty hallway, dark with several doors to either side and little more than peeling paint and chipped tile. The wind slammed the door shut behind them and the sound echoed through the bowels of the factory.

"We might as well have sounded the alarm," he heard Miles whisper. Tyler hoped any listening ears would write it off alongside the rest of the din and clamor from the hurricane.

They moved forward, side-by-side with their weapons drawn. Tyler didn't feel right in the hallway and he was anxious to leave it. If gunfire erupted in that narrow corridor, they would be trading bullets in a funnel that channeled all rounds right into those standing at either end. There was no cover and no room for maneuver.

Then, down the hall and around the corner to the right, Tyler heard the scrape of someone dragging their foot as they walked. Miles grabbed him and gently pushed him into a nearby room. It was pitch black and smelled of rotting wood. They held their breaths as they waited and watched for movement through the crack of the door.

Then the hallway was occupied by the faint footsteps growing closer with each step. Tyler felt a rush of lightning through his veins, as the idea of confrontation was rapidly becoming a reality. He could feel his jaw tightening with the grip around his rifle. He glanced up at Miles, whose countenance appeared to remain unwavering. The man made it look easy, like he didn't care but only because he knew the outcome and had planned accordingly.

When they first met, Tyler thought that Miles was a master at all things tactical, like some kind of ancient ninja or Spartan warrior. Now it occurred to him that everything that Miles knew and had practiced was basic — that all the decisions made in combat were basic, and that ninjas and Spartans probably knew that too. The trick wasn't in the ability to master intricate skillsets, it was the ability to master countless simple tasks and to execute them in a matter of seconds. The difficulty wasn't in the individual tasks, it was in the fact that one simple misstep in any of them could get someone killed The difficulty was in the midst of those thousands of choices within a single moment, a single mistake could get someone killed — Tyler hoped that Miles wouldn't let that happen.

Miles had his hand on Tyler's chest, as if he were ready to release the boy into the fray at the sound of a starting pistol. Two men armed with rifles passed their open door, focused on the exterior door. They didn't think to clear the adjacent rooms.

Just before he moved his hand, Miles poked his head out and glanced the other way down the hallway — yet another maneuver Tyler would have forgotten. Just because two had passed did not necessarily mean a third wasn't in tow.

Satisfied, he released Tyler and they moved back into the hallway toward the guards with their rifles pointed at their backs. Tyler's eyes burned directly through his sights and at the broad shoulders of one of the armed men, meandering thoughtlessly toward the exterior door.

"If you move, I'll shoot," Miles said with unmistakable clarity. He did not have to raise his voice. The two raised their hands, letting their rifles dangle by their frayed, makeshift slings. They didn't even turn around until Miles told them to.

"Put the rifles on the ground," he said, and they complied. "Keep an eye on these two," he told Tyler. "They're going to escort us all the way to HQ."

The two let their weapons clatter to the tile floor.

Tyler stepped behind the two Lakeland sentries. "Move," he said, making his voice sound lower than it was. They moved forward without complaint. Miles waited for them to walk past him and followed behind. As Tyler kept his eye and trigger finger ready for the two in front, Miles's attention was focused on the factory through which they moved. He hunted for any sign of movement.

Miles told the hostages to take them to the mayors, that they had something to discuss with them. That they didn't intend to hurt anyone.

"You're going to get yourselves killed," the man on the left spoke as they moved from one hallway to a flight of stairs.

"Shut up," Tyler said. "Just take us to them."

They weaved through another hallway and pushed into a large room that appeared to have been office storage. Metal cabinets were pressed up against the walls, and moss grew through the stacks of paper and over broken staplers and paper clips. A printer lay on its side, covered in grime and cobwebs.

One wall had been torn away to reveal an adjacent meeting room, which opened up into a floor of offices. Tyler's attention was briefly captured by a pile of dollar bills lying half-burned in a trash can. He guessed that it had been at least a year since he had last seen cash from the old world, and the last time it had been used for tinder as well.

They wove through a maze of cubicles. Most had been soaked over time, disintegrating into powder and melting into the dust on the carpet. As they moved further into the bowels of the factory — the ancient remnants of industry and coin — Tyler could tell they were headed south. The whole building shook under the winds of the hurricane, and with every step toward the damaged end it quivered and rattled more.

"Stop." Miles's voice carried that same authority, though Tyler wasn't sure who he was talking to at first. Miles placed himself strategically behind one man, lifting his rifle up carefully as if he were to shoot just past his hostage's ear, but just far enough away that the man could not turn and grab Miles's rifle.

"Come out," Miles said. "We have two of your own."

A woman stepped forward from the shadows and into the dim light, her rifle raised. Tyler did not recognize her, but he noticed her uniform.

"She's from Gray Platoon," he said. She said nothing and did not give away any expression in the way of fear or defiance.

"What's your name?" Miles asked.

"Callie. Yours?"

"Miles. Pleasure. Look, you probably don't know these two, but they're not much good to you whether they're on team Callie or not. So right now, it's just you," Miles spoke carefully and deliberately. "Sure, if you pull the trigger, you might get me — but my buddy here won't miss you... he doesn't miss anything. Now, we're just here to talk to Mayor Whitley and Mayor Hatch. No sense in everyone dying over a conversation."

"What's to stop you two from just shooting one of them the second you see them?" Callie spoke with equal confidence.

"We might have the drop on you now, but we're outnumbered here. A firefight would go badly for us," Miles said. "We have something they need to see, and it can't wait."

"What is it?"

"We stole some files from Mayor Hatch," Tyler offered.

"I don't care what you stole from Mayor Hatch —"

"Listen," Miles raised his voice. "Either we're going to fucking blow each other away right here, right now, or we're going to talk to your little circle-jerk of local mayors. Up to you."

Callie looked at them for a long, solemn moment. "Alright, but move slow. And if you point your weapons at either mayor, I'm dropping you. I don't care if I can't get both of you before you get me."

"Fair enough."

She didn't lower her weapon; she backed up as they moved forward, glancing briefly at her direction of travel. Miles had the advantage here, and he could have easily moved slightly to the left or right from behind his hostage's head, firing a single shot through hers. But that would alert anyone else inside, ratchet up emotions, and would result in everyone shooting at anything that moved.

Instead, they moved carefully, like a formation of logs drifting down a calm river, gently brushing and altering course around obstacles and through doorways.

This is easy, Tyler thought as they crept forward behind their human barricade. *Things are easy if you just do everything right… it's just a matter of knowing how to do everything right. No mistakes.* The thought sounded right, but he still wasn't sure how they were going to get out safely.

They reached a final door and Callie opened it first, stepping backwards into the next room for them to follow. It was like any other door so far, but as he stepped through, Tyler felt an outside breeze upon his face. They had reached an enormous factory bay, and a freshness filled his nose like he had just stepped out onto an ocean shore.

The door led out to a large platform that was connected to other platforms by a series of catwalks. Two of the catwalks were broken, twisted into jagged shards of metal. While the sturdy walls of the bay were intact, something about the interior of that massive room felt like there was a storm inside of it—when Tyler peeked over the edge of the platform, he realized why.

There was no floor below. Beneath the next level of catwalks and twisted metal, precariously leaning cement slabs and jarring shards of rebar, the bottom floor had completely flooded. Waves pulsated and ravaged the structure below. It was unlikely the water would ever fill the entire bay area, but just peering downward for a moment felt like looking into some hellish abyss. The combination of roaring water and twisted metal would surely thrash and drown a soul in a heartbeat, should they tumble in. Tyler felt very small looking down at all that.

Pale light flickered with the rain through broad, thick windows that had withstood many hurricanes before, and would likely withstand many more to come. They were old panes of glass that would oversee the passing of conflicts and would one day be relics of a forgotten time.

Tyler noticed two figures standing on the center catwalk, illuminated by the windows as the water rose from below. They were facing the newly arrived group and retreating slowly away; a guard ran around them toward Miles and Tyler.

It was mayors Hatch and Whitley. They were unmistakable figures now without the curtain of rain obscuring their faces.

"Hey." Miles snapped his focus off the two mayors, whispering to Tyler so only he could hear. "Keep your weapon on Callie. If we need to keep anyone at bay, it's her. Fuck the rest of these clowns. She's not playin'."

"Okay." Tyler glanced at Callie and another armed Gray Platoon soldier nearby. Two more were stationed on the far side of the catwalks, peering through the mist toward them.

"You hear me?" Miles asked.

"Yeah," Tyler whispered. "Callie first."

He nonchalantly shifted the barrel of his rifle from the two prisoners to Callie, hoping she wouldn't notice the minute transition. Her eyes glared at his muzzle, but there wasn't much she could do. She realized that Miles was by far the most considerable threat, and so she kept her weapon trained on him.

They were technically outnumbered, but Miles had worked them into as advantageous a position as they could have hoped. The pair was hiding behind a human shield, they had Callie on her heels, and they were the ones dishing out the commands. Getting

LUKE RYAN

out of the building alive, should anyone start shooting, would be a whole different story.

Both Hatch and Whitley were soaked — everyone was wet to the bone. Hatch's short hair was matted down to her skull, and her eyepatch glistened in the ambient light. Whitley's hair was more lustrous than ever, but the sight only reminded Tyler of the charming lies the man was constantly vomiting.

The mayors kept about twenty yards away from Tyler and Miles as they approached the catwalk, relying on the two guards ahead and the two guards behind to cover them. The human shield was unarmed, and therefore relatively useless to the mayors beyond the handful of rounds they could absorb first.

Whitley recognized the two before anyone.

"Goddamn, kid. You really fell off the wagon," Whitley mused at the sight of Tyler, his voice less charming than before, un-propped by his signature, counterfeit charm. "Sergeant Santana thought you just ran off into the woods, said you would never join Lakeland like a lot of folks were saying. But I don't think he figured you'd run off and become a… what are you now?"

"We're Marauders," Miles said. Whitley laughed and Tyler's heart swelled in his chest.

"Aren't you all dead?" Whitley asked.

"Marauders… give me a break." Hatch's voice was stern. "What are you here for? I hope you want to return those files of mine."

Tyler kept close watch on Callie. He demanded that his senses not get drawn toward the mayors, and they obeyed. If she fired a

246

shot, dove in any direction, or even twitched wrong, he'd pull the trigger and then move on to the next —

"Dude," Miles said. "Tell 'em what you've got. This is all you."

Just as Tyler understood the necessity of focusing on something small, he was required to focus on something large. He snapped out of his lasered focused and realized that the whole effort was his idea in the first place. Hatch and Whitley were waiting — Hatch's hands were on her hips and Whitley stood behind her, leaning on the railing of the catwalk. The water raged beneath them all.

"We've, uh, we've got your other half of the files — I mean, we've got half of the files here and the other half somewhere safe." Tyler's voice trembled, unused to the weight of responsibility.

"You aren't inspiring me with a whole lot of confidence..." Whitley started.

"— yeah, well, if those files get out, then that's proof that both of you didn't care about any of the people living in Plant City, and you didn't even care about the militiamen who died fighting for you. Every single big mission in the history of Lakeland was never in self-defense — not the way you sold it. It was all about hoarding stuff that wasn't even yours, it was all about the caches of copper. The people in Lakeland and East Tampa would have never gotten on board with those missions if they knew what they were really about, not in a million years. It's all in those files, all the proof in the world.

"And you're literally meeting here, like apparently you do pretty often, and for what, exactly?" Tyler's outrage was beginning to outpace his anxiety — it felt something like confidence, except he knew it could slip away at any second.

"That's our business, not yours," Hatch said.

"Call it our monthly therapy session," Whitley grinned. "But those are Lakeland files, what do they have to do with me?"

Hatch said it before Tyler could: "Where there are positives when we had a surplus in resources after a mission, there are negatives when you and yours got to the stashes first. We annotated what we gained and what we lost."

"Goddamn it, you had to write all that shit down," Whitley groaned, and then he turned back to Tyler. "So what the hell do you want?"

Miles glanced from the two guards on the near side of the catwalks, to the two mayors in the middle, and to the two on the far side.

"I want peace," said Tyler. "You two announce and sign a peace treaty. I'm going to hold onto these files and my friend here is going to hold onto the other half. You swear publicly that you'll rebuild together, and if we so much as think it's not for real… these files get out. And the people bring you down."

Both of the mayors were uncharacteristically silent. The group of assorted politicians, soldiers, and Marauders stood still amidst the din and roar of the hurricane twisting outside and bellowing below.

Then Whitley smirked. It was a crooked sort of smile, one of a school bully who aims to encourage his prey into making desperate comments that will only incite further abuse.

"Alright," he said. "Peace it is."

Tyler cocked his head and glanced at Miles, whose furrowed brow seemed equally surprised with the mayor's response. Perhaps a little perturbed.

"Peace. I love peace. Hatch, how does peace sound?" Whitley said.

"Sounds good to me," she said, her unwavering gaze fixed on Tyler.

Tyler didn't know what to say — he had expected things to be difficult, and he was confounded at how easy things had been, but this was too easy. *Now what? Do we just leave?*

But Miles spoke. "You were already planning on peace."

"Ding, ding, ding!" Whitley still hid partially behind Hatch, but he stretched his neck further out to get a better look at the both of them. "We have a winner. Peace was always the plan, assholes. You'd have known that if you would'a just waited another month or so."

"What?" Tyler felt the flame of indignation within his chest. "Then why go to war at all? My brother died in your war!"

"Because, dipsh —"

Hatch raised a fist and Whitley's lips sealed tight, whitening as he stepped back behind her.

"We don't answer to you," she said.

"You're forgetting what end of this barrel you're on," Miles said.

For a moment, Hatch looked at Miles with a seriousness she had never quite extended to Tyler. *Adults always take each other more seriously than they do teenagers,* he thought. *Even when they're getting a gun pointed at them, they always have to show kids that they don't take them seriously.*

She must have agreed with Miles's position, because she took a deep breath and began to speak. "The National Guard left all sorts of valuables in Plant City. Everyone's trying to get their hands on copper in order to build the electrical grid — either you are the first one to complete the task, or at the very least you build a lucrative business in being the primary source of copper in a post-Red world. Either way, if you have copper, you win. Not to mention all the other valuables the National Guard left behind — antibiotics, quite a bit of food, ammunition — read the lists, you'll see."

"But all that stuff was in Plant City. Not Lakeland, and not East Tampa," Tyler said.

"Exactly," Whitley casually leaned on the railing of the catwalk as if there weren't a seething river of water and metal below him. "You think they're just gonna hand that stuff over? No way, pal."

"So you stage a war," Miles finished the mayor's thought. "And you took turns reaping the benefits of any victorious 'battle' waged in Plant City."

Whitley shrugged. "Don't overcomplicate it, it was more of a casual thing. I think overall we got a little more, but in the end we all won. I mean, there's really not a whole lot left there. Hence the incoming peace process."

"And you two look like the heroes who were able to humble themselves and find peace." Miles gripped his rifle tighter. Tyler's eyes darted from Miles to the mayors, anxious that his tight grip on his weapon would blast off a round and set the whole powder keg of a situation off.

"Everyone loves a hero," Whitley said through his charming smile. "Everyone needs a hero. Why can't it be us?"

"But... you guys are constantly fighting already. I know *you* don't fight alongside your men," Tyler said to Whitley, "but what about you, Hatch? What if you got killed in a firefight or something? Everyone would go on believing your lies about everything, and the fake war would never end."

Whitley turned to Hatch, grinning and pointing. "See? I fuckin' told you. Even the bad guys think your shenanigans are ridiculous." And he turned back to the pair pointing their rifles at their chests. "You know how many times I've told her that? You have no idea how many times I've had to comb the goddamn battlefield — after it's relatively safe, of course — making sure she didn't get whacked or something. All under the pretense of tracking her down, too."

For the first time, Hatch moved her eye from Tyler back to Whitley. "Some of us will always fight next to our own," she muttered. "No matter what we ask them to do."

"Yeah, well, it's a logistical pain in the ass," he spat back.

"Your 'peace' is a lie!" Tyler said, raising his voice and attempting to reassert some sense of dominance.

Callie's eyes shot toward Tyler, and then back to Miles. Tyler repositioned his feet to better suit his weapon's accuracy should the shooting begin.

He could see nervous thoughts roll through Callie's head and betray themselves as she too repositioned her feet. He could see the tendons on her left forearm tighten as they extended to the front of her rifle, gripping the rail just inches before the end of the barrel and pulling it back into her shoulder pocket.

"Alright, sister," he heard Miles's voice. "This doesn't need to turn into a bloodbath."

"That's up to you," she said back.

Hatch's eye turned back to Tyler and Miles. "You talk about peace, but you come in here with weapons raised, threatening a bloodbath. You gloat about ambushing bandits and *our* peace is a lie? When this is over, we'll have a peace people feel they earned. The antagonists — a few rogue soldiers here and there — will shoulder the blame as 'war criminals,' while everyone else focuses on building. Assembling a functioning society from all the pieces scattered around us. So yeah, you can call our peace a lie. Maybe it is, or maybe we're just talking semantics. But at the end of the day, the future I'm striving toward isn't the violent one you're striving toward."

Peace. Tyler thought it sounded nice. But the desperate family in the woods near Miles's cabin —their faces were burned into his psyche. He wondered if that little girl was still alive. He hoped she was.

"And what about Plant City? It just dies?"

"This is the new world, kid," Whitley said, pacing behind Hatch. "Everything dies. But Plant City gives back when it dies. It contributes. It's the fertile land on which peace can grow —"

"I don't want to hear whatever speech you made up for East Tampa. The people need to know what you're doing."

"Why? Why should they know? They haven't exactly expressed a whole lot of interest toward the truth, just that they love to hate Lakeland. You're what, fourteen? Fifteen? That didn't stop you from figuring all this out in a heartbeat — what makes you think they want to know the truth? The truth is complicated, kid. People just want an easy enemy, and they found it in Lakeland."

"Or East Tampa," Hatch added.

"We'll find 'em a new common enemy soon after that, if that's what's needed," Whitley said. "I heard some bandits out east are organizing. You guys like fighting bandits, right? We could organize, we could unify under the banner of peace."

Tyler shook his head. As he was listening, his muzzle had slightly dipped and his mind began to trail into the possible futures Whitley was spinning, but he snapped himself back to reality with a shake of his head. He felt the cool mist of the water below rest on his face and he sucked it into his lungs.

"No. Stop. Just stop. You're building everything on lies. Tell people the truth! Plant City wasn't even a threat to you — you just killed people there because you wanted what they had."

"Listen to yourself, kid," Whitley said. "*You* sound like a fuckin' propaganda poster. We're offering you peace and you're rejecting it. Who's the bad guy now?"

Tyler felt as if spiders were spinning webs in his mind, and he didn't know which way was up and which way was forward.

Hatch and Whitley are smarter than you, he thought. *Does that make them right? What does Miles think? I wish he would speak up. But he's not.*

Focus on the truth, Tyler. Start with the truth, and then we can work out the other stuff later.

"You tell them," he said. "Tell the people what you did, or we will. Then peace will come."

Hatch's face stiffened with his threats; Whitley scowled and rubbed his temples.

"There's two of you…" Whitley growled. "A dozen of us."

"And I've got more," Hatch said.

Staying any longer would only increase the tension and decrease the chances of getting out alive, Tyler thought. He glanced at Miles, whose brow remained furrowed as he kept his rifle forward, unwavering.

"You two are a hell of a lot dumber than you sell yourselves to be," Miles spoke at last. "On top of all your mustache-twisting, maniacally evil misdeeds, killing civilians and jotting it down in your little murder-notebooks, you're just bumbling around like a bunch of fucking idiots. Your security is shit, not to mention your ability to gather resources. You think a few National Guard stashes are going to help you? It's been four years and you're still scraping at the old world. Still scrounging for canned food and trading for water purifiers. You're all hoarding copper for technology you haven't even rebuilt yet. None of it's going to last, and the longer you sit around and continue your dependency on that stuff, the shittier it's gonna be when it all runs out. Things are going to get worse real soon, not better. You aren't preparing for it, and your people are going to suffer."

"Oh please," Hatch interjected. "Copper is the currency of the future. At this point, it's got so much talk behind it that even if you're right, even if it's all for nothing, people will accept it as valuable and fight to the death for it if you ask them to. They used to do it over gold, then paper. Now copper. They want something physical to value, something that shines in one way or another. And don't lecture me on caring for people, you're out there in the woods like some burglar-turned-hermit."

"Miles, we should go." Tyler took a step backward. But he wasn't sure if Miles heard him, as the man stood as firm and steady as ever.

"Look," Whitley spoke with intent, "I don't much like Mayor Hatch here, and she doesn't care for me either. But we play our game of chess with a level of mutual respect, and if 'things get worse' as you so ominously say, we'll just adapt, move the pieces around, and keep going. It's worked for me in the past. It'll work for me in the future."

"Plant City was a means to an end, and we'd do it again," Hatch added. "We're rebuilding empires here, empires that can sustain peace. You two wouldn't understand what it takes to do that. It takes a lot of blood, innocent and otherwise."

As she spoke the words, Miles took a step back. "Yeah, let's go," he said to Tyler without looking at him. "This is over."

And for another moment, there was a fierce silence. The water raged below, and the wind pounded outside, clamoring louder with each ticking second.

Miles and Tyler took several steps backward, keeping their weapons trained intently on those before them. Callie's eyes darted from one to the other, and her thumb tapped the side of her rifle's pistol grip as her finger anxiously rubbed against the trigger. Her expression remained unchanging, like it was made of stone.

"Tell the truth and make peace," Tyler spoke up, as he took another step back. "Or those files go public instead."

"I'm getting kicked around by some punk kid and his hermit buddy from the woods," Whitley spat. "Fuck this; fuck you."

It wasn't slow motion — Whitley's jerk to the small of his back, the yanking of his pistol from his belt — it was like a starting pistol that Tyler's brother Anthony would listen for at his swim meets. And as his brother leapt off the starting block, Tyler pulled the trigger.

Callie hadn't been watching Whitley, so she didn't know he had grabbed his weapon. She buckled to the ground immediately, just as Major Kessler had.

Shots crackled over Miles and Tyler's heads as Whitley fired wildly in their direction, keeping himself half-behind Hatch.

Miles immediately dropped the other guard with four shots in rapid succession to the chest, just as the man drew his weapon. The two from their human shield dove in either direction, unarmed and scrambling to cover.

Without a hint of hesitation, Miles shifted his fire across the factory opening, engaging the men on the opposite side, forcing them behind cover.

Tyler turned to Whitley, who was backing up as he shot recklessly and inaccurately. Hatch reached to her waist as well, stepping toward them as she drew her own pistol. Tyler took aim with his rifle, put the dot from his reticle sight right around her lower neck, and squeezed.

The round went through her chest and struck Whitley square in the gut. Whitley fell to his knees; Hatch leaned on the railing, and her face contorted and twisted with pain.

Miles paid no mind to the mayors, and Tyler knew that when the bullets set the air ablaze, all vendettas and personal emotions were locked in a box and buried far, far away. All Miles concerned himself with were immediate threats, moderate threats, and neutralized threats — Whitley and Hatch were not engaging them so fiercely now that they were wounded, but the men across the factory, whom he harbored no ill will toward, were able to fire on the two of them with deadly accuracy.

Miles didn't turn his weapon toward the wounded mayors until he heard Whitley groan and squeeze off more rounds toward them. The bullets pinged and sparked just behind them. Miles swung his rifle toward them, and just at that moment Hatch intentionally tipped herself over the railing, plunging down toward the tumultuous waters below. Cursing to himself, Whitley slid under the rail and followed her down before either Miles or Tyler could acquire a proper sight on the wounded man.

Tyler craned his neck in an attempt to see where they fell, to determine whether or not they had survived. The roar of Miles's rifle snapped him back to the fight — dead or alive, in that moment the mayors had gone from moderate threat to neutralized, and there were still men on the other side of the factory. Tyler and Miles both fired two more rounds at them each, and they cowered behind cover.

Still, there was a yearning inside of Tyler to follow the mayors down, to see what fate had befell them. He wanted that knowledge,

that assuredness of knowing what happened to his adversaries —
even if it came with a hefty risk.

If you were afraid of risk, you wouldn't have come here in the first place,
he thought. *But that isn't an excuse to do something stupid — is this stupid?*

There wasn't enough time to figure out what was smart and
what wasn't. He turned to Miles, who apparently already knew
what he was thinking. The older man nodded to a pile of I-beams,
structural steel that would laugh at any bullets plinking on its skin.
The I-beams stretched to the edge of the platform and provided a
good view of the floor below.

Tyler slid behind it as Miles followed and stayed at the edge
of the pile, continuing to keep an eye on those across the factory.
Cresting the opposite end and peering down to the lower level
Tyler searched for any sign of human movement.

He first made out Hatch, lying in an awkward position on a
fractured catwalk, swaying about as the currents had already
swallowed half of it. She lay just beyond the submerged portion;
one of her legs, twisted and broken, touched the edge of the
lapping water.

Then he saw Whitley, who had managed to clear the catwalks
and make it to the water. Despite his wounds from the gunshot and
the fall, he clamored and flailed in a desperate attempt to stay
afloat.

Tyler glanced at a ladder descending to a metal stairway that
met on a platform nearby, which would take him right to the
mayors' grasping fingertips.

The two they had used as a human shield were long gone,
having escaped unharmed into the bowels of the factory, exiting

back the way they had come. Tyler figured they were alerting every armed human being in the vicinity of their location.

"We gotta get out of here, man." Miles was peering back through the door from which they had entered the immense factory floor. "It's gonna be a nasty fight out, this place is crawling with Lakeland Militia and Gray Platoon."

"We can't just let them get away," Tyler pleaded. "They'll find a way to get out of this, they always do."

Miles looked as if he were about to refute the boy, but he glanced down at the two, writhing for life among the shards of metal and violent currents, and a thousand calculated thoughts seemed to calmly pass through his mind, one after the other.

"We go down the ladder and fight our way out through the bottom floor. Those two asshole guards got away; everyone will be watching where we came in anyway. Let's go, hurry up." It was the first time Miles had said something that Tyler had already thought. He wondered if that meant he was learning something, or if a lucky thought would just slip into his mind from time to time.

Miles interrupted his train of thought with more shots across the vast space of catwalks toward the others, a reminder to keep their heads down. He reloaded magazines and watched as Tyler climbed down the ladder. Once he was at the bottom, Tyler covered Miles as he too descended. The two of them moved down the stairs, weapons up and their eyes darting around the factory interior.

They reached the lowest point, a crumbling cement platform surrounded by encroaching water and protruding rebar. Tyler could hear the hurricane banging just beyond the walls, like a thousand grizzly bears clawing to get inside. He shuddered to think what it must be like out there.

Hatch was still clutching the perforated catwalk, moaning in pain. Her weight wouldn't quite have been enough to sink the failing bridge if her body hadn't come crashing down into it. Her mangled leg was now almost completely submerged as the catwalk was quickly sinking. Tyler could see bone jutting out from where her shin ought to be. Her eye drifted up toward Tyler and Miles, though it seemed glazed over. He noticed blood streaming down from her hair along the side of her cheek.

Whitley, relatively uninjured from the fall, had grabbed hold of the bottom of Hatch's broken catwalk, fighting furiously against the opposing current. The shot to his stomach undoubtedly hindered his climb as he inched his way forward, gritting his teeth and choking on water. His head had almost reached Hatch's mangled foot.

"Just shoot them. Let's go," Miles said, though he didn't shoot the mayors himself.

"No, not yet. We can give them another chance…"

"Well, make your chances quick."

Tyler inched his way out onto the catwalk, and it swayed and almost buckled under his weight.

"Careful…" Miles said, keeping an eye on the upper levels.

The twisted metal groaned as Tyler stepped forward. He knelt down just outside arm's reach of Hatch, keeping his rifle ready.

Just then, Whitley thrust an arm forward and grabbed onto Hatch's leg. She cried out in pain, and the sound shook Tyler down to his spine — the sound of unbridled human suffering always made his heart wince. While keeping his weapon trained on them, he stretched out his non-firing hand — an offering.

"Take my hand, I'll pull you both out! We can still make peace work," he said, over the roar of the crashing waves and wind.

Whitley spat out a lungful of water toward him. "You dumb fuck! We've got people all over the place here, hers and mine. No way you make it out alive without us escorting you out. Take her hand, or you're taking a bullet."

Tyler looked directly at Hatch, through the blood now beginning to drip over her eyelid on her one remaining eye. She grimaced as Whitley clutched onto her contorted leg for dear life.

"Peace?" he offered directly to her.

Weary, she shook her head. "Peace is gone. Gone with the Red." She started to tremble —tremble with rage. She reached out with a hand and grabbed another handhold in the catwalk. And another. She grunted and heaved herself forward like some machine.

Tyler took a quiet step backward. And then another. And another until he was all the way off the catwalk.

Just for a second, he stared at them. Tyler felt sorry for them both, writhing around like tortured animals, choking on their impending deaths. His eyes began to water.

SLAM! He hammered his foot down onto the mangled catwalk. Hatch and Whitley's heads cocked up, fixating on him.

SLAM! His foot crashed down on it down again. The dwindling thing jolted under his foot. Whitley tried to claw his way past Hatch, but he was met with her elbow crashing into his face.

SLAM! Tyler stepped back on the stable platform and the rest of the catwalk collapsed. It sunk into the violent waters and took the bodies of Hatch and Whitley with them. One of them made a kind of screeching, grunting sound before going under; maybe it was both. They were tossed like ragdolls into the wet inferno of water and twisted metal.

"Is that it?" he asked Miles. He felt as if there should be some sense of completion, but there was nothing.

"That's it, man. They're gone, this isn't some movie. No one's surviving that shit."

Tyler didn't feel any weight off his shoulders. He felt the way he felt back when his brother's murderers were murdered, and his knees suddenly felt weak. His brain began to spin faster and faster and his head felt so heavy and light at the same time... he fell to the ground in that weakness. There was a giant nothingness in his stomach, and it was alive and wriggling with death. His whole body shuddered —

"Stop it." Miles had grabbed both sides of his head and was looking at him directly in the eyes. There was a sense of urgency in his voice, but there was also some distant, deep concern. "Stay on top of it, man. There'll plenty of time for all that later, you just need to push it down right now. Push it down and stay on top. Just until we get out of here, understand?"

He understood, and he choked the nothingness down. Tyler suddenly became very aware of his surroundings — of the factory floor, the rising water level, the ladder and the complex of platforms and catwalks above. He pushed it all down and the physical world became visible again.

"I'm good." It all went to a dark corner of his mind. *Just for now, don't think about it. Just go. Just go.* And they went.

Miles must have spotted someone peeking over the edge, because he fired a shot up toward a platform that towered above them.

"Door behind us, let's go!"

Tyler spotted the door and ran toward it. Suddenly, he didn't feel so weak, though he didn't feel particularly strong either. He felt in sync with Miles, like he was a single cog in a strong machine, and that in turn made him feel like he was a part of something that was strong.

He opened the door and Miles flowed in; Tyler was right behind him. Miles went right and Tyler went left, checking the room's corners first and moving to the sides. It was an intermediate lobby of some kind, though remnants of toolboxes and hand tools were strewn about. Water was up to their ankles now, swirling about, carrying chunks of insulation and cardboard.

A door opened nearby and someone burst in, fixated on the center of the room with their weapon drawn.

Both Tyler and Miles opened fire and the man dropped to the ground, splashing in a heap of flesh and blood. Miles moved to the door and peered through it from a few steps back. He sidestepped, clearing the next room from the safety of this one.

Miles's weapon thundered as more shots were exchanged, and he moved through the next doorway. Tyler followed.

The room's ceiling was low, but it stretched long with several doors to the right side. A dilapidated, indoor crane lay in the corner, and boxes and crates were strewn about. Some kind of system of rails lay at their feet, but it was difficult to make out through the several inches of murky water. As they moved, Tyler made sure to step over them as best as he could.

A shot flew over Tyler, followed by that familiar *CLICK*. Tyler swung around to see another Gray Platoon member fidgeting with a jammed weapon. Tyler pulled the trigger and the weapon lurched in his hands — the rounds slammed harmlessly into the wall behind the man.

The Gray Platoon soldier had cringed at the sound of Tyler's shots, but his hands still worked to clear the malfunction, and he yanked the charging handle back on his rifle, loading a fresh round in. He lifted his rifle and —

Another rifle roared. It was Miles, with his unparalleled accuracy and speed, sending the man to his shallow, watery grave.

Tyler could feel their luck running out like a lit fuse, and it was only a matter of time until it blew up in their faces. He was only alive because of Miles, that much was obvious, but even Miles had been relying on an amount of luck up to this point.

Shots echoed as they ran from room to room, some storage rooms and some offices. Walls were battered down as Tyler, Miles, and their adversaries scurried through the ruinous factory like cockroaches scattering amongst one another. Where Tyler would fire rounds and generally suppress the enemy, Miles would put bullets exactly where he wanted — sometimes it meant suppression, other times it meant a deadly grouping in someone's chest or side.

Tyler lost count of how many men and women Miles had killed already, or at least shot to where they didn't get up again. He wasn't sure if it was something he ought to keep track of, but, like everything else, he locked those thoughts away.

A new feeling of fear crept into Tyler, something that he hadn't felt before. As they endured the reverberating hurricane from the outside and the deafening skirmishes inside, Tyler began to perceive a profound sense of chaos. It was elemental, like he had been thrust into some inescapable hell made of water and fire.

KEEP IT ALL DOWN, Tyler hammered the thoughts as he hammered the trigger. *FOCUS. STAY ALIVE.*

He shifted his mind to his actions. Sometimes he felt that his shots were useful; other times he was not sure if he was shooting at anyone at all. Then, he spotted a rickety exit sign hanging to the ceiling by a couple of wires.

"Exit!" Tyler thrust a finger toward the sign. The two splashed down the hallway and found the door leading outside. The water was now knee-deep. Tyler could hear echoes and shouts throughout the hallways.

"Where the hell are they?"

"Did you see that kid killed both the fucking mayors?!"

"I think they went outside!"

"Check in that next room! I'm with you."

Miles turned to Tyler. "Door," he whispered. Tyler opened the door and Miles flowed out into the storm.

Tyler was about to follow him when what sounded like a dozen guns erupted outside. Miles came crashing back in, his weapon firing indiscriminately out into the hurricane. The steel door sparked and several rounds screamed into the hallway, bouncing off the walls and splashing up the water on the ground.

"Well, looks like that way's blocked." Miles laughed, his voice shaking.

"What was that?" The voices echoed again through the halls.

"Down there! Toward the exit sign. Grab the others!"

Tyler swung his rifle down the hallway, waiting for someone to crest the corner.

"This is what's called a 'fatal funnel,' my friend," Miles said as he changed magazines. "We stay in this hallway, any bullet fired is gonna come flying right into our faces."

"What do we do?" Tyler asked.

"Wanna make a run for it? There's some cover out there like fifty feet away."

"I'm in," Tyler said, ready to commit, whatever it meant.

For the smallest moment, Miles grinned at him. "Goddamn, man. You're a badass dude."

Tyler changed magazines — he would have smiled if he wasn't so focused on trying to catch his breath.

"Let's do it," Miles said, and they stormed out.

Just as the two were passing through the breach, Tyler caught a glimpse of movement in the hallway. He fired several shots, and the enemy leapt back behind cover. He and Miles dove out into the roaring rain.

15

THEY left a place of safety when they left the factory walls.

The roar of the storm made the roar of the interior gunfire seem like fireworks — the rain, thunder, and wind combined into a deafening symphony, twisting around them and tossing bits of tree and gravel in every direction. There was no telling where debris would come from, not while Tyler was moving, trying to identify targets, and shooting all at the same time.

Tyler fought to see. He fought to fire his weapon with any level of passable accuracy. Surely the only reason Gray Platoon and Lakeland Militia were missing them was because of the storm, Tyler understood that.

What he did not understand was Miles; something about the storm invigorated him. In fact, the worse things got, the harder he seemed to fight. And with this biblical storm about them — it was all Tyler could do to keep up.

They made it to the first piece of cover, a chain-link fence that had caught several fallen trees, making it sag almost all the way to the ground. The air roared through the makeshift wall, and the sagging, dying fence bounced up and down like a spring.

Crouching behind one of the fallen trees, Miles fired several shots toward the distant muzzle flashes, and Tyler did the same. He thought there must have been at least five or six shooters out there in the bleary storm, but it was impossible to know for certain. He fired more shots toward them.

A burst zipped past them both, and Tyler felt his head tense and muscles clench, anticipating a hit. But none came, so he continued to shoot back.

Miles turned and fired toward the door they had just left. Tyler turned to see a figure in the doorway, shooting back. He could barely hear the gunshots over the bellow of the hurricane, and he dropped to a knee and fired at the man. Like Miles, his rounds kicked up bits of cement just right of his target. Confused as to why he missed the shot, his first instinct was to glance at Miles — who didn't hesitate or question. Miles shifted left and fired again. In a split second, the figure collapsed to the ground.

"Don't look at me, man! Keep going!" Miles cried out over the pandemonium.

"We gotta go through their lines up there, it's the only way out!" Tyler pointed toward the five or six shooters. They needed to leave the fence line to escape, but the sagging, wavering fence would be impossible to climb and scramble over without getting shot or blown by the hurricane right back into the mud.

"Let's do it!" Miles said, and the two were moving again.

They bounded from the barricade of dead trees to a guard hut just ahead, shooting as they ran. Muzzles flashes and bullets seemed to come from all angles. Tyler was struck in the arm by a small rock or piece of gravel tumbling through the hurricane. The little thing almost took him off his feet and it ripped his arm away from his rifle. There was no time to assess the damage, and his arm seemed to be working just fine. He re-gripped his weapon and continued to fire as they ran.

The two slid into the guard hut. It was being eroded by the storm and gunfire; the roof was already halfway gone. A large piece of sheet metal slammed into the side of the hut, and two rounds flew through a nearby window, ricocheting off a wall just near Tyler's feet off into a pile of rubble.

"I've only got two mags left," Tyler said, changing to his second to last. They were his last two in the world.

"After this one I'm down to one and a half," Miles said. "I feel you." He raised a knee, peeked outside, and ducked back down.

"You gotta stay here and draw their fire. I'm gonna run left and take them up that hill. You should be able to see me just fine from here, so don't shoot me, okay?"

"I won't."

"I'll wave at you when it's time to move up. You can at least see up to the top of the hill, right?"

Tyler peeked out just enough to see. The perimeter fence was to their left, following the high ground right at its edge all the way to the top where the fence had been torn down. There was just enough space that one person could scramble up at a time, hugging the fence as they ascended. There were several dug-out fighting positions and stacks of debris caught against the fence along the incline, though Tyler couldn't tell if they were occupied. The climb would be nothing but mud and torrent, and one wrong step could tumble a man down to the parking lot below.

Down there, lay nothing but a hellish soup of water, tree limbs, leaves, and pieces of brick, metal, and cement. Several battered cars continued to receive a beating down there. All were in perfect firing view of the factory windows, and Tyler knew that if one of them stumbled and fell, that would be the end.

"Yeah, I can see it." He ducked back behind concealment.

"Alright. Listen, if I go down, you book it straight across to that fence, if you can. Then just b-line it into the woods. They're gonna come after you, but turn and shoot every once in a while until they don't know where you are. If you're on the run, just make sure you're moving fast. No one can track you in this thing, but even if they could, they wouldn't be able to do it at a dead sprint. Got it?"

"Got it."

"Let's do this," Miles said, and he gave Tyler a light tap on the shoulder.

The two raised their muzzles back up and fired out the windows every which way before lowering to the safety of the dissolving shed. Miles changed magazines and crept outside.

Tyler could make out at least two shooters from the factory windows to the right — at least, he saw their muzzle flashes from time to time, but with all the rain in his face he couldn't tell exactly from which window they were originating. Suppressing fire was his best bet, he figured.

If Miles "went down," it would be close to suicide to try and climb that fence under fire, but there wouldn't be any better options at that point. The way back was shut and the way forward was closing.

Tyler glanced over just in time to see Miles's momentum send him careening into the fence, and Tyler began to fire as the man scrambled out and slid to another piece of concealment, a stack of scrap wood wedged up against the chain link. Bullets of any significant caliber would undoubtedly cut right through the soaking wood and into Miles.

As Miles started his way up the slope, Tyler could make out three distinct muzzle flashes scattered between him and the freedom of the trees. Not only were they dodging the fire from the factory, but they were scraping up the mud in a literal uphill battle.

Tyler braced himself for his turn to race up the fence line.

Then Miles began to bound uphill. He was completely soaked, but he seemed to move faster and faster, invigorated by every sound of thunder and every passing bullet.

The wind shook the guard shack so violently that Tyler thought he had minutes at best before the whole thing would fold on itself and crush him. He positioned himself nearer to the window, determined to dive out if it fell.

He glanced back at Miles, who was scrambling upward now. Tyler swiveled around and fired at the factory windows to the best of his ability, though something in him knew his shots were not deadly. At best he was keeping the enemy behind the safety of cover.

Shooting at a steady but deadly rate, Miles kept on with his ascent. Tyler had to stop himself from staring in awe at the man as he moved with utter lethality. It was like a fire had been lit within him, ancient and timeless like the hurricane that swallowed them. He wasn't fighting against the hurricane; he was a part of it.

Miles stormed up the ridge, and Tyler made out another figure shooting blindly as he braced for his impending doom. With three shots, Miles dropped the figure, and then slid to a knee behind cover before clearing a malfunction in his rifle. Without skipping a beat, Miles fired toward the another figure slightly further up, catching him in the arm. When he fell, Miles put some rounds toward the third to keep his head down. Tyler saw movement as the third scrambled for better cover, and Miles seized that moment to finish the second off with a bang. He changed magazines and was firing again before the empty mag settled in the mud below.

Tyler would not have believed it had happened, had it not happened right in front of him. It didn't look like an action film from before the Red, but it didn't look like anything he had ever seen in real life either.

Tyler continued to fire upon the factory windows, and he noticed an increase in muzzle flashes appearing from its dark interior. The entire factory was aware of their location now, and they had all picked a spot from which they could join the firing line and take shots out into the rain. The only saving grace was the distortion of the downpour and the power of the wind.

By the time Tyler glanced back at Miles, he had already killed the third figure on the incline.

Then he saw a fourth, a figure shooting in bursts that cut down a small tree behind Miles. The tree had survived the hurricane until now, and with its weakened limbs it cracked into pieces and the wind tossed it right past the shooter.

Diving for cover, Miles must have been out of ammunition. Still, he did not pause to think nor did he hesitate in fear — he snatched an AKM from the last dead shooter and fired several rounds right into the fourth. Like the small tree, the fourth figure cracked into pieces and was taken by the wind.

Miles did not stop. Each movement was connected to the next, an exhausting run-on sentence, and Tyler was afraid he would be left behind. But Miles's next move was to take cover and fire precise shots toward the factory windows with his newly acquired weapon. He waved at Tyler, beckoning him upward.

Tyler clenched his jaw and barreled back out into the rain. At some point he heard what may have been the collapse of the guard shed, but he didn't look back to see. He careened into the fence, clutching at it to keep himself from bouncing right off.

His ears were burning and his senses were as flooded as the parking lot over which he climbed. It was impossible to discern the enemy shots from the thunder, rain, and debris tossed about by the wind — the crack and snap of enemy fire and the pop of splintering trees made his mind cower, but his body knew that it needed to continue up toward Miles. No matter what, he needed to move upward.

At first, Tyler tried to keep both hands on his weapon, firing the occasional round toward the factory. He slipped, his face slamming into the mud, and he used one hand to continue the frantic scramble upward. Soon that one hand turned to two.

The *rat-tat-tat* of Miles's AKM grew closer and closer as Tyler scraped up the same ridge, and as it increased in loudness Tyler began to hope that he may actually make it up the ridge.

His foot slipped in the mud again, and just then he felt the distinct displacement of air as bullets flew over him and tore through the fence. Tyler began to slide toward the edge of the incline, past which he would plummet down into the parking lot.

Tyler clawed at the mud, and he pressed his entire body against the slick ground. The rifle across his chest dug into the muck; he found a foothold against some hard, unknown thing and pressed himself back to all fours.

Again he fell, but again he rose and clambered closer to Miles. He fell to his side and used to the opportunity to fire a couple rounds at the factory, but his rifle malfunctioned — likely from the mud it was covered in — and he continued with the scramble.

And finally, he slid into a defilade at the top of the fence line where he cleared his weapon, wiped way as much of the mud as he could, and replaced its magazine. The ground became luxuriously flat, and Tyler bounded in an all-out sprint to Miles's chosen piece of cover — the foot of a giant, uprooted oak.

"Go-go-go! Keep going! Back to the trees!"

Miles kept firing, providing cover as Tyler slid to the first large tree, turned, and started firing. Miles bounded back as soon as he heard Tyler's shots. Just as they had practiced time and time again in Miles's backyard. Finally, Tyler felt they were a singular, functioning unit again.

The fourth shooter was lying next to Tyler's tree, and she too was holding an AKM. Judging by her uniform, now soaked in water and blood, she was Gray Platoon. Miles picked up any magazines easily accessible from the front and they kept moving.

They bounded back, tree by tree, until eventually Miles told him to join him as they ran together, back toward the shed with the files. Tyler figured he had around five to ten rounds left, and he wished he would have picked up someone else's weapon and ammunition like Miles did.

16

(Due to weather, broadcast unavailable)

THE two stumbled through the woods. The storm was beginning to languish along with the daylight, and the winds transformed from that raw violence to an unusually harsh blowing of the leaves.

Both kept a watchful eye to their rear and maneuvered through the trees, fueled only by spent adrenaline. Tyler wondered, for less than half a second, whether or not he would collapse the moment they stopped and his mind caught up with his body — but then he looked back behind him, scanned the trees, and made sure he had not drifted too far away from Miles, or too close that they could both be hit with a single burst of an enemy rifle. The practical thoughts kept his limbs moving.

It wasn't long before they reached the site of the brick shed.

Tyler felt a lump in his throat when he saw it. A tree had fallen through the side and the rest of that wall had been ripped apart. The entire building had flooded, and most of the debris inside had washed out the door, which was nowhere to be seen. Wherever their extra files were, they were long gone.

"Holy shit, I guess we should've thought of that," Miles said, characteristically casual. Both stood and stared at the rubble for a moment as the rain let up for the first time all day. The sun was peeking its last rays over the treetops.

Miles shook his head, snapping himself back to reality. "How much ammo do you have left?"

"Uh…" Tyler glanced down. "Just what's left in this mag."

"I've got two, but it's with this AK. Won't… won't be compatible." His voice faltered. "Check each other."

"Check each other?"

Miles approached him and looked him close over, promptly patting him down methodically. "Dude."

Tyler looked at him, expectant.

"You got shot in the arm, man."

"What? No, I just got hit with a rock —" He glanced over. It must not have been flying gravel after all: a streak of mutilated flesh crossed his upper arm, but up until now he had felt no pain. If there was pain to be felt, his brain hadn't gotten the memo. His whole arm from shoulder to elbow was covered in blood, and suddenly he felt its warmth.

And finally, with his awareness of the wound, that warmth turned to the searing heat of pain.

"Your arm still work?" Miles asked.

Tyler grimaced. "Yeah, I've been shooting with you the whole time… oh, man…"

As the pain began to well up, he started to breathe heavier and his thoughts began to race faster. He shuddered as he took that pain and shoved it down into his gut, next to his rampant emotions and the storm of conflicted thoughts. *Stifle the pain, stifle it all. Push it all down. This isn't over yet.*

"I need to check you too, right?"

"Yeah."

He saw it almost immediately. On Miles's lower chest, which was busy with its labored inhaling and exhaling, a distinct spot of soaked red lay in contrast to the rest of his rain-soaked body.

"You're shot too."

Just then, Tyler focused on Miles's face — it was paler than usual, and his eyes seemed to be scanning the trees while looking at nothing at all.

"Really?" Miles asked, peering down at the hole in his lower chest, right where it met the top of his abdomen. He immediately slapped the palm of his hand on the wound and applied pressure.

"Check the rest of me, look for an exit wound."

Tyler walked around him, patting him down. He found no signs of any other wounds, exit or otherwise, past the expected scrapes and bruises.

"Well, shit." Miles said, and he fell to his knees, stabilizing himself with one hand on the ground. He clutched the hole in his body with the other, and the AKM lay at his side.

"In my bag. My med-kit," he said.

Tyler knew where it was. He rifled through the small pack strapped to his back. A round had torn into the bag and through the files, exposing them to the wet outside world. They too were ruined, but there was no time to think about that, and he put those thoughts away with the rest. *One thing at a time.*

He pulled out a sealed bag filled with aid supplies and ripped it open, handing Miles some sterile gauze. Miles placed it over the wound, retrieved a cravat, and wrapped it around himself.

"Don't think it hit the lung, but I might need the plastic… the plastic…" he mumbled. "Nevermind, we gotta keep going, we're not far enough away yet… wrap your arm up too."

Tyler took some of the gauze and packed it as deep in his wound as he could bear, gritting his teeth as he did it. He felt the pain rumble through his head like an earthquake made of fire, but accepted it as a separate part of his mind. His ability to move his emotions, feelings, thoughts — to cordon them off and partition them away — he realized then how useful that was, as he shoved gauze into his arm. Tyler pushed the fabric up against his bone and wrapped a cravat over it as neatly as he could. Turning to Miles, he wrapped another cravat around Miles's midsection, holding the gauze in his lower chest wound in place as well.

Tyler remembered what Miles had told him under the shade of his cabin, using strips of old blankets as pretend gauze. Any chest wound like this was either going to be a problem with breathing, or a nasty wound that may have damaged his intestines or some other vital process in the mess of organs around the gut. Either way, he was watching to make sure Miles didn't start stuffing the gauze into his wound, and therefore into his chest or abdomen. Of course, on any other day, Miles wouldn't make a mistake like that, but on this day he seemed to be drifting someplace else. Some place far away.

They continued to hike on. Miles's breathing became increasingly labored, like he had to use every muscle in his body to push each breath out. Tyler took Miles's bag, slung it over his shoulder, and they pushed forward, though Miles wouldn't let him take his weapon.

The forest was a jumbled mess of fallen limbs and scattered leaves, so Tyler searched for structures and hills that would not be moved by a hurricane. When they came across an overhead pipeline jutting over an unusually open portion of swampland, he knew they had at least several miles to go before they reached Miles's cabin, if it was still standing. If the Lakeland Militia or the hurricane hadn't toppled it to the ground.

Maybe we can find shelter before then. Something standing so we can rest.

Miles put his hand on a nearby tree at the edge of the clearing, on a patch of dry dirt jutting forth from the swamp. His head weighed downward, and his shoulders sagged like an invisible pack had been strapped to his back. Tyler took Miles's AKM and slung it across his back — Miles didn't seem to notice now. They slogged through the swamp, stepping on roots where they could through the bog, under the overhead pipeline and to the other side.

"Hey, you know what?" Tyler asked, his voice lightening.

"What's that?"

"It's my birthday today."

"...for real?"

"Yeah," Tyler laughed to himself. "I'm sixteen today."

"No shit."

"Finally, old enough to join the East Tampa Militia."

Miles laughed, grimacing in pain. Tyler laughed with him.

"You know, that hurricane really wasn't that bad," Miles said. "I mean, we had to run around and shoot people in the middle of it, so I guess that made it a lot worse, but all in all, not too bad. I mean look, it's already clearing up. Just sayin'…"

As they passed through the clearing and delved back into the trees, Tyler glanced up and thought he caught a patch of blue amidst the swirling clouds, but it was getting too dark to be sure. They plodded back into the thick brush and began to move uphill. The incline was slight and the earth was getting dryer with each step, but Miles's feet grew heavier, and he barely managed to keep from tripping over fallen branches.

"You know…" Miles said, catching his breath between words. "I was a firefighter before the Red."

"I didn't know that."

"Yeah… I think I was pretty good, too. I got out of the military when I got married, and it just seemed like a good job to get after." He looked deep into the trees at something very far away. "I think I just liked helping. Giving. I did a lot of taking in the years after the Red, but firefighting was better. What we did today was better." Miles gazed down at his own broken flesh. "Giving for a little while is better than taking for a long time, I think."

Miles slowed to a stop. Tyler gazed upon him and his heart felt like a hopeless, useless weight in his chest. *What can I do?* Miles turned and looked up at the darkening sky through the thick canopy. He leaned back against a tree and slid down, so that he was sitting on the wet ground.

Tyler scanned their surroundings and knelt next to him. He retrieved an intact water bottle from the bag and gave it to him. Miles sipped.

"I want to help too," Tyler said. "I wanted to, anyway. But all the files are gone. All the evidence got washed away." Tyler felt a lump in his throat and he choked down tears as he spoke.

Miles smirked. His teeth were stained with blood.

"What?" Tyler prodded. He would almost be offended if the man weren't so terribly wounded.

"Well," Miles said, "then it's a good thing they shot me and not this thing."

He pulled out a tape recorder. It was wrapped in a plastic bag, but the microphone was poking out of the corner. It was *the* tape recorder.

"You…" Tyler's eyes grew wide. "You taped them? Everything they said?"

"Sure did. I hope it worked. And I hope this piece of shit didn't get all jacked up from the rain."

"It probably did, knowing our luck."

Miles laughed again, his face contorting in pain soon after. "Probably." He handed it to Tyler. "Worth giving it a listen."

Tyler unwrapped it from the plastic bag. The small microphone plugged into it was soaked and had been stripped down to the wire, likely during their gunfight outside and all the agitation thereafter. However, the recorder itself seemed to be intact.

"What do I do? How does this thing work?"

"Buttons… on the side… you got fast-forward and rewind, and the pause and play button. That's it, just don't hit the record button. It's a tape, old-school… sixteen and can't even work a tape recorder." He tried to laugh again. "You're way too young for this shit, man," he said, his eyes growing very sad and falling to the forest floor.

"Wait…" Tyler held the precious recorder in his hand. "This is… this is the tape with your…" *With your family. Your wife and your daughter.* He couldn't even say the words.

Miles just nodded. "It's okay."

Tyler felt those familiar, unknown emotions bubble up within him. He knew he had to keep them buried; they were in a volatile situation and might need to move at the sound of a snapping twig. If he stopped and cried then both of their deaths would be on his hands. Miles still needed medical attention, and Tyler needed to be ready if there was anything that he could possibly do to help Miles survive. But this, this gift of Miles's, it crept past all the other things, and crept out through Tyler's eyes in the form a few, quiet tears.

"It's okay, the past is important, but the future is… more…" Miles said, struggling to finish his sentence. "Just play it. Besides, it's the second tape. It's not the treehouse one. I like the treehouse one too much…"

Tyler rewound the tape recorder and played. Nothing but static, as he expected. He rewound more. Nothing.

Did he erase their memory for nothing? Tyler thought.

Miles stared at the wet leaves on the ground, unable to lift his eyes to anywhere else. Unable to keep his head held up. He breathed as best he could. The indiscernible static from the tape recorder echoed through the woods, scratching at the emptiness of the Red. That emptiness that consumed the planet, and now threatened to consume them too.

"Ding, ding, ding — we have a winner. Peace was always the plan, assholes. You'd have known that if you would'a just waited another month or so." The recorder crackled to life. Tyler could barely hear Whitley's voice — but he could hear it. Tyler almost dropped his weapon. He fast-forwarded just for a moment and hit play again.

"Plant City was a means to an end, and we'd do it again. We're rebuilding empires here, empires that can sustain peace. You two wouldn't understand what it takes to do that. It takes a lot of blood, innocent and otherwise." It was the damning voice of the former Mayor Hatch.

Tyler almost wept at the sound of it. This was better than files or the word of any witnesses. This was the crime coming from the mouths of the criminals.

He listened further, and it was all there. Segments were flooded with static or sounds of the storm — as soon as they started moving, the scratching from Miles's chest and the rain outside made it impossible to make out, but the important part, the stand-off with Hatch and Whitley — it was all there.

Tyler held the recorder in his hands like it was made of gold. But what was more precious? In the moment of victory, Tyler wondered if hearing the voice of his wife and child one last time would be more valuable to Miles than any triumph on Tyler's account.

But the decision had already been made.

Tyler carefully wrapped up the recorder in the plastic bag, tightly sealing it from the elements, and he put it the bag where there was newfound room in the old aid kit.

He zipped the bag up carefully, treating it as the most cherished thing he had ever been responsible for. Tyler wondered, for a moment, if that was true. After all, he had held his parents as they died slow and agonizing deaths, one by one. He held what was left of his brother's body in his arms in his parents' old bedroom, just after the departure of the red truck. *No*, he thought, *not more precious than those.*

And yet this thing, this inanimate and lifeless object designed to record sound on magnetic tape — it held something the dead did not. What, exactly, he could not say.

Tyler sat there motionless for a moment, on both knees with the small pack in front of him.

"I can't keep going, Tyler. I'm done," Miles said. "You take that tape, and you keep going."

Tyler didn't have the strength to look at him. He didn't have the strength to speak. He knew he couldn't drag Miles further than a mile, certainly not all the way back to the cabin.

"Hey," Miles rolled his head upward and admired him with his little remaining strength. Tyler looked back, partly out of respect and partly because he knew he wouldn't be able to look at the man much longer. "Keep those other tapes, will you? Of my daughter and my wife. What's left of 'em, anyway."

"I will."

Miles seemed to nod, but Tyler wasn't sure if he was just too weak to keep his head up.

"I've said it before, but I'll say it again… things aren't going to get better, Tyler. They're going to get worse. Resources are running out… it's a miracle people have been living off of canned beans this long. Once people start starving, and I mean really starving… then things will get bad. They're picking up all this copper for a world that's never actually coming back. Not anytime soon."

"What do I do?" Tyler asked.

"I don't know, man. But the world only ends when people give up on it. Just don't… don't give up."

"I understand."

"I know you do…" Miles said. "You're stronger than me. And you have a talent for tactical thinking… but you've been lucky, up until this point. I'd be willing to guess that for every hundred guys with your story, ninety-nine are facedown in some ditch. Like I always told you before, train. All the dumb stuff — mag changes, room clearing, react to contact, wrapping a goddamn chest wound… you need to get good at that stuff." He choked the words out, knowing there would not be many more. "Promise me you'll get good at that stuff."

"I will." Tyler could barely speak.

"But those… those are all things you can learn. And those books in the library, those are all things you can learn, too. Right there —" He dug a finger into Tyler's chest. "You can't learn that shit. Don't forget it, and don't lose it."

"I won't," Tyler said. "I promise I won't."

"I have so many things to say, I wish I had more time to say them… but the faster I talk, the worse… the worse it…" Miles looked at him for a long time, blood in his mouth and a deep sorrow in his eyes. He lifted himself to Tyler's ear and whispered.

He whispered so no one could hear but the trees and great empty night air.

Finally, they separated. "Time for me to go, Tyler," Miles said. "Time for you to go too."

"Go where?"

"See if the cabin's still up. It's yours, if you want it. You earned it."

A well of tears was bubbling up from Tyler's heart. From his throat and under his eyes. It was all he could do to keep it from bursting forth. "Thank… thank you…" was all he could muster.

"You're welcome," Miles said, with that paternal voice that also told him that he was heard. "Go." Miles looked as if he had so much more that he wanted to say, but the wounded man could barely muster the single word. He pointed in the rough direction of the cabin.

Tyler turned and started to walk. If Gray Platoon were tracking them, the night would slow them down considerably. Once he downloaded his gear and stripped away all evidence of combat, he would just look like a teenager who had survived the Red — not like the man who killed two mayors with the stomp of his foot.

He looked back at Miles, slumped over and gazing at the ground, breathing slow, labored breaths. It was in that moment of weakness that Tyler regarded him as the strongest person he would ever know. That opinion would never change.

"Hey," Miles said, tightening his voice and lifting his chin just as Tyler departed. "The radio station. The mines. The gun positions and the tripwires. The bloodthirsty criminals… it's all bullshit.

Smoke and mirrors, just like everywhere else. You can walk right up to that place and the old man inside won't know what hit him. I've done it a couple times." He almost chuckled.

Tyler glanced back at him. The two exchanged sad smiles before Tyler left.

"Just sayin'..."

17

"Looks like we're back on the air, folks. We had some trouble during the storm, but it seems like we're through the worst of it. Funny how after a storm you don't feel like you won anything, you just sorta pick up and keep on keepin' on.

"Speakin' of, I got a busted window to attend to, so I'll leave y'all with some tunes for the occasion — tunes about keepin' on. Just remember, you heard 'em on 101.7, the soundtrack to the end of the world."

TYLER'S eyes were dry for the walk home. He trudged through swamps that at times rose to his chest; he ploughed through thickets and over the plethora of fallen limbs and branches. He found rest in the solace of physical labor, despite his burning feet and fresh blisters. The night air was getting colder by the minute and being soaked to the bone only made it colder.

He walked and he walked, until the back of his right heel felt like it would just dissolve into the murky waters, and then he walked a little further. The pain was rhythmic and it didn't matter much to him, like the groaning pain in his stomach or the famished weakness that spread to every muscle in his body — none of it mattered as long as he kept plodding forward.

He was unsure as to his exact location, but he knew that if he just kept north, he would eventually hit an old highway, and then from there he would turn right and move west until he found an overpass over a creek that was probably a river after all the flooding. From there he couldn't remember if it was north or south, but it was only a thirty-minute walk either way. He figured he would go half an hour one way, and if he had no luck then he would turn around and walk an hour the other way.

A part of him hoped he got it wrong, and that he would just keep on walking forever until his entire body turned into one big blister and he disintegrated into the deep, black woods. Another part of him remembered Miles's words, that he needed to learn more practical skills. No doubt navigating these woods were one of them.

But the cabin eventually came, and he couldn't remember which direction he had even picked. He knew Miles had offered him the cabin, but Lakeland knew exactly where the cabin was as Allie had given up their location, and he was sure that they would be after him.

Just as Tyler expected: the cabin was ransacked. Under the moonlight, he could make out the front door — it had been torn open and he could see clothes and boxes spilling out it. The wind and sporadic bursts of rain were still gently blowing the trees, and he found it unlikely that anyone would actually be there — the hurricane probably took precedence in the minds of Lakeland militiamen, not some teenager in a cabin in the woods.

Once their families are safe, they'll be back.

Still, he lifted his rifle and approached the cabin. It had withstood the storm with little damage, and no trees had fallen on it. One tree about a foot in diameter had collapsed just near the door, but other than that it was just a sporadic littering of limbs. The scraps of wood hammered over the windows remained intact — Miles's preparations had worked. The thought made his heart heavy.

Tyler reached the front door and opened it the rest of the way with one hand, pointing the muzzle of his rifle inside with his other. The wound on his upper arm stung, but he didn't mind the pain anymore.

Step by step, Tyler cleared as much of the home as he could from the safety of the outdoors. Then he moved indoors, checking the corners and crannies that couldn't be cleared from the outside. After that, he ensured no one was hiding in the latrine.

He stood outside for no longer than thirty seconds, scanning his surroundings. Then he returned indoors.

The house had been ransacked, but not much had been taken. He figured they left in a hurry once they realized the place was empty and a hurricane was headed their way.

Tyler found another, larger pack and consolidated the one on his back into it. He took essential food, an on-the-go water purifier, iodine tablets, some dry food, lighters and batteries, two small solar panels, three empty bottles that he intended to fill on the road, and some dry clothes from a sealed bag. He changed into another pair of dry clothes he had washed a few days prior. Tyler snagged any piece of camping equipment he could find — Miles had aggre-gated quite the stockpile over the years.

He dug through the trunk under Miles's bed and found the other tape of his family. Tyler put it in a hard container and wrapped that in a plastic bag.

Once everything was stowed away in his pack, Tyler had no desire to linger. He tore open a bag of dried fruit and ate as he walked. There were no thoughts to return, and he did not pause at the threshold of the tree line and gaze at his lost home. He just walked back into the dark woods and melted into the wind.

18

"You know what they say: love hurts. Oh baby, does it hurt. I've been stabbed before, and I gotta say I'd rather get stabbed with a knife again than get metaphorically stabbed in the 'ol heart. Though my ex-wife was responsible for both, but that's another story for another day.

"And no, before you ask — I ain't fixin' to play you the tunes of pre-Red teenagers whinin' on an electric guitar about some boy or girl that left 'em in the dust. Nope, not today. I'm fixin' to play y'all some opera. You heard me, straight up opera. No, I don't know what year it's from.

"After it's done, I'll tell ya what he's goin' on about, but suffice to say... he's bent outta shape, whinin' about some boy or girl that left 'em in the dust.

"Just remember, you hear these tales as old as time on 101.7, the soundtrack to the end of the world."

ALLIE was far enough away that she was about the size of his watch face. His watch ticked and she toiled, shoulder-to-shoulder with a group of Lakeland men and women carting a heap of cement blocks from one pile to another. The first pile had been a shed before the hurricane, and it had toppled in the wind and rain and they appeared to be digging for some precious item beneath the mess of cement and tile.

Tyler was leaning in the darkened bay of a car wash across an overgrown field of weeds and orange wildflowers and a wide street. The car wash had been overwhelmed with trees and vines and grass; that brush had been blanketed by old world climbing fern, an invasive species that had begun to make the area northeast of Lakeland look something like a single green mass. The fern, the weeds, and wildflowers all hung their heads heavy at the weight of the hurricane that was now a thing of the past.

His heart extended to Allie, from his concealed spot in the shade out to her in the light under the overcast field. He knew he wouldn't speak to her, but he longed to feel the warmth of her smile and voice, to know that contrast to the wind that was still biting at them all. He wanted to hear talk about Ivy the alligator and he wanted to follow her up another Tampa hill that she called a mountain. He knew he should be angry with her, but a part of him was too tired to be angry.

Tyler stared at them from that dark place, wondering why they dug and what they were digging for. Rubble covered so much in the world after the Red, and more rubble just meant more lost things.

Maybe they're after food or weapons. Maybe they're digging up the body of someone they love.

Seeing her, even from that distance, had tempered the seeth-ing rage he felt at everyone and everything. The air in his lungs felt heavy at even the thought of Allie having to unearth someone she cared for, to see someone from her post-Red family cut down to a broken bag of skin and bones. To see those eyes with that look that only the dead wore. He knew she had seen it before, and he hated that she might have had to see it again.

"I got it!" Allie's voice was faint but unmistakable. It shook with excitement and Tyler squinted to see what it was that she had found.

First, he could see the shimmer — it was a brilliant brown and gold even without a sun to shine on it. She pulled it from the rubble and held it high over her head, and then she kept pulling like she was yanking on a ball of yarn and passing the string to the man next to her.

The group shifted angles for better leverage and Tyler knew what he was seeing: it was copper. An older man hobbled over and tossed Allie a pair of gloves. She put them on and continued to tug at the spool of copper wire buried beneath the ruins.

Tyler's heart retracted. There was no body. He wasn't disappointed in that particular fact, but for the sake of his own image of humanity he wished it had at least been weapons or food or even some sentimental memorabilia.

Copper. The word made Tyler's stomach turn. He felt sick at the thought of the blood spilled over such petty things. He felt sick that Allie, a soul that shone with independence and good will, would wind itself up in shiny wire just because the others around her were doing the same. They told her that its shine had value, like it could reflect some distant image of an old world that was now nothing more than ash.

As he watched Allie pull the remaining stretch of copper from the coil stuck below the broken bits of cement, a thought surfaced in Tyler's mind that he had kept away from the light.

She followed you to Miles's cabin one of those days you were together. That's how she knew you were there. That's how she knew where to send Lakeland troops after you escaped Hatch's office. She always kept that in her back pocket, that idea to turn you over.

His heart and his mind were in agreement; the heart turned hard and the mind turned away. Soon his eyes and body followed, and he backed out of the car wash bay and walked through an overgrown, abandoned town behind it, sticking to the tall underbrush and low-hanging trees.

Tyler hoped that he would never see Allie again.

You're not here for her, just keep walking to where you're going. Miles is gone, but we set out to do something and it's not done yet. You've still got work to do.

19

"I don't know about you, but I feel like the last few years made me a whole lot older than I ever intended to be. They got to this Americana folk artist who released her very first album, just a year before the redness hit, and she might be young, but brother... does she pack a punch right in the gut with her songs about growin' up just a lil' bit too fast.

"Listen to her sing the truth on 101.7, the soundtrack to the end of the world."

As he hiked in the darkness of the early, early morning, Tyler had begun to wonder if the hill would ever end. *How did mountain climbers in the Rockies or the Alps do it?* After all, this was just some hill in Florida. It was taller than the one that he and Allie had climbed, allegedly the tallest bump in the land around, but Florida was supposed to be a flat place. He just never actually walked it until now.

Flat seems a lot less flat when you're the one who has to walk it, he thought.

Tyler paused and sat amidst the waist-high underbrush. He took off his shoe and checked his heel; it was rubbed raw, and a spot of blood had appeared on his sock. His thighs burned alongside his lungs as they struggled for each breath of air. Tyler suppressed the pain and continued up. Up, up, and up.

The trees were thick and the footpath he had chosen wound through the jungle like a maze. The switchbacks were so sharp, he may have thought he was going in circles if it weren't a continuous uphill climb. Entire sections of the trail had been washed away, and at times he doubted whether or not he was on the right hill at all.

No, other hills around here aren't like this. Just keep going up.

Up, up, and up.

Tyler stumbled several times, and he hoisted himself up by grasping bunches of leaves or low branches. He felt no jolts of frustration as it happened; he simply rose back up and carried on. Up, up, and up again.

In an attempt to heave himself up a boulder, the rubber of Tyler's shoe slipped on the rock and his hip slammed right into its rough surface. Pain seared from his hip through his pelvis and around his waist, but he did not cry out. Instead, Tyler lay there and considered never getting up again. He thought perhaps he ought to wait until someone came by and took his things and maybe shot him. He thought maybe he could just roll down the hill to be skewered by some protruding branch or break his neck on some lonely rock.

He thought those things and then got up again and continued the climb.

The woods were starting to thin and the morning began to make itself known. There were no breaking rays of sunshine, just a gradual increase of light across the sky, heavily spotted with clouds. A wave of cold blanketed itself through the Floridian jungle. Tyler's clothes were soaked with sweat now, and with the dawn they were matted to his skin, wet and cold like frozen rags.

He arrived at a clearing, and his path continued directly through its center. The radio tower loomed over him from the middle of the field, which was at the highest point of what felt like a mountain. He gazed up at its colossal metal scaffolding, and at the red blinking light on top. The light didn't seem much closer, even from up there — it just blinked on and off like it always had.

A small compound lay beneath the tower itself. Several buildings with blown-out windows and doors knocked off their hinges provided a teetering foundation to the radio tower, but one particular building grabbed Tyler's attention. Heavy pieces of wood were screwed securely to its exterior windows, and a bulky steel door stood as the only perceivable entrance.

Tyler's mind began to turn as it used to; it revived the stories he had heard not so long ago from the other children of East Tampa, of all the mines and the machine-gun positions and tripwires. Of the maniacal group of serial killers who ambushed the unwary wanderers. Several signs were posted throughout the clearing, reading in crudely written spray paint: "WARNING: MINES!"

Miles's voice played in his head: *"The radio station. The mines. The gun positions and the tripwires. The bloodthirsty criminals… it's all bullshit. Smoke and mirrors, just like everywhere else."*

Tyler decided to do the same thing he'd been doing for the last several months: he kept moving forward.

A part of him expected to feel that flash of heat he felt back at the barracks in East Tampa, followed by an enveloping darkness. A part of him expected to feel the rock that had hit him in the upper arm at the factory, except it would be several rocks and they would slam into his chest. And then the enveloping darkness. And maybe light afterward? He wondered.

He stepped forward, one foot and then the other.

Before he knew it, he was at the heavy steel door. The outside was adorned with stickers of all brands and symbols, of animals and stars and butterflies, many of which were worn and shredded, but many that seemed new and colorful. Some were of skating and surfing companies, others were made for children to decorate their rooms. Now they graced the entrance to this fortress.

His eyes drifted to a latch on the front. It was half-cocked, and he gently lifted it to see if it was secured. It moved freely in his grasp. That may have surprised him several months ago, but it did not surprise him now.

Tyler gripped his rifle and pressed the door open.

The inside of the room was lit by a single candle. Extinguished candlesticks lay strewn about the room, melted down to varying heights with tiny, wax glaciers pouring over onto their respective surfaces.

The burning candle flickered as it illuminated the hunched body of an old man, curved over his desk, writing with a broken pencil on a piece of paper. His long, unkempt beard was entangled with bits of dirt, and his skin was wrinkled like old leather. The cutoff t-shirt he wore revealed sleeves of tattoos, all of which were faded beyond recognition. His lips, however, were red and young.

"Sir."

The man whirled around, almost teetering out of his seat. His mouth was agape, and his eyes grew wide, but he did not speak.

"Sir, I'm here with a tape. I'd like to play it over your radio station."

The old man still couldn't quite find his speech, but Tyler waited patiently.

I've got nowhere in the world to be but here.

Finally, the old man spoke. "Is it classic rock? I need some more classic rock, brother."

It was that familiar voice he had heard almost every day for the last four years. The voice that preceded music and had sent both him and his brother drifting off to sleep, and in person it rung with a clarity he hadn't expected.

"I know," Tyler said with a smile. "But it's not classic rock."

The old man looked behind Tyler. "You made it past the mines and the guns, huh?"

"Yeah. It was tough, but I made it," he said, and he wanted to chuckle but nothing came.

"So what'chya got, then?"

"News."

"News? Brother, I haven't aired news since the Redness hit."

"Well now's your chance to get back on the horse."

"Is it good news?"

"No."

"I don't think people can take any more bad news, brother."

"How would you know? You're all the way up here."

"It's just… it's just there's an awful lot of bad news out there goin' on all the time already. The Redness, all the fightin', you know. It never ends. The world's fallin' apart, brother."

"There's always something going on down there, one way or another. But this is the truth, and that's always in short supply. They can get on with things from there themselves, you don't worry about that. You can stay up here. It's not like you really care anyway, right? Hiding up here like you do."

"Why would you say that? Of course I care, brother…"

"Are you gonna play my tape or not?"

"Alright, alright. I'll play it."

Tyler pulled out the tape recorder from the bag and handed it to the man.

"I don't have a tape deck, brother, how am I going to play that?"

"Just play the speaker into the microphone," Tyler was beginning to raise his voice. "And play it over and over. All day. For a couple days. I'm gonna stay up here while you do. I've got plenty of extra batteries I can feed into this thing."

"People are going to get real bored of that, brother…"

"Then they'll get bored of it. Let me see that paper, if you don't mind."

The old man handed him the paper and pencil. Tyler wiped his hand dry on one of the man's nearby jackets that hung on a coat hook fixed to the wall. He started scratching the pencil to paper and then handed it back to the old man. "What's your name? You never say it on air."

"Fairchild. Johnny Fairchild."

"My name's Tyler. Nice to meet you."

"Nice to meet you too, I guess…"

"I need you to read these bullet points, Mister Fairchild. You can word them however you want, but I need that information clearly communicated. Is that alright?"

Fairchild looked over the notepad. "Holy shite, brother. Things are really goin' on down there, aren't they?"

"Will you read it?"

"You really did all that? Who the hell are you?"

"Are you gonna read it or not?"

"I'll read it. And I'll play your tape. You're the one with the gun."

Tyler stood and thought in silence. He closed the door behind him, placed his rifle to the side, unslung Miles's AKM, and also placed it to the side. He put down his bag, grabbed a nearby stool, and slumped down onto it. His shoulders felt very heavy — heavier even, now that the bag was off of them. He felt dreadfully tired, down to his soul and down to his bones.

"Damn, brother. You're just… how old are you?"

"I'm not making you do anything. I'm just asking you. If you don't do this, then it's shit. It's all shit."

Fairchild studied Tyler, the way an elderly man might look at a young, sick child in hospice. "I'll play it. I'll read it."

"Thank you."

"You're welcome."

The man went back to his work, and Tyler just sat on the stool. He watched the man for a while, then stared off into space for a while longer.

He did not feel angry at Hatch and Whitley, or Gray Platoon or whoever fired the shot that killed Miles. He did not feel rage toward God or fate or Tampa or Lakeland. He wasn't angry at himself, and he knew he did his best with what he had. He did not have violent flashbacks of combat, and if a shelf were to fall over or if someone were to fire a shot in the air, he would react as he always would have. He felt no burning hatred or confusion or restlessness in his heart.

He was just very sad, and very tired.

20

"Some of you may be asking why I've been playin' these tapes over and over. You might say, 'Brother we get it, but I just wanna hear that sweet music one more time. Play me Mozart, play me rock n' roll — hell, play me your screamo mumbo jumbo, just quit it with this real world shit.'

"I get it. I really do, believe me, and I will never stop playin' these tunes 'till one of y'all comes up here, gets past the tribe-a crazies livin' 'round these woods, weaves through these mines, and gets past the other three traps I ain't spillin' the beans about. 'Till one of you does all that and forces me to stop, I ain't gonna stop sendin' those succulent tunes over the airwaves.

"But brothers, I gotta tell ya. Ya can't listen to music 24/7—sometimes ya need a little truth thrown in the mix. Hell, maybe ya need a break from music just so ya really know why music was good to listen to in the first place.

"So for the millionth time, I'm playin' the 'Mayors' Tapes' again, courtesy of one Tyler Ballard. Just remember: you heard it on 101.7, the only soundtrack around, baby."

TYLER switched off the radio. He retrieved the tape recorder from the bag, and it glistened in the sunlight as he pressed play.

"Be careful!" Miles's voice laughed and crackled to life. *"We gotta build this thing, but how about we build it without falling to the earth and breaking all of our bones?"*

"Daddy, you're too big to fit up there! I'm the only one."

"Listen —"

"Miles, just stand under. You're a good catch, right?" Miles's wife's voice was both sweet and strong. They laughed.

"Oh no, you're not getting out of this one. We're both standing under, if she falls it's on both of us."

"Fine by me."

His heart swelled as he heard laughter and hammering and the scraping of someone climbing up a tree.

Tyler pressed stop and basked in the sounds of Florida's daylight nature. The cicadas, the chirping birds, and the natural gusts of wind in the trees that did not originate from a hurricane.

He was seated next to his makeshift lean-to, a piece of tarp crudely fashioned between several trees. As he studied it, he realized that it would probably fall apart at the slightest rainfall, though it hadn't rained in several days now. He was glad no one saw how long it took him to put such a pathetic structure up, and he figured he would be taking it down soon enough. *Just because you know how to shoot a gun doesn't mean you know all this other stuff,* he reminded himself. *You need to find shelter, and today. Abandoned houses are easy to find; you just need to find the right one.* And he thought he needed to return to that library in hopes it would teach him something about building homes.

The small radio lay beside him, and he turned it on again to hear Fairchild's voice repeat the same words that had been airing over and over for days. The old man had decided to run with Tyler's notes, and the next day he had even asked Tyler more questions. Before he left, Tyler felt like he had begun to warm up to the man, though he wondered if liking someone was a doorway to trust, and he wasn't sure how freely he wanted to dole that out.

Tyler also couldn't figure out why Fairchild would block himself off to the world at large, but then express so much interest in something as soon as he was forced exposure to it. *Maybe that's what made it real. Maybe before it was all just a bunch of things that ants did down the hill, but hiking up there brought it to his doorstep.*

Whatever the reason, he was miles away from Fairchild now and what was done was done. Besides, it worked. Tyler had been up there for days while the DJ replayed the tape and read through the notes that Tyler had given him. Most of it just spoke to what had happened; most of it left out Tyler, and none of it mentioned Miles. *Miles wouldn't have wanted that.*

Before Tyler left, he told the old man that smoke and mirrors wouldn't save him forever, and that, especially if he started involving himself in the world beyond music from his distant tower, he had better set up some legitimate defenses. It was a wonder how he had lasted that long without anyone knocking on his door, completely based on the man's big mouth and bigger lies. It was a wonder *anyone* lasted with the security he had seen in the past few months.

To be fair, I suppose they really haven't lasted at all.

As Fairchild's voice blithered on, "brother-ing" this and that, he thought of what East Tampa and Lakeland must look like right now. Both had lost their valiant heroic mayors, and Tyler had destroyed any chance they had of martyrdom by airing the tape. Their heroes were exposed as cheaters and liars. He wondered if even now Santana and Allie were telling themselves stories to retain the illusions they spent so long constructing. He wondered what he would say if he ever saw them again.

Tyler retrieved a flask from his rucksack. It was the same, dented flask Miles had given him before, the one they had taken from the bandits. He unscrewed the lid and put the small opening to his mouth. He took a hefty gulp, and this time he barely winced.

Tyler studied the flask like he was looking at a headstone, and then he poured the contents on to the ground, wiping the rest off his face. He put the flask back in its pouch.

The thought of the dead mayors did not give him satisfaction, but he did feel that he had done something at least remotely right. Still, he did not feel victorious. Too much had been lost for that.

His train of thought was interrupted by the distant *rat-tat-tat* of gunfire. His hand instinctively reached for the M4 by his side, and he whirled his head around to try and discern the direction from which the gunfire originated.

A round was already in the chamber, so he threw on his chest rack, which held four full magazines, and looked around again.

Rat-tat!

Two more gunshots, probably a rifle, but not here, and not meant for him. They were far, or at least far enough away that he wasn't in danger quite yet. He threw on his socks and shoes, momentarily feeling and appreciating their dryness, and shoved a water bottle in an empty magazine pouch.

Tyler recognized most every tree in this particular patch of woods. It was an area he and his brother had frequently explored when they were younger, and every odd-looking tree and every misplaced knot was like an old, familiar face. The hurricane had broken and shuffled, but in the end, it was the same forest.

He raced as fast as he could effectively keep track of his surroundings, dodging thickets and fallen trees. There were still endless piles of fallen debris from the storm, and he didn't expect it would go away any time soon. No one would organize to clean it up; it would just rot and wither with time.

The rifle shots were getting closer. Tyler knew a road would appear soon. It was a dirt road, seldom used before the Red, but Plant City refugees had frequented it prior to the tape going on air. There was still traffic over the last couple of days, but it was going both ways. No doubt bandits from the Orlando area would notice the recent changes. No doubt they already had.

When he saw the break in the treetops, he began to slow down. He knew he would find the road just beneath the incoming gap in the canopy.

Tyler gripped his rifle and peered over its optic, keeping it low enough that his peripheral vision would not be blocked and he would not fixate on his sights. He had just changed its battery, and he had several more, and having a freshly powered sight on his small, cheap reflex optic made his whole body feel refreshed.

Just ahead, he spotted several figures beyond the break in the trees. There was a wagon of some kind, and an assortment of people were frantically shuffling around while a few others stood still.

Something within him jolted, almost prompting him to run out into the midst of them and figure out what was going on, to save anyone who needed saving. Instead, he waited.

One figure had a rifle pointed in the air, and he fired a shot.

"Let's go! Let's go! Let's see what you got, hurry up!" the voice roared, a deep, grating voice with a thick New England accent. Tyler spotted another armed figure, what looked like a woman, moving between kneeling hostages.

As Tyler inched forward, he could make them out: the man was larger and slightly overweight. The woman was scrawny hunched forward. Both wore decrepit Halloween clown masks over their faces with tattered, stained clothes and wraps lazily twisted around their arms intended to protect their skin from the sun, though they wouldn't do the pair much good with gaps like that. Miles had told Tyler once that some bandits wore masks like this to instill fear or surprise, but ultimately it just hindered their vision and sometimes hearing, and that they should be seen as a hindrance to his enemy.

"Y'all make any quick moves," the woman screeched, "and I'll blast 'yer head right off."

Tyler began to shift to a more advantageous vantage point. He counted five on their knees, all young except for one woman in her sixties. Besides her, there were two girls and two boys, and he figured the oldest of them must have been in her twenties. Most were crying and shaking, except for one girl. She sat on her knees with her hands in the air and waited patiently. Her hair was long and red, her skin was freckled and slightly sunburned. Her eyes were dejectedly fixed on the ground.

He made out two bodies in the dirt; a pistol lay near one of them, but he couldn't make out what kind.

"What's gonna happen," the woman said, waving her clown mask and sawed-off shotgun in their faces, "is we're gonna take you out northeast of here. Good fer you, right? You was already headed up north, sorta. But there's no need to be lookin' for a job no more, we already got you one. And we're gonna get ourselves a nice lil' referral fee, and y'all are gonna do everything that we say until that happens. Understand?"

Two of the girls acknowledged her with frantic cries; one of the boys let out a whimper.

"She asked if you understand!" The man's voice rumbled through the vegetation as Tyler climbed through it, careful to make no noises of his own.

"We understand," said the redheaded girl, who remained unwavering.

"Okay… we understand," said the whimpering boy, attempting to echo her confidence.

"Good," said the man.

"Honey." The woman grabbed the tallest girl by the arm. As she stood, Tyler realized she may have even been close to thirty; she was lanky and had mud caked across the front of her shirt — *she must have dove to the ground at some point*, Tyler thought.

The redhead's eyes moved as the assailants moved, quietly tracking them.

The clown-masked woman picked up the pistol on the ground, put a hand on the tall girl's shoulder, and then shot her in the head.

Just when Tyler thought his heart was no longer capable of shaking in horror, the death rattled him like it was the first time.

Several of the hostages cried out in terror, and the man paced around them, ready to slam the butt of his rifle into someone's nose. The older woman looked frantically around, possibly for some kind of weapon, but she found none.

The woman bent over the corpse and pulled a knife from the girl's belt. "This right here is liable to get you kilt. She was fingerin' it like she wanted to do somethin' with it. Let that be a lesson to y'all. Heroes got no place here."

Tyler buried his elbows into the ground. The sand caved to them, but he quickly nestled in deep until they rested on solid earth below. He lay prone, fixing the red dot of his optic directly at the man's chest, whose rifle was more of a threat since the woman had slung her primary weapon and toted the pistol.

Tyler breathed in deeply, waited for a moment, and exhaled. He waited until his lungs emptied themselves of air, waited a hair longer, and he pulled out the slack in his trigger.

The weapon lurched in his hands. He waited a split second for the sights to settle again on the target and fired twice more. The man careened backward, toppling as he hit the wagon with his shoulder — he fell to the ground and did not move again.

The woman let out a yelp and didn't even look for Tyler before bolting for cover. She headed for the tree line while she unslung her shotgun —

Three rounds and she was on the ground too.

The redheaded girl leapt up. She sprinted over to the fallen pistol, picked it up, and put a round in both of their heads before anyone else thought to flinch.

Tyler waited for a moment. He scanned the surrounding area and listened. Everyone had dropped their faces to the dirt road again, hugging the ground like they were on a jet spiraling out of control, clinging on for dear life.

Everyone except the redhead. She stood, breathing heavily now. Her head whirled around, looking for the shooter who had saved their lives.

Still, he waited. He would not get caught again like he had after his conversation with Allie and her Lakeland friends.

Once he was satisfied, Tyler rose from his position of concealment. He stepped forward into the sunlight, only to be met by the muzzle of the redhead's newly acquired pistol.

"Don't shoot me. I mean, if you don't mind," he said.

She lowered her weapon and studied him carefully, but she said nothing.

The older woman moved toward him. "Thank you, sir. You saved us."

"You guys are all a group?"

"Just him and me." The older woman pointed at the boy who had been whimpering. "He's my nephew. We met the others just yesterday — the fighting is dying down, but it's just a matter of time before it all starts again. We have to leave before that happens, you understand."

"You don't have to leave," Tyler said. "The offensive to Plant City was the idea of the mayors, and they're both dead now. That's why the fighting died down, and I'm hoping it'll stay that way."

"So what the radio was saying… it's true? That they're both dead?"

"Yes."

"How do you know?"

"I just know."

"Well, maybe we could camp outside of town for a while. See how things go. If I can manage to stay, I will. I know a lot of good people who are still there, and leaving is… well, you know. Always a risk. I would like to stay, if I can."

"That sounds smart. You should probably keep the others here close to you."

"I will." The woman's eyes softened, and she smiled warmly and put a hand on his cheek. He felt like he might cringe under her affectionate touch, but the second the skin of her hand touched his face, it just about broke his heart.

He thought of his mother and her sweet, gentle touch. He thought of his father and the soft, reassuring hand he'd put on his arm. He thought of his brother, with his arm over his shoulder. He thought of his dog Lacey, and how she'd snuggle up to any one of the family and sleep peacefully.

But his heart did not break; he didn't let it. He was still in the wilderness, and he felt that there was no time for that. He was used to pushing these kinds of things down, and so that's what he did.

One day, he thought, *one day someone will touch me. Be it a mother or a girlfriend or even just a friend. And then I'll let myself break. One day, but not today. Today these people need to get off the road and make it back to Plant City.*

"You guys should get out of here," he said. "Gunfire might bring someone curious."

She turned to the others. "Gather your things, let's get going." She turned back to Tyler. "You're a good man. Thank God for people like you."

They moved to the small wagon, pulled by two of them with straps on their backs and loaded with food and supplies. They stripped the friendly dead of essential equipment and loaded them onto the wagon as well.

"We'll bury them properly when we get back."

Then they threw the bandits to the side of the road to decay at the mercy of the sun.

Tyler watched as they did it. They looked at the criminals with disgust, but he felt no such contempt for them. They needed killing at the time, sure, and he didn't think he would lose any sleep over the act. But he wondered what brought them here, what made them do the things that they did. They wore masks, but there were faces under those masks, just as there are faces under every mask.

The redhead just stood and watched. She was maybe a year or two older than Tyler, like many of the others in her group, but she did not seem to belong to them. She meandered his way.

"Hey."

"Hey," he said back.

"What are you? You're not a bandit."

"I'm… I'm a Marauder." He said it with pride, though he wasn't sure why. Marauders were considered glorified bandits who all wound up dead. Miles included.

"What is that?"

"You haven't heard of a Marauder?"

"No. I came from further south, near Fort Myers. Is it like your group or something?"

"Sure."

"What do you do?"

"Save people on roads, I guess."

"Oh. Yeah, that makes sense. Cool. How many people have you got?"

"Just me."

"Just you? Shit, that's not a very big group."

"I guess not."

"Huh," She paused. "You want help?"

"Help?" He turned to her quizzically.

"Yeah, help." She stepped over the two bodies and disappeared into the woods. Seconds later she returned with two chest racks and another rifle in her hands. She tossed him one of the racks, which was stripped of pouches but had shotgun shells lined in the webbing.

"I saw those assholes stash these in the woods while they worked. Not sure why exactly, probably just lazy and didn't want to carry them while kicking us around in the dirt. Can't blame them, they're pretty bulky."

"What's your name?" he asked.

"May."

"I'm Tyler."

She told the others that she would not be joining them, and as they began to roll their wagon of supplies and bodies away, she watched them go with a deep and profound sadness. It was buried under her rough demeanor, but Tyler could see it because it was familiar.

He wondered what roads had led her here, what terrible things she had suffered to grow such old eyes in such a young face — though he knew the same expression was sculpted onto him. He was sorry that others had endured the same misery and heartbreak he had endured, just with different names and different voices.

And yet, something told him that she was no stranger to gluing the pieces back together and carrying on.

As they stood in the road and watched the caravan drift back toward Plant City, the older woman glanced back at the two and nodded in solemn appreciation. Tyler felt a stab of warmth in his heart and thought that that was a feeling he could get used to.

COLLECTIVE

DEAD RECKONING COLLECTIVE is a veteran owned and operated publishing company. Our mission encourages literacy as a component of a positive lifestyle. Although DRC only publishes the written work of military veterans, the intention of closing the divide between civilians and veterans is held in the highest regard. By sharing these stories it is our hope that we can help to clarify how veterans should be viewed by the public and how veterans should view themselves.

Visit us at:

deadreckoningco.com

 @deadreckoningcollective

@deadreckoningco

@DRCpublishing

Check out Luke Ryan's poetry
surrounding the topic of war:

The Gun and the Scythe
A Moment of Violence

Available on amazon.com

For signed copies go to deadreckoningco.com
(while supplies last)

Follow Luke Ryan

@lesgingerables

@LesGingerables

@Les_Gingerables

LUKE RYAN grew up overseas, the son of aid workers, where he spent 9 years in Pakistan and 5 years in Thailand. He eventually joined the U.S. military and became an Army Ranger for the 75th Ranger Regiment, where he went on four deployments to Afghanistan and left the service as a team leader. After a brief nomadic period, Luke attended the University of South Florida where he got a degree in English Literature. From there he worked a number of jobs as a journalist, videographer, copy editor, creative services producer, and social media manager. In the United States, he's bounced around between Arkansas, Georgia, California, Florida, New York, and now Texas, where he works for Black Rifle Coffee Company. He lives with his love, Kenna, a dog, and two cats.